VINTAGE

INTERNATIONAL

RAINER MARIA RILKE

THE NOTEBOOKS OF MALTE LAURIDS BRIGGE

TRANSLATED BY STEPHEN MITCHELL

VINTAGE INTERNATIONAL

Vintage Books
A Division of Random House, Inc.
New York

VINTAGE INTERNATIONAL EDITION, DECEMBER 1990

Translation copyright © 1982, 1983 by Stephen Mitchell
Introduction copyright © 1985 by William H. Gass

Grateful acknowledgment is made to Random House, Inc., for
permission to reprint excerpts from *The Selected Poetry of Rainer
Maria Rilke* by Rainer Maria Rilke, edited and translated by
Stephen Mitchell. Copyright © 1982 by Stephen Mitchell.
Used with permission.

Library of Congress Cataloging-in-Publication Data
Rilke, Rainer Maria, 1875-1926.
[Aufzeichnungen des Malte Laurids Brigge. English]
The notebooks of Malte Laurids Brigge / Rainer Maria Rilke ;
translated by Stephen Mitchell. — 1st Vintage International ed.
p.   cm. — (Vintage international)
Translation of: Die Aufzeichnungen des Malte Laurids Brigge.
ISBN 0-679-73245-4
I. Mitchell, Stephen, 1943-   . II. Title.
PT2635.I65A83   1990
833'.912—dc20   90-50272
CIP

Manufactured in the United States of America
10 9 8 7 6

ACKNOWLEDGMENTS

In the course of my work I have consulted
the John Linton and M. D. Herter Norton
translations, and especially the French
version by Maurice Betz.

Introduction

When Rilke arrived in Paris on August 28, 1902, and found a room at 11, rue Toullier, he believed he had come there to collect himself, to study in the libraries with one dreamy eye on a distant degree, and to meet the controversial sculptor, Auguste Rodin, whose work he had received a commission from a German publisher to write about. Rilke had recently married and fathered a child; his own father was no longer paying him the small stipend which had supplied Rilke for some years with the simplest of essentials; so that the commission, scarcely munificent, nevertheless seemed at least like a life ring if not a rescue launch. He not only needed an immediate income, he found it necessary, now, to think of the future, of a career of some kind, a useful pursuit. But Rilke had begun to slip out of the knot of his marriage in the moment that he tied it; and as time went on his habit of letting go of things even as he reached out for them would become firmly established; although, when he wrote about such "partings" later, it suddenly seemed to be the objects themselves or the beckoning women who broke the lines of attraction and connection.

How I have felt it, that nameless state called parting,
and how I feel it still: a dark, sharp, heartless
Something that displays, holds out with unapparent hands,
a perfect union to us, while tearing it in two.

With what wide-open eyes I've watched whatever
was, while calling to me, loosening its hold,
remaining in the road behind as though all womankind,
yet small and white and nothing more than this:

a waving which has blown the hair beyond its brow,
a slight, continuous flutter—scarcely now
explicable: perhaps the tremor of a plum tree
and the bough a startled cuckoo has set free.

When Rilke went to Paris, he was in full retreat from the noise of infants and their insistent needs; from the dull level of everyday life he had reached the instant his romance with the country cottage had subsided and intimacy's repeated little shames had reasserted their reality. He was returning, he felt, to the world of his work, and the prospect of going to Paris for the first time, as it would be, was therefore welcome to more than one of his selves. If Rilke approached Paris with eagerness and relief, however, and found Rodin, indeed, a genius he could quite decently idolize, Paris grasped his outstretched spirit with a pair of gnarled and beggarly hands which wrung nothing but outcry out of him, mercilessly squeezing him until body and soul were only a dry husk around rented air.

Rilke had written poems on poverty and death, but up to now he had really known neither. From the first, he had possessed, as a poet, enormous technical facility. Sentiment's superficial song came easily to him. Heine had held his heart longer than was necessary to warm it. While waiting for the muse, he struck his poses, and handed out pamphlets containing his work to passers-by on Prague's more notable streets as if giving away bread to the poor in spirit. At 26, Rilke still seemed an adolescent youth and selfstruck poet whose glibness was no longer a gift to either his art or his attitudes. It was as if he saw the people, actions, and objects of the world as basins into which he might empty the apparently boundless bladder of his being.

Now he was alone, in effect a runaway, nearly friendless, fearful, living in a shabby rented room in a squalid neighborhood: the pale fleck of a fly's egg in spoiling meat; and as poor as the poor all about him were poor, the poor who were dying nearby him in pallid strips like sprayed weeds. When he walked the mile or two to Rodin's atelier on the rue de l'Université; or took, from the Gare Montparnasse, the twenty-minute train ride to Meudon, Rodin's modest villa in the country; or crossed a few streets to the Bibliothèque Nationale where he was reading about the architecture of the great medieval cathedrals; he encountered everywhere figures like himself: lonely, grubby, ill, forlorn, although by now they were so at home in their hopelessness the furniture of their fate seemed almost comfortable (for what else would there ever be but this? *this* was the world; and then, at Rodin's, the master would suddenly appear, larger than duty, to draw Rilke into a crowd of dazzlingly white plaster casts, against which one's dark trousers threw an insipid shadow. In one moment, the sculptor's purposeful presence would replace an otherwise empty "now" with creative life. There would be folios of sketches to examine, a model also, odd lunches taken in the company of the sculptor's addled wife; there would be Rodin's laugh, his open and intense gaze on every surface and every hollow like an exploratory hand; his unfinicky, robust lust for the visible and invisible alike; and there would be his direct and simple advice: to watch, work, and have patience; for work was a continual necessity, he said: to work and to have a woman; but it was certainly dismaying as well—this unashamed physicality, this utter concentration upon a piece of stone to whose shape he would gradually give the undulating surface of some soon-to-be-living thing.

On other days, Rilke would turn in from the noisy streets to enter the public quiet in which books are read or significant objects contemplated: a space which equally enclosed the spaces of texts and dusty cabinets of sleeping things. Sometimes the poet would try to rest in his room, to write, where an unsteady table, sagging bed and single window indifferently surrounded what remained of a soul which had fled into the interior of the self, and came up occasionally to peer cautiously out of the ports of the eyes.

While in Rodin's studio, he was in a vibrant and creative present; while in the library, he could visit an equally creative and living past; but in his room or out in the streets of Paris, or even in himself, it seemed, there were only the failed, the sick, the pitiable, the threatening, the ugly. Rodin showed him who he ought to be; Paris demonstrated where and what he really was. The difference was the width of a wound.

If Rilke had fled his family, it was with his wife's leave,

for she was soon to follow him, after depositing little Ruth on Granny's stoop like a basket packed with orphan; still, his guilt, the relatively petty quality of his accomplishments, his lack of ordinary skills, his poverty and consequent dependency, made him an outcast, a stranger in a world of strangers, as he would later write. More and more, there was less and less difference to be discerned between himself and *les misérables* around him. "Regard! Observe!" came the command, but it was difficult indeed to face one's face reflected from the sooty stones, the soiled eyes, the pebbled skin, the unclean clothes one saw in the streets. Features followed him—buildings, hoardings, windows, watched—or they parted like wet paper or adhered like paint to distraught palms. "I sometimes press my face against the iron fencing of the Luxembourg in order to feel a little distance, stillness, and moonlight," Rilke writes his wife, Clara, "but in that place, too, is the heavy air, heavier still from the scents of the too many flowers they have crowded together in the constraint of the beds . . ." Thus Rilke, as if obeying Rodin's advice, visits the Jardin des Plantes, where he will find the panther's gaze so worn from passing through the bars that it sees nothing more; he also frequents fountains, tosses breadcrumbs from benches, watches the pigeons peck about in the gravel; he searches desperately inside himself for some spiritual strength (as in his letters he advises his wife to do when she arrives); he goes to Cluny where he sees the celebrated unicorn tapestries, to the Trocadéro, the Louvre. For the lonely, they invented museums.

There was no painter's autumn for the dessicated leaves which had begun to fall in August, so that now, in September, they are rattling down the dry paths in the parks, uttering, as if insects were calling out to one another, that brittle and bitter sound that signifies the irreversible absence of life.

The leaves are falling, falling from far away,
as though a distant garden died above us;
they fall, fall with denial in their wave.

And through the night the hard earth falls
farther than the stars in solitude.

We all are falling. Here, this hand falls.
And see—there goes another. It's in us all.

And yet there's One whose gently holding hands
let this falling fall and never land.

Rilke writes long letters to Clara about Rodin, about his reading, about Botticelli, about Leonardo, about a Paris brimming with sadness. He is beginning to prepare for a book whose beginning has not yet arrived. We sometimes forget, thinking of him as a poet, which is certainly natural enough, that Rilke was a master of German prose; that he wrote far more prose than he did poetry; that much of it is as astonishingly beautiful as prose can be, and as terrifying too; not simply in his notorious essay on dolls (which frightened females), or in the theoretical fancies of "Primal Sound" (which charmed them), or with the angry eloquence of "The Young Workman's Letter," or in the painful, and painfully prepared, pages of this singular novel; but in those countless, carefully composed, ample, and always elegantly indited lines drawn out of his loneliness like silk threads unwound from a cocoon: the correspondence which kept him, in his isolation, a social being.

These letters are sometimes shaded by self-pity. They are sometimes too supplicating, dandified, indulgent (the poseur is the other side of this poet); but they are invariably sensitive and thoughtful, often full of the unexpected in being raw, direct, and harsh. Certainly, they are rich, intense, frequently breathtaking: letters that could create a passion and stimulate an affair, for real acts of love occasionally covered the white sheets, and his skillful writer's hand could manage to touch even the most guarded heart. They are letters it must have taken—sometimes—more than a day to compose and copy over; and for their recipients, hours of rereading and rest before they would be able to recover. Rilke's writing *is* breathtaking: it falls upon the center of the spirit like a blow.

By early spring—ill in every element and tatter—Rilke leaves for Viareggio, an Italian resort near Pisa which he favored for a time; and then, for the summer, and still wan, he decides to return to Worpswede, the art colony close to Bremen where he had met his wife. It is here, with Paris safely over several hills on the calendar, that he is finally able to find a voice for his fears; and he begins to send to Lou Andreas-Salomé, his former lover and now a faithful and most valued friend, those stupendous letters which are the actual origin and part of the early text of *The Notebooks of Malte Laurids Brigge*. These long letters to Lou could not have been dashed off. They clearly come from notes, from prose trials and errors, so that when Rilke revises sections of them for inclusion in the novel, they are already in their third kind of existence.

It is in Rome, however, on the 8th of February, 1904 (always a propitious, hard, deep month for Rilke's work), that the project at last takes the sort of shape that begs for a name. Rilke had initially thought to title these pages, *The Journal of my Other Self*, and in many ways it is a better choice than the one he settled on. The novel we have now is made of two notebooks of nearly equal length, yet none of these entries is very notelike, unless a musical meaning is meant. The prose is too polished, the thought too refined, the sentiments too considered. The prose is constantly pushing at its edges, enlarging its capacities for expression. There can be little doubt, either, that the work is therapeutic and projective; that in its pages Rilke endeavored to confront, and overcome, the nightmares of his present life. True, it is about another self, because even if his surrogate's name has the same phonological shape as his own, it is the northern, Dane-touched Rilke who appears as a character in the novel, not the sensual, southern one; it is not the Malte who sees and speaks of ghosts, but the Rilke who harkens to the Angels, who writes it, and, in writing it, succeeds in escaping its protagonist's ambiguous fate.

Nonetheless, the word 'journal' suggests that these spoon-sized paragraphs are likely to contain doses of daily life's more commonplace medications; and that a familiar temporal progression is going to give a straightforward course to the work; when it is the psychological climate and not the clock that counts. It is a felt world which arises around us. At the same time, the phrase 'of my other self' identifies the author with his fictional agent so narrowly that the wider reaches of neither can be appreciated. Even if every observation in the text has been brought up from its low birth in rude fact, and every thought and feeling is one which Rilke at one time entertained like a guest for lunch; even if some of the transformations come to no more, immediately, than making an address ("11 rue Toullier") into a date ("September 11th, rue Toullier"); the sum of the alterations, omissions, and additions is significant, because Rilke saw and thought and felt strongly about far more things than he permits Malte to see and think and feel. Rilke (as any fine novelist must) will see "all round" his hero the way Henry James once arrogantly claimed to see "all round" Flaubert.

Malte's extraordinary lucidity may mislead us about the bars which frame his vision. There is no Rodin in this book to humble Malte's artistic claims; there is no mention of the glory and the menace of Cézanne, who meant so much to the development of Rilke's art during the time he spent writing this book; there is no intimation of success or greatness; there are no passages, such as those which occur in his letters to Clara, for all their gloomy remonstrances, which evoke the vitality and sensuality of the city.

There is simply a sudden end to the notebooks, as if their author had no interest in beginning a third, or as if the third were lost, or as if Malte Laurids Brigge were no longer alive.

No. Rilke is not Malte. Yet Malte *is* Rilke. Just as matter and mind, for Spinoza, were essential but separate aspects of one natural whole, so Malte is an aspect of Rilke—Rilke seen with one "I". And Malte, when he describes the remaining interior wall of a demolished house (to choose a celebrated example), is penetrating more fully into things than Rilke or Rodin or any one of us would, if we were merely walking by on some Parisian sidewalk, because this vision, like so many others, is an observation taken home, and taken to heart, and held warmly there until it rises like bread. Anyone can stand still and take notes. Quite a different eye or recording hand *constructs one thing out of its response to another*. It is the artful act of composition that creates the emotional knowledge which such passages contain—the metaphors of misery and shame and decay which arise like imagined odors from the wall. Thus Rilke comes into possession of this knowledge in the same moment Malte does; but he does so (and consequently suffers a stroke of synethesia, smelling the ugliness he has just seen) because he is imagining Malte; and Malte, to be Malte, must make these discoveries; must run in horror from this wall which he feels exposes his soul to every passerby like a flung-open coat. One probably cannot say it too often: writing is, among other things, an activity which discovers its object; which surprises itself with the meanings it runs into, and passes sometimes with apologies, or recognizes with a start like an old friend encountered in a strange place.

Rilke has little idea where his project is heading. It has no head: that is the trouble. Bits and pieces of his book are accumulating. They have a thematic and emotional unity. They are uncentered insights. That's all. And the pain of Paris has receded somewhat. To finish his work he will have to return to Paris eventually, but the old wounds won't open as widely as before. How to continue? Worse: why continue? The difficulty is familiar. To rebleed isn't easy.

Rilke has recently reviewed the posthumous writings of an obscure Norwegian poet. It is a collection of scratched-over jottings and aborted beginnings, a jumble that he says was at bottom just movement, nervous twitches of attention: "and this world of moods and voices trembled and revolved around the peculiar silence left behind by one who has died." At first, Rilke has thought he would attach a small preface to the notebooks indicating to the reader how they had presumably been acquired, but later decided against it, which was wise: first, because to pretend to honesty by calling a mess by its right name will not remove it; second, because the fragmentary and chaotic condition of the text at that time needed no further emphasis (even the suggestion of looseleafery in the novel's name is enough to mislead many critics), and because now Malte's body, as well as the fate of his soul, lies in a deeper darkness than mere dirt or damnation can contrive.

Fictions have large but brittle bones, and suffer frequent fractions and dislocations. Their legs limp a long time after the bones have knit. Unfortunately, Rilke was an accomplished interrupter. He travels: first to pillar, then to post. He becomes a professional guest; he lives in other people's houses, in hotels, in rented rooms. Unfamiliar mirrors become his temporary friends. For a time, he resides in Rome. Then he visits Scandinavia. He complains about the uglification of Capri. He lectures: first hither, then yon. In Vienna, before a reading of "the death of the Chamberlain" section of *Malte,* he has a nosebleed. Hofmannsthal is solicitous and offers to substitute himself if necessary. At Meudon, he watches Rodin work on the bust of George Bernard Shaw. He occupies himself with his so-called "thing poems," but the truth is that he is avoiding the failure he fears. He is filling his life with inconsequence. And if the novel cannot be completed; if some sort of whole cannot be made of it, Rilke will become his other self.

Back in Paris (it is now 1907), his book begins to mature and to assume a shape, but there is an important change of tone. The second part, or afterhalf, is a progressive transformation of the thematic material of the first. Malte's early obsessions (with alienation, fear, poverty, loneliness, art, disease, death) continue to occupy his thoughts, and figures from the past are still called up; but Malte's meditations on death, for instance, are first mingled with, and then gradually replaced by, his reflections on the notion of a non-possessive passion (the idea of one's own *Tod* is supplanted by an ownerless *Liebe*); loneliness is more and more that emancipating distance between lovers which we have already seen symbolized in the wave which is both greeting and goodby; alienation begins to look like a defiant freedom; other kinds of dreams, and different ghosts, preoccupy Malte now: the indistinct forms of saintly women, temporally distant kings; while his graphic impressions of Parisian lowlife are overshadowed by his equally intense experiences of ancient texts, often equally grim and macabre, particularly demonstrated by his grisly description of the maggot-infested, rosette-shaped wound in the center of the chest of Charles VI. What is said, early in the first notebook, to be "the main thing" (that is, to survive), is no longer, in the second, "the main thing" at all ("the main thing is just to keep drawing," to remain faithful to one's art). And the initial commandment: to learn to see, is followed by another, later: to take on and learn the task of love.

The final section of the first notebook, and the initial section of the next, are both given over to a description of the *Dame à la Licorne* tapestries which are on display in the Cluny Museum, and to the girls who come to contemplate and sketch them. These pages form a hinge between the novel's two halves. The girls are from good families, Malte imagines, but they have left their homes; no one any longer takes care to see that all the buttons down the backs of their dresses are properly fastened. They are prodigal daughters, entranced momentarily by emblems, by this ethereal, floating, simultaneous, enigmatic world . . . a woven world, static, pictorial, plastic, even as this novel is, although its images are rarely so benign. And the young girls, enamored, begin to draw. The objects they wish to reflect on their tablets, perhaps as the mirror which the woman holds reflects the unicorn and the unicorn's lone white horn back at itself, are, in their way, eternal objects—images which can be safely, purely, loved. Here all passions come to rest like a splash caught by a camera so the wild drops glint like gems, and their frantic rush remains serenely in one place, in the path of a few threads.

In their families, Malte remarks of the girls, religion is no longer possible. "Families can no longer come to God." And in families, if one shares an end or object equally with all its other members, "each gets so shamefully little." And if one tries to gain a little more of liberty or local love or leisure of one's self, disputes will arise. Such thoughts, again, approach those of Spinoza. These girls, before they have known the fat but actually fragile pleasures of the flesh, are able to lose themselves in their drawings for a moment; lose themselves, and thereby realize another kind of love: a love which allows them to take into an almost unfolded soul, like a bee between hesitant petals, "the unalterable life that in these woven pictures has radiantly opened in front of them." Of course, as ordinary girls— as anybody's kids—they want to change, grow up, have their loneliness embraced by another's loneliness; they believe they want to enjoy that promised world where one pleasure is supposed to follow another like sweetmeats tamely to the mouth. Yet not in all young women is the shining, still image of this other—ethereal—love suppressed. And Malte begins to recite the names of his "saved ones," his "blessed"—those whose dedication survives all indifference, cruelty, or rejection, because it contains a love which refuses to enslave or possess its object, but paradoxically insists upon increasing the selfhood, the freedom, the plenty, the being, of what is loved.

Rilke was a rather accomplished caricaturist, even as a child, and his eye is a painterly and plastic one. It is his punishment as a poet not to be able to shape and fondle and bring forth *things*. The lyric poem, too, of which he was one of the last great masters, is only typographically a linear event. Its words interact in all directions to produce an entity whose nature it is to occupy a space—a space which song sings us through like a gracious guide from room to room, but whose structure we grasp as a single simultaneity.

The eyes, the lips, of the reader move, then, and as they move, the music of the work begins; those moving lips sustain it; but, for this great novel, it is as if the eyes were lighting here, then there, upon the surface of a series of tapestries, observing in each place the signs: symbols like the figures of the lion and the lady, the little dog, the silver moons, sung above an oval island. Another significant clue to the character of this fiction is contained in the passage which almost immediately follows Malte's meditation upon *la Dame à la Licorne*; namely, the section in which Malte remembers when his mother unrolled for him the antique pieces of lace she had collected. Malte, even more susceptible to "ecstacy" and loss of self as a child than he will be as an adult, is gratefully absorbed into the realms their lacelight shapes create. He becomes enmeshed in the luxurious leaves and tendrils of one design; he crosses the bleached fields of another, suffering from its chill white winds, its frost. And in the weave where he is happily caught are also the women who sewed and directed and knotted the threads—there, in the linen, in lieu of a lesser heaven. These epitomal pages, which are so occupied with ghostlike, archetypal, and mystical episodes, also include this epiphany of their novel's slow unspooling movement.

Like the tapestries, the laces have a fixed yet enrapturing esthetic design, and their delicate art redeems, from a life of merely "what's expected," those women who might have been otherwise wholly wasted.

And if one day all we do and suffer done
should seem suddenly trivial and strange,
as though it were no longer clear
why we should have kicked off our childhood shoes
for such things—would not this length
of yellowed lace, this densely woven swatch
of linen flowers, be enough to hold us here?
See: this much was accomplished.

A life, perhaps, was made too little of, who knows?
a happiness in hand let slip; yet despite this,
for each loss there appeared in its place
this spun-out thing, not lighter than life,
and yet perfect, and so beautiful that all our so-be-its
are no longer premature, smiled at, and held in abeyance.

Rilke has basely encouraged and nobly earned the affection of many fine women by the time his novel appears in

1910, although their numbers will increase, and although he is fully aware of what these feelings normally mean. His conception of an intransitive love is certainly a defense of his own needs and an apology for his own behavior, but that does not lessen its interest or even increase its novelty, since it is at least as old as the average idea.

Because you are loved, Rilke found (and he interprets the parable of the Prodigal Son in these terms when he chooses to conclude *Malte Laurids Brigge* with it), you are expected to serve your lover, whose feelings have been left like a kitten in your care. Because you are loved, you become the victim of many benevolences which your lover wishes to bestow upon you, but which you are scarcely prepared to receive. Because you are loved, your work, which is a rival much admired but not more jealously betrayed for all that, will have to step aside so that the loving one can be comforted by your attention, assured of your devotion by the degree to which you are prepared to neglect yourself, abandon your principles, release your dreams. Because you are loved you will be offered a physical intimacy which will be perceived as conferring spiritual rights. Because you are loved, you are now fuel for another's fire; and the Prodigal Son does not wish to burn from outward, in. The Prodigal Son flees the embrace of the world, and when he returns he does not desire to be forgiven his departure. *To be loved means to be consumed in flames. To love is to give light with inexhaustible oil. To be loved is to pass away; to love is to endure.* These are Malte Laurids Rilke's hard words. And they have provoked rather stern, angry, and anquished responses.

However, to anyone whose work has to do with the unity of heart and mind in the service of some truth, or the pursuit of some distant ideal of justice or beauty, these words do not seem wide of the mark but rather its eye; for when one compares the concern of the poet for poetry, the philosopher for the good, or that of the physicist for the more abstractly material formulation of what's finally real, all other adorations (now that the love of the gods has got the go by) come to resemble merely plant or animal appetites; and how well we know those plant and animal appetites! and how they put the objects of their solitude in immediate danger of their teeth, in more distant, slower danger, of their roots.

"Who speaks of victory?" Rilke writes in one of his poems. "To endure is all." The love of God which Malte Laurids Brigge yearns for is actually a license for his own love. Even when the courtly poet loves, in love with love itself and each of its amorous rites, the object of that love, already half imaginary, must nevertheless be worthy. Its pursuit, its contemplation, must furnish the inspiration necessary to sustain the poet's efforts. It need not *do* anything, but it must *be*. Spinoza cannot call "God" some ignominious thing; and although Nature, as that divinity, is certainly indifferent to him, God *is* God, and deserving of the devotion of such a mind as his. When Art or God or the Good return one's love, permission is the substance of it: they have allowed that service simply by meriting it. Rilke's saintly women, who begin by worshipping vain men—earthly objects, leafless twigs—end by transubstantiating them. There is no other way. Malte's choice of deity, it would appear when the novel subsides, has not yet offered him that opportunity. Hence this strenuous attempt, to substitute for his obsession with death the practice of a liberating love, cannot be deemed a success.

The Notebooks' last words make a dismal sound. *He* [Malte in the guise of the Prodigal Son] *was now terribly difficult to love, and he felt that only One would be capable of it. But He was not yet willing.* Here, the second book breaks off.

It may be that the love which this work asks for is also of the non-possessive kind, although it has certainly received a surfeit of the other sort. In any case, by writing it, Rilke succeeded in furthering the art of fiction so far as to make its continued practice forbidding if not impossible. From its readers, as well, *Malte* requires a wholly different dedication; it requires a *gaze*. Paradoxically, it is just such difficulties which drive us on, so that the novel has become more beguilingly daunting for every age of its existence. As readers too—*look!*—brought to a standstill before the page—how wide, now, we must widen our eyes.

WILLIAM H. GASS

Washington University
St. Louis,
May 6, 1984

[Note: of the poems quoted in this Preface, "Autumn" and "Parting" have been previously published in *River Styx*, No. 11 (1982).]

xxiv

THE NOTEBOOKS OF
MALTE LAURIDS BRIGGE

September 11th, rue Toullier

So this is where people come to live; I would have
thought it is a city to die in. I have been out. I saw:
hospitals. I saw a man who staggered and fell. A
crowd formed around him and I was spared the rest.
I saw a pregnant woman. She was dragging herself
heavily along a high, warm wall, and now and then
reached out to touch it as if to convince herself that
it was still there. Yes, it was still there. And behind
it? I looked on my map: maison d'accouchement.
Good. They will deliver her—they can do that. Farther along, on the rue Saint-Jacques, a large building
with a dome. The map said: Val-de-grâce, hôpital

3

militaire. I didn't really need to know that, but all right. The street began to give off smells from all sides. It smelled, as far as I could distinguish, of iodoform, the grease of pommes frites, fear. All cities smell in summer. Then I saw a house that was peculiarly blind, as if from a cataract; it wasn't on the map, but above the door there was an inscription, still fairly legible: Asile de nuit. Beside the entrance were the prices. I read them. It wasn't expensive.

And what else? A child in a baby-carriage standing on the sidewalk: it was fat, greenish, and had a clearly visible rash on its forehead. This was apparently healing and didn't hurt. The child was sleeping with its mouth open, breathing iodoform, pommes frites, fear. That is simply what happened. The main thing was, being alive. That was the main thing.

— ••• —

To think that I can't give up the habit of sleeping with the window open. Electric trolleys speed clattering through my room. Cars drive over me. A door slams. Somewhere a windowpane shatters on the pavement; I can hear its large fragments laugh and its small one giggle. Then suddenly a dull, muffled noise from the other direction, inside the house. Someone is walking up the stairs: is approaching, ceaselessly approaching: is there, is there for a long time, then passes on. And again the street. A girl screams, Ah tais-toi, je ne veux plus. The trolley races up excitedly, passes on over it, over everything. Someone calls out. People are running, catch up with each other. A dog barks. What a relief: a dog. Toward morning there is even a rooster crowing, and that is an infinite pleasure. Then suddenly I fall asleep.

— ••• —

These are the noises. But there is something here that is more dreadful: the silence. I imagine that during great fires such a moment of extreme tension must sometimes occur: the jets of water fall back, the firemen stop climbing the ladders, no one moves. Soundlessly a black cornice pushes forward overhead, and a high wall, with flames shooting up behind it, leans forward, soundlessly. Everyone stands and waits, with raised shoulders and faces contracted above their eyes, for the terrifying crash. The silence here is like that.

— ••• —

I am learning to see. I don't know why it is, but everything enters me more deeply and doesn't stop where it once used to. I have an interior that I never knew of. Everything passes into it now. I don't know what happens there.

Today, while I was writing a letter, it struck me that I have been here just three weeks. Three weeks anywhere else, in the country for example, would be like one day; here they are years. And I don't want to write any more letters. What's the use of telling

5

someone that I am changing? If I'm changing, I am no longer who I was; and if I am something else, it's obvious that I have no acquaintances. And I can't possibly write to strangers.

— ••• —

Have I said it before? I am learning to see. Yes, I am beginning. It's still going badly. But I intend to make the most of my time.

For example, it never occurred to me before how many faces there are. There are multitudes of people, but there are many more faces, because each person has several of them. There are people who wear the same face for years; naturally it wears out, gets dirty, splits at the seams, stretches like gloves worn during a long journey. They are thrifty, uncomplicated people; they never change it, never even have it cleaned. It's good enough, they say, and who can convince them of the contrary? Of course, since they have several faces, you might wonder what they do with the other ones. They keep them in storage. Their children will wear them. But sometimes it also happens that their dogs go out wearing them. And why not? A face is a face.

Other people change faces incredibly fast, put on one after another, and wear them out. At first, they think they have an unlimited supply; but when they are barely forty years old they come to their last one. There is, to be sure, something tragic about this. They are not accustomed to taking care of faces; their last one is worn through in a week, has holes in it, is in many places as thin as paper, and then, little by little, the lining shows through, the non-face, and they walk around with that on.

But the woman, the woman: she had completely fallen into herself, forward into her hands. It was on the corner of rue Notre-Dame-des-Champs. I began to walk quietly as soon as I saw her. When poor people are thinking, they shouldn't be disturbed. Perhaps their idea will still occur to them.

The street was too empty; its emptiness had gotten bored and pulled my steps out from under my feet and clattered around in them, all over the street, as if they were wooden clogs. The woman sat up, frightened, she pulled out of herself, too quickly, too violently, so that her face was left in her two hands. I could see it lying there: its hollow form. It cost me an indescribable effort to stay with those two hands, not to look at what had been torn out of them. I shuddered to see a face from the inside, but I was much more afraid of that bare flayed head waiting there, faceless.

— ••• —

I am afraid. One must take some action against fear, once one has come down with it. It would be horrible to get sick here, and if someone thought of taking me to the Hôtel-Dieu, I would certainly die there. It is a

7

pleasant hotel, with an enormous clientele. You can hardly look at the façade of Notre-Dame without the risk of being run over by one of the many vehicles that cross the open square, as quickly as possible, to disappear inside. They are little omnibuses which incessantly clang their bells, and the Duke of Sagan himself would have to stop his carriage if one of these little people who are dying had decided to drive straight into God's Hotel. The dying are pigheaded, and all of Paris stops when Madame Legrand, junk dealer from the rue des Martyrs, is driven toward a certain square in the Cité. It is to be noticed that these fiendish little carriages have extraordinarily intriguing windows of frosted glass, behind which you can picture the most glorious agonies; even the imagination of a concierge could do that. If your imagination is more lively and you let it develop in other directions, the possibilities are truly endless. But I have also seen open horse-cabs arrive, hired cabs with their hoods folded back, which drove at the usual rate: two francs per death-hour.

— ••• —

This excellent hotel is very ancient; already in the time of King Clovis people were dying here, in a few beds. Now there are 559 beds to die in. Like a factory, of course. With production so enormous, each individual death is not made very carefully; but

8

that isn't important. It's the quantity that counts. Who is there today who still cares about a well-finished death? No one. Even the rich, who could after all afford this luxury, are beginning to grow lazy and indifferent; the desire to have a death of one's own is becoming more and more rare. In a short time it will be as rare as a life of one's own. Because, my God!, it is all there. You come, you find a life, ready-made, you just have to slip it on. You leave when you want to, or when you're forced to: anyway, no effort: Voilà votre mort, monsieur. You die as best you can; you die the death that belongs to the sickness you have (for since all sicknesses are well known, it is also known that the various fatal endings belong to the sicknesses and not to the people; and the sick person has, so to speak, nothing more to do).

In the sanatoriums, where people die so willingly and with so much gratitude to the doctors and nurses, it is one of those deaths which are attached to the institution; that is looked on favorably. But when people die at home, it is natural they should choose that polite, genteel death by which a first-class funeral has, as it were, already begun, with the whole sequence of its admirable customs. Then the poor stand in front of the house and look till they are full. *Their* death, of course, is banal, without fuss. They are happy if they find one that more or less fits. No matter if it's too large: you always keep growing a little. Only if it doesn't meet around the chest, or if it strangles, is there a problem.

— ••• —

When I think back to my home, where there is no one left now, it always seems to me that things must have been different back then. Then, you knew (or perhaps you sensed it) that you had your death *inside* you as a fruit has its core. The children had a small one in them and the grownups a large one. The women had it in their womb and the men in their chest. You *had* it, and that gave you a strange dignity and a quiet pride.

It was obvious that my grandfather, old Chamberlain Brigge, still carried a death inside him. And what a death it was: two months long and so loud that it could be heard as far away as the manor farm.

The long, ancient manor-house was too small for this death; it seemed as if new wings would have to be added on, for the Chamberlain's body grew larger and larger, and he kept wanting to be carried from one room to another, bursting into a terrible rage if, before the day had ended, there were no more rooms that he hadn't already been brought to. Then he had to go upstairs, with the whole retinue of servants, chambermaids, and dogs which he always had around him, and, ushered in by the chief steward, they entered the room where his dear mother had died. It had been kept exactly as she had left it twenty-three years before, and since then no one had ever been allowed to set foot in it. Now the whole pack burst in. The curtains were pulled back, and the robust light of a summer afternoon examined all the shy, terrified objects and turned around clumsily in the forced-open mirrors. And the people did the same. There were maids who, in their curiosity, didn't know where their hands were loitering, young servants who gaped at everything, and older ones who walked around trying to remember all the stories they had been told about this locked room which they had now, incredibly, entered.

But it was especially the dogs who were excited by this place where everything had a smell. The tall, slender Russian wolfhounds loped busily back and forth behind the armchairs, moved across the rug swaying slightly in long dance-steps, stood up on their hind legs like the dogs on a coat-of-arms, and, leaning their slender paws on the white-and-gold windowsill, with sharp, attentive faces and wrinkled foreheads gazed right and left into the courtyard. Small, glove-yellow dachshunds sat on the large silk easychair by the window, looking as if everything were quite normal. A wire-haired, sullen-faced setter rubbed its back on the edge of a gilt-legged table, and on the painted top the Sèvres cups trembled.

Yes, it was a terrible time for these drowsy, absent-minded Things. Down out of books which some careless hand had clumsily opened, rose leaves fluttered to the floor and were trampled underfoot; small, fragile objects were seized and, instantly broken, were quickly put back in place; others, dented or bent out of shape, were thrust beneath the curtains or even thrown behind the golden net of the fire-screen. And from time to time something fell, fell with a muffled sound onto the rug, fell with a clear sound onto the hard parquet floor, but breaking here and there, with a sharp crack or almost soundlessly; for these Things, pampered as they were, could not endure a fall.

And if anyone had thought of asking what had caused all this, what had called down such intense destruction upon this anxiously protected room, —there could have been only one answer: death.

The death of Chamberlain Christoph Detlev Brigge at Ulsgaard. For he lay on the floor in the middle of the room, enormously swelling out of his dark blue uniform, and did not stir. In his large, strange face, which no one could recognize now, the eyes had closed: he no longer saw what was happening. At first they had tried to lay him on the bed, but he had put up a fight, for he hated beds ever since those nights when his illness had first grown. Besides, the bed in this room had turned out to be too small, so there was nothing left but to lay him on the rug; for he refused to go downstairs.

So now he lay, and one might think that he had died. As it slowly began to grow dark, the dogs had one after another slipped out through the half-closed door. Only the stiff-haired setter with the sullen face sat beside its master, and one of its wide, shaggy forepaws lay on Christoph Detlev's large gray hand. Most of the servants were now standing outside in the white hallway, which was brighter than the room; but those who had stayed inside sometimes stole a glance at the large darkening heap in the middle of the room, and they wished that it were nothing more than a large blanket over some rotten inanimate object.

But there was something more. There was a voice, the voice that, seven weeks before, no one had known: for it wasn't the Chamberlain's voice. This voice didn't belong to Christoph Detlev, but to Christoph Detlev's death.

Christoph Detlev's death was alive now, had already been living at Ulsgaard for many, many days, talked with everyone, made demands. Demanded to be carried, demanded the blue room, demanded the small salon, demanded the great banquet-hall. Demanded the dogs, demanded that people laugh, talk, play, stop talking, and all at the same time. Demanded to see friends, women, and people who had died, and demanded to die itself: demanded. Demanded and screamed.

For, when night had come and, exhausted, those of the servants who didn't have to sit up tried to get some sleep, Christoph Detlev's death began screaming, it screamed and groaned, it howled so long and continuously that the dogs, which at first had howled along with it, fell silent and didn't dare to lie down and, standing on their long, thin, trembling legs, were afraid. And when, through the huge, silvery Danish summer night, the villagers heard it howling, they got up out of bed as if there were a thunderstorm, dressed, and stayed seated around the lamp, without a word, until it was over. And the women who would soon give birth were brought to the most remote rooms and to the most inaccessible alcoves; but they heard it, they heard it, as if it were screaming from inside their own bodies, and they begged to be allowed to get up, and came, white and heavy, and sat down among the others with their blurred faces. And the cows that were calving then were helpless and miserable, and the dead fruit had to be torn out of one of them, along with all the entrails, since it refused to come out at all. And everyone did their daily work badly and forgot to bring in the hay because they spent the day dreading the arrival of night and because they were so worn out by the sleeplessness and the terrified awakenings that they couldn't concentrate on anything. And when on Sunday they went to the white, peaceful church, they prayed that there might no longer be a master at Ulsgaard: for this one was a terrifying master. And what they were all thinking and praying, the minister said out loud up in the pulpit, for he too had no nights anymore and could no longer understand God. And the church-bell said it, having found a terrible rival which boomed out all night long and against which, even when it rang with all its metal, it could do nothing. Indeed, they all said it; and one of the young men dreamed that he had gone to the manor-house and killed the master with his pitchfork; and they were so exasperated, so overstrained, that they all listened as he told his dream and, quite unconsciously, looked at him to see if he were really brave enough to do that. This is how people felt and talked in the whole district where, just a few weeks before, the Chamberlain had been loved and pitied. But though there was all this talk, nothing changed. Christoph Detlev's death, which had moved in at Ulsgaard, refused to let itself be hurried. It had come for ten weeks, and for ten weeks it stayed. And during that time it was master, more than Christoph Detlev Brigge had ever been; it was like a king who is called the Terrible, afterward and for all time.

This was not the death of just any old man with dropsy; this was the sinister, princely death which the Chamberlain had, all his life, carried inside him and nourished with his own experiences. Every excess of pride, will, and authority that he himself had not been able to use up during his peaceful days, had passed into his death, into the death that now sat squandering these things at Ulsgaard.

How Chamberlain Brigge would have looked at anyone who asked him to die any other death than this. He was dying his own hard death.

— ••• —

And when I think about the others I have seen or heard of: it is always the same. They all had a death of their own. Those men who carried it in their armor, inside themselves, like a prisoner; those women who grew very old and small, and then on an enormous bed, as if on the stage of a theater, in front of the whole family and the assembled servants and dogs, discreetly and with the greatest dignity passed away. The children too, even the very small ones, didn't have just any child's death; they gathered themselves and died what they already were and what they would have become.

And what a melancholy beauty this gave to women when they were pregnant and stood there, with their slender hands instinctively resting on their large bellies, in which there were *two* fruits: a child and a death. Didn't the dense, almost nourishing smile on their emptied faces come from their sometimes feeling that both were growing inside them?

— ••• —

I have taken action against fear. I sat up all night and wrote; now I am as tired as after a long walk through the fields of Ulsgaard. Still, it is hard for me to think that that world no longer exists, that strangers are living in the ancient, long manor-house. It may be that in the white room up in the gable the maids are sleeping now, sleeping their heavy, moist sleep through the night until morning comes.

And you have nobody and nothing, and you travel through the world with a trunk and a carton of books and truly without curiosity. What kind of life is this: without a house, without inherited Things, without dogs. If at least you had your memories. But who has them? If childhood were there: it is as though it had been buried. Perhaps you must be old before you can reach all that. I think it must be good to be old.

— ❖ —

Today we had a beautiful autumn morning. I walked through the Tuileries. Everything that lay toward the East, before the sun, dazzled; was hung with mist as if with a gray curtain of light. Gray in the gray, the statues sunned themselves in the not yet unveiled garden. Single flowers in the long parterres stood up to say: Red, with a frightened voice. Then a very tall, thin man came around the corner from the Champs-Elysées. He was carrying a crutch, but it was no longer thrust into his shoulder-pit: he was holding it out in front of him, lightly, and from time to time he hit the ground with it, firmly and loudly, as if it were a herald's staff. He couldn't repress a joyful smile, and smiled, past everything, at the sun, the trees. His step was as bashful as a child's, but extraordinarily light, filled with memories of an earlier walking.

— ••• —

How much a small moon can do. There are days when everything around you is luminous, scarcely intimated in the bright air, and yet quite distinct. The foreground takes on the colors of distance, is remote and merely shown from far away, not given to you. And everything related to expanse—the river, the bridges, the long streets, and the extravagant squares —has taken that expanse behind it, is painted on it as if on silk. It is impossible to say what a bright-green carriage on the Pont-Neuf can then become, or a red so vivid that it can't be held back, or even a simple poster on the division wall of a pearl-gray group of houses. Everything is simplified, brought onto a few correct, clear planes, like the face in a Manet portrait. And nothing is trivial or superfluous. The booksellers on the quai open their stalls, and the fresh or worn yellow of the books, the violet brown of the bindings, the larger green of an album: everything is in harmony, has value, everything takes part and forms a plenitude in which there is nothing lacking.

— ••• —

In the street below there is the following group: a small wheelbarrow, pushed by a woman; lengthwise across the front of it, a barrel-organ. Behind that, a small crib in which a baby is standing on firm legs, chuckling with delight under its bonnet, not wanting to be sat down. From time to time the woman turns the organ handle. Then the baby immediately stands up again, stamping in its crib, and a little girl in a green Sunday dress dances and beats a tambourine lifted up toward the windows.

— ••• —

I think I should begin to do some work, now that I am learning to see. I am twenty-eight years old, and I have done practically nothing. To sum it up: I have written a study of Carpaccio, which is bad; a play entitled "Marriage," which tries to demonstrate a false thesis by equivocal means; and some poems. Ah, but poems amount to so little when you write them too early in your life. You ought to wait and gather sense and sweetness for a whole lifetime, and a long one if possible, and then, at the very end, you might perhaps be able to write ten good lines. For poems are not, as people think, simply emotions (one has emotions early enough)—they are experiences. For the sake of a single poem, you must see many cities, many people and Things, you must understand animals, must feel how birds fly, and know the gesture which small flowers make when they open in the morning. You must be able to think back to streets in unknown neighborhoods, to unexpected encounters, and to partings you had long seen coming; to days of childhood whose mystery is still unexplained, to parents whom you had to hurt when they brought in a joy and you didn't pick it up (it was a joy meant for somebody else—); to childhood illnesses that began so strangely with so many profound and difficult transformations, to days in quiet, restrained rooms and to mornings by the sea, to the sea itself, to seas, to nights of travel that rushed along high overhead and went flying with all the stars,—and it is still not enough to be able to think of all that. You must have memories of many nights of love, each one different from all the others, memories of women screaming in labor, and of light, pale, sleeping girls who have just given birth and are closing again. But you must also have been beside the dying, must have sat beside the dead in the room with the open window and the scattered noises. And it is not yet enough to have memories. You must be able to forget them when they are many, and you must have the immense patience to wait until they return. For the memories themselves are not important. Only when they have changed into our very blood, into glance and gesture, and are nameless, no longer to be distinguished from ourselves—only then can it happen that in some very rare hour the first word of a poem arises in their midst and goes forth from them.

But all my poems had a different origin; so they are

not poems.—And when I wrote my play, how far I wandered from the point. Was I an imitator or a fool, that I needed a third person in order to present the fate of two people who were making life difficult for each other? How easily I fell into the trap. And yet I should have known that this third person who passes through all lives and literatures, this ghost of a third person who has never existed, has no meaning and must be disavowed. He is one of the pretences of Nature, which is always careful to divert men's attention from her deepest mysteries. He is the partition behind which the play is performed. He is the noise at the entryway to the voiceless silence of a true conflict. It could be said that every playwright up to now has found it too difficult to speak of the two whom the drama is really about. The third person, just because he is so unreal, is the easiest part of the problem; they have all been able to manage him; from the very first scene you can feel their impatience to have him enter; they can hardly wait. The moment he appears, everything is all right. But how tedious when he's late. Absolutely nothing can happen without him; everything slows down, stops, waits. Yes, and what if this delay were to continue? What, my dear playwright, and you, dear audience who know life so well, what if he were declared missing—that popular man-about-town or that arrogant youth, who fits into every marriage like a skeleton-key? What if, example, the devil had taken him? Let's suppose this. All at once you feel the unnatural emptiness of the theaters; they are bricked up like dangerous holes; only the moths from the rims of the box-seats flutter through the unsupported void. The playwrights no longer enjoy their elegant townhouses. All the detective agencies are, on their behalf, searching in the remotest corners of the world for the irreplaceable third person, who was the action itself.

And all the while they are living among us—not these "third persons," but the two about whom so incredibly many things might be said, about whom not a word has ever yet been said, though they suffer and act and don't know how to help themselves.

How ridiculous. I sit here in my little room, I, Brigge, who am twenty-eight years old and completely unknown. I sit here and am nothing. And yet this nothing begins to think and thinks, five flights up, on a gray Paris afternoon, these thoughts:

Is it possible, it thinks, that we have not yet seen, known, or said anything real and important? Is it possible that we have had thousands of years to look, meditate, and record, and that we have let these thousands of years slip away like a recess at school, when there is just enough time to eat your sandwich and an apple?

Yes, it is possible.

Is it possible that despite our discoveries and advances, despite our culture, religion, and science, we have remained on the surface of life? Is it possible that even this surface, which might still have been something, has been covered with an incredibly tedious material, which makes it look like living-room furniture during the summer vacation?

Yes, it is possible.

Is it possible that the whole history of the world has been misunderstood? Is it possible that the past is false, because we have always spoken about its masses, just as if we were telling about a gathering of many people, instead of talking about the one person they were standing around because he was a stranger and was dying?

Yes, it is possible.

Is it possible that we thought we had to retrieve what happened before we were born? Is it possible that every one of us would have to be reminded that he had his origin in all who have gone before, that consequently he contains this past and has nothing to learn from those who assert that their knowledge is greater?

Yes, it is possible.

Is it possible that all these people know, with perfect accuracy, a past that never existed? Is it possible that all realities are nothing to them; that their life is running down, unconnected with anything, like a clock in an empty room—?

Yes, it is possible.

Is it possible that we know nothing about young girls, who are nevertheless living? Is it possible that we say "women," "children," "boys," not suspecting (despite all our culture, not suspecting) that these words have long since had no plural, but only countless singulars?

Yes, it is possible.

Is it possible that there are people who say "God" and think that this is something they have in common?—Take a couple of schoolboys: one buys a pocket knife, and the same day his friend buys another exactly like it. And after a week they compare knives, and it turns out that there is now just a very distant resemblance between them—so differently have they developed in different hands. ("Oh," says the mother of one, "you can't own *any*thing without wearing it out in a day . . .") In the same way: Is it possible to believe we could have a God without using him?

Yes, it is possible.

But if all this is possible, if it has even a semblance of possibility,—then surely, for the sake of everything in the world, something must be done. The first comer, the one who has had these alarming thoughts, must begin to do some of the things that have been neglected; even though he is just anyone, certainly not the most suitable person: since there is no one else. This young, insignificant foreigner, Brigge, will have to sit down in his room, five flights up, and keep writing, day and night. Yes, he will have to write; that is how it will end.

— ••• —

I must have been twelve then, or at most thirteen. My father had taken me with him to Urnekloster. I don't know what the occasion was for this visit to his father-in-law; the two men hadn't seen each other for years, not since my mother's death, and my father had never been inside the ancient manor-house that Count Brahe had retired to in his old age. I never again saw that remarkable house, which passed into strangers' hands after my grandfather's death. As I find it in the memorics of my childhood, it isn't a complete building; it has been broken into pieces inside me; a room here, a room there, and then a piece of a hall-way that doesn't connect these two rooms, but is preserved as a fragment, by itself. In this way, it is all dispersed inside me—the rooms, the staircases that descended so gracefully and ceremoniously, and other narrow, spiral stairs, where you moved through the darkness as blood moves in the veins; the tower rooms, the high, suspended balconies, the unexpected galleries you were thrust onto by a little door—all this is still inside me and will never cease to be there. It is as if the image of this house had fallen into me from an infinite height and shattered upon my ground.

The only area that has remained complete in my

heart, I think, is the banquet-hall where we used to assemble for dinner every evening at seven o'clock. I never saw this room by day; I can't even remember if it had windows or where they faced. Whenever the family entered, the candles would be burning in the heavy branched candlesticks, and in a few minutes you forgot the time of day and everything you had seen outside. This high and, I suspect, vaulted room was more powerful than everything else. With its darkening height and its never fully illuminated corners, it sucked all images out of you, without giving you anything definite in return. You sat there as if you had disintegrated—totally without will, without consciousness, without pleasure, without defense. You were like an empty space. I remember that at first this state of annihilation almost made me feel nauseated; it brought on a kind of seasickness, which I only overcame by stretching out my leg until my foot touched the knee of my father, who was sitting opposite me. It didn't strike me until later that he seemed to understand this strange gesture, or anyway seemed to tolerate it, although between us there was an almost cool relationship, which wouldn't have accounted for such behavior. Nevertheless, it was that slight contact which gave me the strength to sit through the long meal. And after a few weeks of tensed endurance, I had, with a child's almost limitless adaptability, gotten so very used to the eeriness of those gatherings that it no longer cost me any effort to sit at table for two hours; now the time even passed more or less quickly, because I was busy observing the dinner-guests.

My grandfather called them "the family," and I also heard the others use this term, which was completely arbitrary. For although these four people were distantly related to one another, they in no way belonged together. My uncle, who sat next to me, was an old man, whose hard, sunburned face had several black spots on it, the result (as I later found out) of a gunpowder explosion. Sullen and embittered, he had retired from the army with the rank of major, and was now conducting alchemical experiments in some region of the house where I had never been. He was also, as I heard the servants say, in communication with a prison, from which once or twice a year corpses were sent to him; he would lock himself in with them for days and nights, dissecting and preparing them in some mysterious way so that they could withstand putrefaction.

Opposite him was Miss Mathilde Brahe. She was a person of uncertain age, a distant cousin of my mother's. Nothing was known about her, except that she kept up a very active correspondence with an Austrian spiritualist who called himself Baron Nolde and to whom she was so completely devoted that she would not undertake even the most trivial action without first obtaining his consent or, rather, something like his blessing. She was at that time exceptionally plump, of a soft, lazy fullness that looked as if it had been carelessly poured into her loose, brightly colored dresses. Her movements were tired and uncertain, and her eyes watered constantly. And yet there was something about her that reminded me of my frail, slender mother. The longer I looked at her, the more I discovered in her face all those delicate features which since my mother's death I had never been able to remember clearly; only now that I was seeing Mathilde Brahe every day did I again know what she had looked like; perhaps I had even come to know it for the first time. Only now did the hundreds and hundreds of details come together inside me to form an image of my dead mother, the image that accompanies me everywhere I go. Later it became clear to me that all the details which determined my mother's features were actually present in Miss Brahe's face— only they seemed forced apart, distorted, no longer connected to one another, as if some stranger's face had thrust itself among them.

Beside this lady sat the small son of a female cousin, a boy about as old as I, but smaller and more delicate. His pale, slender neck rose out of a pleated ruff and disappeared beneath a long chin. His lips were thin and closed tightly, his nostrils trembled a bit, and only one of his beautiful dark-brown eyes was movable. It sometimes glanced peacefully and sadly in my direction, while the other eye remained pointed toward the same corner, as if it had been sold and was no longer being taken into account.

At the head of the table stood my grandfather's huge armchair, which a servant who had no other duty pushed beneath him, and in which he took up very little room. There were people who addressed this deaf and imperious old gentleman as "Your Excellency"; others called him "General." And, to be sure, he had a right to be addressed that way; but it had been so long since he had held any position that such titles were now barely intelligible. It seemed to me, at any rate, as if no definite name could adhere to his personality, which was at certain moments so sharp, and yet, again and again, without any precise outline. I could never manage to call him Grandfather, though he was occasionally quite friendly to me and sometimes would even summon me to him, trying to give a playful intonation to my name. For the rest, the whole family acted toward the Count with a mixture of veneration and fear. Little Erik was the only one who lived in any degree of intimacy with him; his movable eye at times cast quick glances of understanding at the old man, which were just as quickly answered. Sometimes too, during the slow afternoons, you would see them appear at the end of the long gallery, and you could observe how they walked, hand in hand, past the dark, ancient portraits, in total silence, apparently understanding each other without needing to say a word.

I would spend nearly the whole day in the garden and outside in the beech-woods or on the heath. Fortunately there were dogs at Urnekloster, who would accompany me on my walks; here and there I would come across a tenant's house or farm, where I could get milk, bread, and fruit. I think I enjoyed my freedom in a fairly carefree way, without letting myself, at least during the next few weeks, be frightened by any thought of the evening meals. I hardly talked to anyone, for I found my greatest joy in being alone; only with the dogs did I now and then have short conversations: we understood one another perfectly. Taciturnity was, in any case, a kind of family trait. I was used to it in my father, and wasn't at all surprised that during the long dinners hardly a word would be spoken.

In the early days after our arrival, however, Mathilde Brahe was extremely talkative. She questioned my father about old acquaintances in foreign cities; she reminisced about events in the distant past; she even moved herself to tears by recalling friends who had died and a certain young man who, she intimated, had been in love with her, though she hadn't cared to respond to his urgent and hopeless passion. My father listened politely, now and then nodding in agreement, and answering only when necessary. The Count, at the head of the table, sat with a contemptuous smile on his lips. His face seemed larger than usual, as if he had put on a mask. He also at times entered the conversation himself, without speaking to anyone in particular; but though his voice was very soft, it could be heard all through the room. It reminded me of the regular, indifferent motion of a pendulum; the silence around it seemed to have a strange, empty resonance, the same for each syllable.

Count Brahe believed he was doing my father a particular courtesy by speaking to him of his deceased wife, my mother. He called her Countess Sybille, and all his sentences ended as if he were inquiring about her health. Indeed, it appeared to me, I don't know why, as if he were talking about a very young girl in white, who might enter the room at any moment. I heard him speak in the same tone about "our little Anna Sophie." And one day, when I asked who this young lady was, whom Grandfather seemed so particularly fond of, I was told that he was referring to the daughter of High Chancellor Conrad Reventlow: the second, morganatic wife of Frederick IV, who had been reposing in one of the tombs at Roskilde for nearly a century and a half. The passing of time had absolutely no meaning for him; death was a minor incident which he completely ignored; people whom he had once installed in his memory continued to exist, and the fact that they had died did not alter that in the least. Several years later, after the old gentleman's death, I heard stories about how, with the same obstinacy, he experienced future events as present. It was said that on one occasion he had spoken to a recently married young woman about her sons, in particular about the travels of one of them, while the young woman, who was in the third month of her first pregnancy, sat almost fainting from bewilderment and horror as the old man talked on and on.

But it began with my laughing. I laughed out loud and couldn't stop. What had happened was that one evening Mathilde Brahe hadn't appeared for dinner. The old, almost totally blind butler nevertheless held out the serving-dish when he came to her seat. He remained in that attitude for a few moments; then, content and dignified, and as if everything were in order, he moved on. I had watched this scene, and for the moment, as I looked, it didn't seem at all funny. But a few moments later, just as I was about to swallow a mouthful of food, a fit of laughter rose to my head so quickly that I choked and caused a great commotion. And even though I myself found this situation painful, even though I tried with all my might to be serious, the laughter kept bubbling up in little fits and in the end completely took control of me.

My father, as if to divert attention from my bad manners, asked, in his broad, muffled voice: "Is Mathilde sick?" Grandfather smiled his peculiar smile and then answered with a sentence which, occupied as I was with myself, I paid no attention to, but which sounded something like: No, she merely does not wish to meet Christine. Nor did I realize, therefore, that it was these words which made my uncle, the brown-faced major, get up and, with a mumbled apology and a bow in the Count's direction, leave the room. It only struck me that he turned around again at the door, behind my grandfather's back, and began waving and nodding to Erik and suddenly (to my utter amazement) to me as well, as if he were urging us to follow him. I was so surprised that my laughter stopped. Beyond that, I paid no further attention to the major; I found him unpleasant, and I saw that Erik took no notice of him either.

The meal dragged on as usual, and we had just reached the dessert when my eye was caught by something moving in the semi-darkness at the other end of the room. A door there, which I thought was always kept locked and which I had been told led to the mezzanine, had opened little by little, and now, as I looked on with a feeling, entirely new to me, of curiosity and alarm, a slender woman in a light-colored dress stepped into the shadows of the doorway and slowly walked toward us. I don't know whether I made any movement or sound; the noise of a chair being overturned forced me to tear my eyes from the apparition, and I saw my father: he had leapt up from the table and now, his face deathly pale and hands clenched at his sides, was walking toward the woman. She, meanwhile, kept moving toward us, quite untouched by this scene, step by step, and was already not far from the head of the table when the Count suddenly stood up, seized my father by the arm, pulled him back to his seat and held him there, while the strange woman, slowly and indifferently, continued across the space that had now been left clear, moving step by step, through an indescribable silence in which only a glass clinked trembling, and vanished through a door in the opposite wall. At that moment I noticed that it was Erik who, with a deep bow, closed the door behind her.

I was the only one left sitting at the table. I had become so heavy in my chair that I felt I would never be able to get up again by myself. For a few moments I saw without seeing. Then I thought of my father, and I became aware that the old man was still holding him by the arm. My father's face was now angry, swollen with blood, but Grandfather, whose fingers clutched his arm like a white claw, was smiling his mask-like smile. Then I heard him say something, syllable by syllable, though I couldn't understand the meaning of his words. Nevertheless, they must have fallen deeply into my hearing, for about two years ago I discovered them one day at the bottom of my memory, and I have known them ever since. He said: "You are violent and uncivil, Chamberlain. Why don't you let people go about their business?"

"Who is that?" my father shouted, interrupting.

"Someone who has every right to be here. Not a stranger. Christine Brahe."

Then there was again that same peculiarly thin silence, and again the glass began to tremble. But with an abrupt movement my father tore himself away and rushed out of the room.

All night long I heard him pacing back and forth in his bedroom; for I couldn't sleep either. But suddenly, toward morning, I woke out of a sleep-like drowsiness and saw, with a horror that made my bones freeze, something white sitting on my bed. Despair finally gave me enough strength to bury my head under the covers, and there, from fear and helplessness, I began to cry. Suddenly I felt something cool and bright above my tear-filled eyes; I kept them closed so I wouldn't have to see what it was. But the voice which was now speaking to me from quite nearby touched my face with its warm, sweetish breath, and I recognized it: it was the voice of Miss Mathilde. I immediately grew calm, and even when I was quite composed I continued to let myself be comforted. I did feel that this kindness was rather effeminate, but I enjoyed it even so, and thought I had somehow deserved it.

"Aunt," I said at last, trying to assemble in her face the scattered features of my mother: "Aunt, who was the lady?"

"Ah," answered Miss Brahe with a sigh that seemed to me ludicrous, "an unfortunate woman, my child. An unfortunate woman."

That same morning I noticed a few servants in one of the rooms, who were busy packing some trunks. I thought this meant that we would be leaving, and it seemed quite natural to me. Perhaps my father actually did intend to leave then. I never found out what made him stay on at Urnekloster after that evening. But we didn't leave. We remained in that house for eight or nine weeks more, we put up with its oppressive eeriness, and we saw Christine Brahe three more times.

In those days I knew nothing about her story. I didn't know that she had died a long, long time before, as she was giving birth to a second child, a boy, who grew up to a terrifying, cruel fate: I didn't know that she was a dead person. But my father knew. Had he wanted to force himself, precisely because he was of such a passionate nature and yet so invested in logic and clarity, to endure this adventure calmly and unquestioningly? I saw, without comprehending, how he struggled with himself, and how, in the end, he triumphed.

It was the evening when we saw Christine Brahe for the last time. On this occasion Miss Mathilde had come to dinner; but she was in an unusual mood. As in the first few days after our arrival, she talked incessantly, without any clear sequence, and continually getting entangled in her own words, while some physical restlessness forced her to keep adjusting something in her hair or her dress—until unexpectedly she jumped up with a shrill cry of lament and vanished.

At the same moment my eyes involuntarily turned toward that particular door, and indeed: Christine Brahe was entering. The major, in his seat next to me, made a short, violent movement that passed on into my own body, but he apparently no longer had enough strength to stand up. His old, brown, spotted face turned from one person to another, his mouth hung open, his tongue writhed behind his decaying teeth; then all at once this face was gone, and his gray head lay upon the table, and his arms lay over it and under it as if in pieces, and from somewhere a withered, spotted hand emerged, quivering.

And then Christine Brahe walked past, step by step, slowly, like a sick person, through an indescribable silence interrupted only by a single whimpering sound, as if from an old dog. But then, to the left of the large silver swan filled with narcissus, the large mask of the old Count thrust forward with its gray smile. He lifted his wine-glass toward my father. And then I saw how my father, just as Christine Brahe was passing behind his chair, seized his glass and lifted it, as if it were something extremely heavy, a handsbreadth above the table.

And that same night we left.

I am sitting here reading a poet. There are many people in the room, but they are all inconspicuous; they are inside the books. Sometimes they move among the pages, like sleepers who are turning over between two dreams. Ah, how pleasant it is to be among people who are reading. Why aren't they always like this? You can go up to one of them and touch him lightly: he feels nothing. And if, as you get up, you happen to bump against the person sitting next to you and you apologize, he nods in the direction your voice is coming from, his face turns toward you and doesn't see you, and his hair is like the hair of someone sleeping. How good that feels. And I am sitting here and have a poet. What a fate. There are perhaps three hundred people reading in this room; but it is impossible that each one of them has a poet. (God knows what they have.) There can't *be* three hundred poets. But just imagine my fate: I, perhaps the shabbiest of all these readers, and a foreigner: I have a poet. Even though I am poor. Even though the jacket I wear every day has begun to get threadbare in certain spots; even though my shoes are not entirely beyond criticism. True, my collar is clean, my underwear too, and I could, just as I am, walk into any café I felt like, possibly even on the grands boulevards, and confidently reach out my hand to a plate full of pastries and help myself.

No one would find that surprising; no one would shout at me or throw me out, for it is after all a genteel hand, a hand that is washed four or five times a day. There is no dirt under the nails, the index finger isn't ink-stained, and the wrists especially are irreproachable. Poor people don't wash so far up; that is a well-known fact. Certain conclusions can therefore be drawn from the cleanliness of these wrists. And people do draw these conclusions. For example, in the shops. Though there are still one or two individuals, on the Boulevard Saint-Michel for example, or on the rue Racine, who are not fooled, who don't give a damn about my wrists. They look at me and know. They know that in reality I am one of them, that I'm only acting. After all, it's carnival time. And they don't want to spoil my fun; they just grin a little and wink at me. No one sees them do it. For the rest, they treat me like a gentleman. If someone happens to be nearby, they even become servile, behave as though I were wearing a fur coat and my carriage were following along behind me. Sometimes I give them two sous and tremble that they'll refuse; but they take them. And everything would be all right if they hadn't grinned a little and winked at me. Who are these people? What do they want of me? Are they waiting for me? How do they recognize me? It's true that my beard looks somewhat neglected and very, very slightly resembles their own sick, faded beards, which have always made a deep impression on me. But don't I have the right to neglect my beard? Many busy men do that, and no one ever thinks of numbering them, for that reason, among the outcasts. For it's obvious they are outcasts, not just beggars; no, they are really not beggars, there is a difference. They are human trash, husks of men that fate has spewed out. Wet with the spittle of fate, they stick to a wall, a lamp-post, a billboard, or they trickle slowly down the street, leaving a dark, filthy trail behind them. What in the world did the old woman want of me, who had crawled out of some hole carrying a night-table drawer with a few buttons and needles rolling around inside it? Why did she keep walking at my side, keep looking at me? As if she were trying to recognize me with her bleary eyes, which looked as though some diseased person had spat a greenish phlegm under the bloody lids. And how did that small, gray woman come to be standing at my side for a whole quarter of an hour in front of a store window, showing me an old, long pencil that pushed infinitely slowly up out of her wretched, clenched hands. I pretended that I was busy looking at the display in the window and hadn't noticed a thing. But she knew I had seen her; she knew I was standing there trying to figure out what she was doing. For I understood quite well that the pencil in itself was of no importance: I felt that it was a sign, a sign for the initiated, a sign only outcasts could recognize; I sensed that she was directing me to go somewhere or do something. And the strangest part was that I couldn't get rid of the feeling that there actually existed some kind of secret language which this sign belonged to, and that this scene was after all something I should have expected.

That was two weeks ago. Since then, hardly a day has passed without a similar encounter. Not only in the twilight, but at noon, in the busiest streets, a little man or an old woman will suddenly appear, nod to me, show me something, and then vanish, as if everything necessary were now done. It is possible that one fine day they will decide to come as far as my room; they certainly know where I live, and they'll manage to get past the concierge. But here, my friends, here I am safe from you. One must have a special card in order to get into *this* room. And I have the advantage of possessing this card. I walk through the streets a little shyly, as you can imagine; but finally I stand in front of a glass door, open it as if I were at home, show my card at the next door (just the way you show me your things, except that the guard understands me and knows what I mean—), and then I am among these books, am removed from you, as if I had died, and sit reading a poet.

You don't know what a poet is?—Verlaine . . . Nothing? No recollection? No. You didn't see a difference between him and the people you knew? You make no distinctions, I know. But it is another poet I'm reading: a poet who doesn't live in Paris, a very different one. One who has a quiet house in the mountains. Who rings like a bell in the clear air. A happy poet, who tells about his window and the glass doors of his bookcase that pensively reflect a dear, solitary distance. This poet is the one I would have liked to be. He knows so much about young girls, and I too would have known much about them. He knows about girls who lived a hundred years ago; it no longer matters that they're dead, for he knows everything. And that is the main thing. He says their names, those soft, gracefully written names with old-fashioned loops in the long letters, and the grown-up names of their older friends who are almost young women, in which you can already hear a little bit of fate echoing, a little bit of disillusionment and death. Perhaps in a compartment of his mahogany desk you might find their faded letters and the loose leaves of their diaries, where birthdays are recorded, summer picnics, birthdays. Or it may be that in the potbellied dresser at the back of his bedroom there is a drawer in which their spring dresses are kept—white dresses worn at Easter for the first time, dresses of dotted tulle, which really belong to the summer they couldn't wait for. What a happy fate, to sit in the quiet room of an ancestral house, among calm, sedentary Things, and to hear the wrens trying out their first notes in the airy, bright-green garden, and far away the chimes of the village clock. To sit and look at a warm streak of afternoon sun, and to know a lot about young girls who have passed away, and to be a poet. And to think that I too would have been a poet like this if I could have lived somewhere, anywhere in the world, in one of the many closed-up country houses that no one cares about. I would have used just one room (the bright room in the attic), and I would have lived there with my old Things, the family portraits, the books. I would have had an armchair and flowers and dogs and a strong walking-stick for the stony paths. And nothing else. Just a book bound in yellowish, ivory-colored leather with an old flowered design on the endpaper: on its pages, I would have written. I would have written a lot, for I would have had many thoughts, and memories of many people.

But life has turned out differently, God knows why. My old furniture is rotting in the barn where I left it, and I myself, yes, my God, I have no roof over me, and it is raining into my eyes.

— ••• —

Sometimes I pass little shops—in the rue de Seine, for example. Dealers in second-hand furniture, small used-book sellers, specialists in engravings, with over-crowded windows. No one ever walks through their doors; they apparently don't do any business at all. But if you look in, you can see them sitting there, sitting and reading, without a care in the world; they don't think about the future, don't worry about success, have a dog that sits in front of them, wagging its tail, or a cat that makes the silence even greater by gliding along the rows of books, as if it were trying to rub the names off their bindings.

Ah, if only that were enough: I sometimes wish I could buy myself a crowded shop-window like that and sit down behind it, with a dog, for twenty years.

— ••• —

It is good to say it out loud: "Nothing has happened." Once again: "Nothing has happened." Does that help?

That my stove began to smoke again and I had to go out isn't really so terrible. That I feel tired and cold is unimportant. That I have been wandering in the streets all day is my own fault. I could just as well have sat in the Louvre. Though actually, I couldn't have done that. There are certain people who go there to warm themselves. They sit on the velvet benches, and their feet stand side by side, like large empty boots, on the hot-air grates. They are extremely modest people, and they are thankful that the guards in the dark-blue uniforms studded with medals let them stay there. But when I enter, they grin. Grin and nod slightly. And then, when I walk back and forth in front of the pictures, they watch me, they keep watching me, with their cloudy, multiple gaze. So it was just as well that I didn't go to the Louvre. I have been walking and walking. Heaven knows how many towns, districts, cemeteries, bridges, and entryways I passed. Somewhere or other I saw a man who was pushing a vegetable cart. He was shouting: "Chou-fleur, chou-fleur," pronouncing the *fleur* with a strangely flat *eu*. An ugly, angular woman walked beside him, nudging him from time to time; and when she nudged him, he shouted. Sometimes he also shouted on his own, but then it was wasted, and he immediately had to shout again, because they were in front of a customer's house. Have I already said that he was blind? No? Well, he was blind. He was blind and he shouted. I am not telling the truth when I say that; I haven't included the cart he was pushing; I am pretending I didn't notice that he was crying out "cauliflowers." But is that essential? And even if it were, isn't the main thing to say what it all meant for me? I saw an old man who was blind and shouted. That is what I saw. Saw.

Will people believe that there are houses like this? No, they'll say I am not telling the truth. But this time it *is* the truth; nothing has been left out, and of course nothing has been added. Where would I get it from? People know that I'm poor. People know that. Houses? But, to be exact, they were houses which no longer existed. Houses which had been demolished from top to bottom. It was the other houses that were there, the ones that had stood along-side them, tall neighboring houses. Apparently they were in danger of collapsing, since all support had been removed; a whole scaffolding of long, tarred poles had been rammed diagonally between the rubble-strewn ground and the bared wall. I don't know if I have already said that this is the wall I am talking about. It was, so to speak, not the first wall of the existing houses (as you would have supposed), but the last of the ones that were no longer there. You could see its inside. You could see, at its various stories, bedroom walls with wallpaper still sticking to them; and here and there a piece of floor or ceiling. Near these bedroom walls there remained, along the entire length of the outer wall, a dirty-white space through which, in unspeakably nauseating, worm-soft, digestive movements, the open, rust-spotted channel of the toilet pipe crawled. The gaslight jets had left dusty gray traces at the edges of the ceiling; they bent here and there, abruptly, ran along the walls, and plunged into the black, gaping holes that had been torn there. But the most unforgettable things were the walls themselves. The stubborn life of these rooms had not let itself be trampled out. It was still there; it clung to the nails that were left, stood on the narrow remnant of flooring, crouched under the corner beams where a bit of interior still remained. You could see it in the paint which it had changed, slowly, from year to year: blue into moldy green, green into gray, yellow into a faded, rotting white. But it was also in the places that had been kept fresher behind mirrors, paintings, and wardrobes; for it had traced their outlines over and over, and had been with cobwebs and dust even in these hidden places, which were now laid bare. It was in every flayed strip of surface; it was in the damp blisters on the lower edges of the wallpaper; it fluttered in the torn-off shreds, and oozed from the foul stains which had appeared long before. And from these walls, once blue, green, and yellow, and now framed by the broken tracks of the demolished partitions, the air of these lives issued, the stubborn, sluggish, musty air which no wind had yet scattered. There the noons lingered, and the illnesses, and the exhalations, and the smoke of many years, and the sweat that trickles down from armpits and makes clothing heavy, and the stale breath of mouths, and the oily smell of sweltering feet. There the pungent odor of urine lingered, and the odor of soot, the gray odor of potatoes, and the heavy, sickening stench of rancid grease. The sweet smell of neglected infants lingered there, the smell of frightened schoolchildren, and the stuffiness from the beds of pubescent boys. And all the vapors that had risen from the street below, or fallen down from above with the filthy urban rain. And many things brought there by the weak house-winds, which always stay in the same street; and much more whose origin would never be known. I said, didn't I, that all the outer walls had been demolished except the last one—? It is this wall that I have been talking about all along. You would think

I had stood looking at it for a long time; but I swear I began to run as soon as I recognized this wall. For that's what is horrible—that I did recognize it. I recognize everything here, and that's why it passes right into me: it is at home inside me.

After all this, I was rather tired—I would even say, exhausted—and so it was really too much that *he* had to be waiting for me. He was waiting in the little crémerie where I meant to have two poached eggs. I was hungry. I had gone the whole day without eating. But even now I couldn't wait there for the eggs; before they were ready, something drove me out again into the streets, which rushed toward me in a viscous flood of humanity. It was carnival-time, and evening, and the people, with time on their hands, were roaming through the streets, rubbing against one another. Their faces were full of the light that came from the carnival booths, and laughter oozed from their mouths like pus from an open wound. The more impatiently I tried to push my way forward, the more they laughed and crowded together. Somehow a woman's shawl caught onto me; I dragged her along, and people stopped me and laughed; I felt I should have laughed too, but I couldn't. Someone tossed a handful of confetti into my eyes, and it stung like a whip. On the street-corners, people were wedged in, flattened together, with no way to move forward, just a gentle back-and-forth motion, as if they were copulating. But though they stood there and I ran like a madman along the edge of the pavement where there were gaps in the crowd, it was actually they who were moving, while I stood still. For nothing changed; when I looked up, I saw the same houses on one side, and on the other, the booths. Perhaps everything was stationary, and it was just a dizziness in me and in them that seemed to make everything whirl. I didn't have time to think about that; I was heavy with sweat, and a stupefying pain was circulating inside me, as if something too large were rushing through my blood, distending the veins wherever it passed. And I also felt that the air had long since been exhausted and that I was breathing only stale exhalations, which my lungs refused.

But now it's over. I have survived. I am sitting in my room, near the lamp. The room is a bit cold, but I don't dare try the stove. What if it smoked and I had to go out again? I am sitting and thinking: if I weren't poor, I would rent another room, a room with furniture that isn't so worn out and full of former tenants as this furniture is. At first I found it really difficult to lean my head on the back of this armchair; for there is a certain greasy-gray hollow in its green slipcover, which all heads seem to fit into. For a long time I took the precaution of putting a handkerchief under my hair, but now I am too tired to do that; I have discovered that it's all right the way it is and that the small hollow fits the back of my head perfectly, as if it had been custom-made.

But if I weren't poor, I would first of all buy myself a good stove, and burn good sturdy logs from the mountains, not these miserable little lumps of cheap coal, whose fumes make your head so dizzy and your breathing so forced. And then I would need someone who could come and clean up without making noise, and keep the fire the way I like it. For often when I have to kneel in front of the stove and poke for a quarter of an hour, my eyes tearing and my forehead scorched by the close flames, I exhaust all the strength I have stored up for the day, and when afterward I appear among people, they have an easy time with me. Sometimes, when there is a large crowd, I would take a carriage and drive past; I would eat every day in a Duval . . . and wouldn't have to slink into crémeries . . . Would *he* have been sitting in a Duval? No. He wouldn't have been able to wait for me there. They don't permit dying people to enter. Was he actually dying? I am in my own room now; now I can calmly try to think about what happened. It's good not to leave anything in the realm of the uncertain. So: I walked in and at first I saw only that the table where I usually sit was occupied by someone else. I nodded in the direction of the little counter, ordered, and sat down at a nearby table. But then I felt him, though he didn't move. It was precisely this immobility of his that I felt, and I understood it in an instant. The bond between us was established, and I knew that he was numb with terror. I knew that terror had paralyzed him, terror at something that was taking place inside him. Perhaps one of his blood-vessels had burst; perhaps, just at this moment, some poison he had long been afraid of was trickling into a ventricle of his heart; perhaps a large abscess had risen in his brain like a sun, transforming the whole world for him. With an indescribable effort I forced myself to look at him, for I still hoped it was all my imagination. But finally I had to jump up from the table and rush out; for I hadn't been mistaken. He was sitting there in a thick black winter coat, and his gray, tense face was buried in a woolen scarf. His mouth was tight, as if it had fallen shut with great force, but it was impossible to tell whether his eyes could still see: they were hidden by smoke-gray glasses, which trembled slightly. His nostrils were chapped, and the long hair over his devastated temples looked wilted, as if from too intense a heat. His ears were long and yellow, with large shadows behind them. Yes, he knew that he was now withdrawing from everything in the world, not merely from human beings. One more moment, and everything would lose its meaning, and this table and the cup and the chair he was clinging to would become unintelligible, alien and heavy. So he sat there, waiting for it to happen. And no longer bothered to defend himself.

And I am still defending myself. I am defending myself though I know that my heart has been torn out and that even if my torturers left me alone I couldn't live. I tell myself: "Nothing has happened," and yet I was able to understand this man just because inside me too something is taking place that is beginning to withdraw and separate me from everything. I have always shuddered to hear that a dying person could no longer recognize anyone. I would imagine a solitary face that lifted itself up from the pillow and looked, looked for something familiar, looked for something seen before; but there was nothing there. If my fear weren't so great, I would find some consolation in the thought that it's not impossible to see everything differently and still remain alive. But I am frightened, I am unspeakably frightened of this change. I have not yet grown accustomed to this world, which seems good to me. What would I do in another? I would so much like to remain among the meanings that have become dear to me, and if something has to change, I would at least want to live among dogs, who have a world that is related to our own, with the same Things in it.

For the time being, I can still write all this down, can still say it. But the day will come when my hand will be distant, and if I tell it to write, it will write words that are not mine. The time of that other interpretation will dawn, when there shall not be left one word upon another, and every meaning will dissolve like a cloud and fall down like rain. In spite of my fear, I am still like someone standing in the presence of something great, and I remember that I often used to feel this happening inside me when I was about to write. But this time, I will be written. I am the impression that will transform itself. It would take so little for me to understand all this and assent to it. Just one step, and my misery would turn into bliss. But I can't take that step; I have fallen and I can't pick myself up. Until now I have always believed that help would come. There they are, in my own handwriting: the words that have been my prayer, evening after evening. I copied them from the books I found them in, so that they would be right in front of me, issued from my hand as if they were my own words. And now I want to write them again, kneeling here before my table I want to write them; for in this way I can have them with me longer than when I read them, and every word will last and have time to echo and fade away.

"Mécontent de tous et mécontent de moi, je voudrais bien me racheter et m'enorgueillir un peu dans le silence et la solitude de la nuit. Âmes de ceux que j'ai aimés, âmes de ceux que j'ai chantés, fortifiez-moi, soutenez-moi, éloignez de moi le mensonge et les vapeurs corruptrices du monde; et vous, Seigneur mon Dieu! accordez-moi la grâce de produire quelques beaux vers qui me prouvent à moi-même que je ne suis pas le dernier des hommes, que je ne suis pas inférieur à ceux que je méprise."

— ••• —

"The children of despised men, who were the vilest in the land. And now I am their song, and I have become their legend.

. . . they have built a road over me . . .

. . . it was easy for them to injure me; they needed no help.

. . . but now my soul is poured out upon me, and the days of affliction have seized me.

My bones are pierced in the night, and my tormentors do not sleep.

Through their power my clothes have been changed, and I am bound as if by the collar of my coat . . .

My intestines boil without ceasing; the days of affliction have caught me . . .

And my harp is tuned to lament now, my flute to the sound of tears."

— ••• —

The doctor didn't understand me. At all. And certainly my case was difficult to describe. They wanted to try electrotherapy. Good. I was given a slip of paper: at one o'clock I was supposed to be at the Salpêtrière. I appeared. I had to walk past a long row of barracks and through several courtyards, where people in white hats that made them look like convicts were standing here and there under the bare trees. Finally I entered a long, dark, corridor-like room, which had four windows on one side, made of a dull, greenish glass and separated from one another by an expanse of black wall. There was a wooden bench in front, along the whole length of the wall, and on this bench they were sitting and waiting. Yes, they were all there, and they knew me. When I had gotten used to the dim lighting, I noticed that among these people sitting shoulder to shoulder on an endless line, there were also a few others, insignificant people, artisans, housemaids, teamsters. Down at the narrow end of the corridor, two fat women had spread themselves out on special chairs and were talking—concierges, probably. I looked at the clock; it was five minutes to one. In five or, say, ten minutes, my turn would come; so it wasn't so bad. The air was foul, heavy, filled with clothing and breath. At a certain spot the strong, heightening coolness of ether blew in through a crack in a door. I began to pace back and forth. It occurred to me that I had been directed *here*, among these people, to this overcrowded, public waiting-room. It was, so to speak, the first official confirmation that I belonged to the category of outcast. Had the doctor known by my appearance? Yet I had gone to his office in a fairly decent suit; I had even sent in my card. In spite of that, he must have somehow discovered it; perhaps I had given myself away. However, now that it was a fact, I didn't find it so terrible after all. The people were sitting still and paid no attention to me. Some of them were in pain, and moved one leg a bit, to endure it more easily. Several men had leaned their heads against their palms; others were fast asleep, with heavy, fatigue-crushed faces. A fat man with a red, swollen neck sat bent over, staring at the floor. From time to time he spat loudly at a point that he seemed to find suitable for this purpose. A child was sobbing in a corner; it had pulled its long skinny legs in, onto the bench, and was now holding them tightly to its body in an embrace, as if it would soon have to take leave of them forever. A small, pale woman, who was wearing a crêpe hat, slightly askew, adorned with round black flowers, had the grimace of a smile about her gaunt lips, but her eyelids were constantly overflowing. Not far from her they had put a girl with a round, smooth face and bulging eyes that were totally expressionless; her mouth hung open, so that you could see the white, slimy gums with their stunted teeth. And there were many bandages. Bandages wrapped around a whole head, layer by layer, until just a single eye remained that no longer belonged to anyone. Bandages that hid, and bandages that revealed, what was under them. Bandages that had been opened and in which, as if in a filthy bed, a hand lay now, that was no longer a hand; and a bandaged leg that stuck out of the line on the bench, as large as a whole man. I walked back and forth, trying hard to remain calm. I spent a good deal of time observing the wall opposite me. I noticed that it contained a number of single doors and that it didn't reach the ceiling, so that this corridor was not entirely separated from the rooms adjoining it. I looked at the clock: I had been pacing back and forth for an hour. A few moments later, the doctor came. First a couple of young men, who walked past with indifferent faces; then the one I had been to see, in light-colored gloves, chapeau à huit reflets, impeccable topcoat. When he saw me, he tipped his hat and smiled inattentively. I was hoping I would be called in right away, but another hour passed. I can't remember how I spent it. It passed. An old man in a soiled apron came in—an attendant, apparently— and tapped me on the shoulder. I went into one of the side rooms. The doctor and the young men were seated at a table and looked at me. Someone gave me a chair. Good. And now I was supposed to describe what was the matter with me. As briefly as possible, s'il vous plaît. For the gentlemen did not have much time. I felt very uncomfortable. The young men sat and looked at me with the condescending, professional curiosity that they had learned. The doctor I knew stroked his black goatee and smiled inattentively. I thought I would burst into tears, but I heard myself say in French: "I have already had the honor, monsieur, of giving you all the information I can give. If you think it is necessary for these gentlemen to be initiated, you are certainly able, from our conversation, to do that in a few words, while I would find it very difficult." The doctor stood up, with a polite smile, walked to the window, followed by his assistants, and said several words, which he accompanied with a vague, horizontal movement of his hand. Three minutes later, one of the young men, near-sighted and perfunctory, came back to the table and said, trying to look at me severely: "Do you sleep well, monsieur?" "No, badly." At this, he hurried back to the group at the window. They deliberated for a few more moments, then the doctor turned to me and informed me that I would be called in again. I reminded him that my appointment had been for one o'clock. He smiled and made a few quick, jerky motions with his small white hands, which were meant to indicate that he was extremely busy. So I returned to my corridor, where the air had become much more oppressive, and began to pace back and forth again, though I felt dead-tired. After a while, the stale, musty odor set my head spinning; I stopped at the entrance door and opened it slightly. I saw that it was still afternoon outside, and rather sunny, and this made me feel much better. But I had been standing there for barely a minute when I heard someone calling me. A female, who was sitting at a small table two or three steps away, hissed something at me. Who had told me to open the door? I said that I couldn't stand the air. Well, that was my own business, but the door had to be kept shut. Wouldn't it be possible, then, to open a window? No, that was forbidden. I decided to start pacing again, because it had a calming, anesthetic effect and wouldn't bother anyone. But now this too displeased the woman at the small table. Didn't I have a seat? No, I didn't. Walking around was not permitted; I would have to find myself a seat; there ought to be one. The woman was right. In fact, there was now a seat next to the girl with the bulging eyes. I sat there feeling that something terrible was about to happen. On my left was the girl with the rotting gums; what was on my right I couldn't recognize for a few moments. It was a huge, immovable mass, which had a face and a large, heavy, inert hand. The side of the face that I saw, was empty, without features and without memories; and it was eerie to notice that the clothes were like the clothes a corpse laid out in a coffin might be wearing. The narrow black necktie was fastened around the collar in the same loose, impersonal way, and it was obvious that the jacket had been placed over this will-less body by someone else. The hand had been positioned on the pants exactly where it was lying now, and even the hair looked as if it had been combed by undertakers; it was stiffly arranged, and bristled like the hair of a stuffed animal. I observed all this very carefully, and it occurred to me that this must be the seat I had been destined for: I had finally arrived at the place in my life where I would remain forever. Truly, the paths of fate are wondrous and beyond understanding.

Suddenly, right near me, I heard the screams of a terrified, struggling child, one scream after another, and then a low, suppressed sobbing. While I strained to find out where this sound was coming from, there was again a little scream, and I could hear voices questioning, a voice whispering orders, and then some kind of machine started, and hummed on indifferently. I remembered that half-wall, and realized that all these sounds were coming from the other side of the doors and that the doctors were working there now. From time to time the attendant with the soiled apron appeared and signaled to someone. I had given up thinking that this could be directed at me. Was it? No. Two men came in with a wheelchair; they lifted the mass onto it, and I now saw that it was an old paralytic, who had another, smaller side to him, worn out by life, and an open, dim, sorrowful eye. They took him inside, and now there was a large space next to me. And I sat and wondered what they would do to that idiot girl and whether she too would scream. Behind the wall, the machines made a pleasant, mechanical hum; there was nothing upsetting about it.

But suddenly everything was quiet, and a vain, condescending voice, which I thought I knew, said:

"Riez!" A pause. "Riez. Mais riez, riez." I was already laughing. It was incomprehensible why the man in there didn't want to laugh. A machine rattled, and immediately stopped; words were exchanged; then the same energetic voice ordered: "Dites-nous le mot *avant*." Spelling it: "A-v-a-n-t" . . . Silence. "On n'entend rien. Encore une fois: . . ."

And then, as I listened to the warm, flaccid babbling on the other side of the door: then, for the first time in many, many years, it was there again. What had filled me with my first, deep horror, when I was a child and lay in bed with a fever: the Big Thing. That's what I had always called it, when they all stood around my bed and felt my pulse and asked me what had frightened me: the Big Thing. And when they sent for the doctor and he came and tried to comfort me, I would just beg him to make the Big Thing go away, nothing else mattered. But he was like all the others. He couldn't take it away, though I was so small then and it would have been so easy to help me. And now it was there again. Later, it had simply stayed away; it hadn't come back even during the nights of fever; but now it was there, though I wasn't at all feverish. Now it was there. Now it was growing out of me like a tumor, like a second head, and was a part of me, although it certainly couldn't belong to me, because it was so big. It was there like a large dead animal which, while it was alive, used to be my hand or my arm. And my blood flowed through me and through it, as through one and the same body. And my heart had to beat harder to pump the blood into the Big Thing: there was barely enough blood. And the blood entered the Big Thing unwillingly and came back sick and tainted. But the Big Thing swelled and grew over my face like a warm bluish boil, and grew over my mouth, and already my last eye was hidden by its shadow.

I can't remember how I got out through the many courtyards. It was evening, and I lost my way in the unknown neighborhood, and walked up boulevards with endless walls in one direction and, when there was no end to them, walked back in the opposite direction until I reached some square or other. Then I began to walk down one street, and other streets came that I had never seen before, and still others. Electric trolleys, too brightly lit, raced up and past, their harsh bells clanging into the distance. But on their signboards were names I couldn't recognize. I didn't know what city I was in, or whether I had a room somewhere, or what I had to do so that I could stop walking.

— ••• —

And now this illness again, which has always affected me so strangely. I'm sure it is underestimated. Just as the importance of other illnesses is exaggerated. This illness doesn't have any particular characteristics; it takes on the characteristics of the people it attacks.

With the confidence of a sleepwalker, it pulls out their deepest danger, which seemed passed, and places it before them again, very near, imminent. Men who once, in their schooldays, tried the helpless vice that has as its duped partner the poor, hard hands of boys, find themselves doing it again; or an illness they had overcome when they were children begins again inside them; or a lost habit reappears, a certain hesitating turn of the head that was characteristic of them years before. And with what comes, a whole tangle of confused memories arises, hanging from it like wet seaweed on a sunken boat. Lives that you would never have known about bob to the surface and mingle with what really happened, and drive out a past that you thought you knew: for in what rises there is a new, rested strength, while what was always there is tired out from too much remembrance.

I am lying in my bed five flights up, and my day, which nothing interrupts, is like a clock-face without hands. As something that has been lost for a long time reappears one morning in its old place, safe and sound, almost newer than when it vanished, just as if some-one had been taking care of it—: so, here and there on my blanket, lost feelings out of my childhood lie and are like new. All the lost fears are here again.

The fear that a small woolen thread sticking out of the hem of my blanket may be hard, hard and sharp as a steel needle; the fear that this little button on my night-shirt may be bigger than my head, bigger and heavier; the fear that the breadcrumb which just dropped off my bed may turn into glass, and shatter when it hits the floor, and the sickening worry that when it does, everything will be broken, forever; the fear that the ragged edge of a letter which was torn open may be something forbidden, which no one ought to see, something indescribably precious, for which no place in the room is safe enough; the fear that if I fell asleep I might swallow the piece of coal lying in front of the stove; the fear that some number may begin to grow in my brain until there is no more room for it inside me; the fear that I may be lying on granite, on gray granite; the fear that I may start screaming, and people will come running to my door and finally force it open, the fear that I might betray myself and tell everything I dread, and the fear that I might not be able to say anything, because everything is unsayable,—and the other fears . . . the fears.

I prayed to rediscover my childhood, and it has come back, and I feel that it is just as difficult as it used to be, and that growing older has served no purpose at all.

— ❖ —

Yesterday my fever was better, and this morning the day began like spring, like spring in paintings. I want to go out to the Bibliothèque Nationale and spend some time with my poet, whom I haven't read for many weeks, and afterward perhaps I can take a leisurely walk through the gardens. Perhaps there will be a wind over the large pond which has such real water, and children will come to sail their little red boats.

Today I really didn't expect it; I went out so bravely, as if that were the simplest and most natural thing in the world. And yet something happened again that took me up and crumpled me like a piece of paper and threw me away: something incredible.

The Boulevard Saint-Michel lay in front of me, empty and vast, and it was easy to walk along its gentle slope. Window-casements overhead opened with a clear, glassy sound, and their brilliance flew over the street like a white bird. A carriage with bright red wheels rolled past, and farther down someone was carrying something green. Horses in their glittering harnesses trotted along the dark, freshly sprinkled boulevard. The wind was brisk and mild, and everything was rising: odors, cries, bells.

I came to one of those cafés where false red gypsies perform in the evening. From the open windows, the air of the previous night crept out with a bad conscience. Sleek-haired waiters were busy sweeping in front of the door. One of them was bent over, tossing handful after handful of yellowish sand under the tables. A passerby stopped, nudged him, and pointed down the street. The waiter, who was all red in the face, looked sharply in that direction for a moment or two; then a laugh spread over his beardless cheeks, as if it had been spilled across them. He gestured to the other waiters, turned his laughing face quickly from right to left several times, to call everyone over without missing anything himself. Now they all stood there, seeing or trying to see what was happening down the street, smiling or annoyed that they hadn't yet found out what was so funny.

I felt a slight fear beginning inside me. Something was urging me to cross the street; but all I did was start to walk faster; and when I looked at the few people in front of me, I didn't notice anything unusual. I did see that one of them, an errand-boy with a blue apron and an empty basket slung over one shoulder, was staring at someone. When he had seen enough, he turned around toward the houses and gestured to a laughing clerk across the street, moving his finger in front of his forehead with that circular motion whose meaning everyone knows. Then his dark eyes flashed and he came toward me, swaggering and content.

I expected that as soon as I had a better view I would see some extraordinary and striking figure; but it turned out that there was no one in front of me except a tall, emaciated man in a dark coat, with a soft black hat on his short, faded-blond hair. I was sure there was nothing laughable about this man's clothing or behavior, and was already trying to look past him down the boulevard, when he tripped over something. Since I was walking close behind him I was on my guard, but when I came to the place, there was nothing there, absolutely nothing. We both kept walking, he and I, with the same distance between us. Now there was an intersection; the man in front of me hopped down from the sidewalk on one leg, the way children, when they are happy, will now and then hop or skip as they walk. On the other side of the street, he simply took one long step up onto the sidewalk. But almost immediately he raised one leg slightly and hopped on the other, once, quite high, and then again and again. This time too you might easily have thought the man had tripped over some small object on the corner, a peach pit, a banana peel, anything; and the strange thing was that he himself seemed to believe in the presence of an obstacle: he turned around every time and looked at the offending spot with that half-annoyed, half-reproachful expression people have at such moments. Once again some intuition warned me to cross the street, but I didn't listen to it; I continued to follow this man, concentrating all my attention on his legs. I must admit I felt very relieved when for about twenty steps the hopping didn't recur; but as I looked up, I noticed that something else had begun to annoy the man. His coat collar had somehow popped up; and as hard as he tried to fold it back in place, first with one hand, then with both at once, it refused to budge. This kind of thing can happen. It didn't upset me. But then I saw, with boundless astonishment, that in his busy hands there were two distinct movements: one a quick, secret movement that flipped up the collar, while the other one, elaborate, prolonged, exaggeratedly spelled out, was meant to fold it back down. This observation disconcerted me so greatly that two minutes passed before I recognized in the man's neck, behind his hunched-up coat and his nervously scrambling hands, the same horrible, bisyllabic hopping that had just left his legs. From this moment I was bound to him. I saw that the hopping was wandering through his body, trying to break out here or there. I understood why he was afraid of people, and I myself began to examine the passersby, cautiously, to see if they noticed anything. A cold twinge shot down my spine when his legs suddenly made a small, convulsive leap; but no one had seen it, and I decided that I would also trip slightly if anyone began to look. That would certainly be a way of making them think there had been some small, imperceptible object on the sidewalk, which both of us had happened to step on. But while I was thinking about how I could help, he himself had found a new and excellent device. I forgot to mention that he had a cane; it was an ordinary cane, made of dark wood, with a plain, curved handle. In his anxious searching, he had hit upon the idea of holding this cane against his back, at first with one hand (who knows what he might still need the other hand for), right along his spine, pressing it firmly

into the small of his back and sliding the curved end
under his collar, in such a way that you felt it standing behind the cervical and first dorsal vertebrae like
a neck-brace. This posture didn't look strange; at
most it was a bit cocky, but the unexpected spring
day might excuse that. No one thought of turning
around to look, and now everything was all right.
Perfectly all right. True, at the next intersection two
hops escaped, two small, half-suppressed hops, but
they didn't amount to anything; and the one really
visible leap was so skillfully timed (just at the spot
where a hose was lying across the sidewalk) that
there was nothing to be afraid of. Yes, everything was
still all right; from time to time his other hand too
seized the cane and pressed it in more firmly, and
right away the danger was again overcome. But I
couldn't keep my anxiety from growing. I knew that
as he walked and with infinite effort tried to appear
calm and detached, the terrible spasms were accumulating inside his body; I could feel the anxiety *he* felt
as the spasms grew and grew, and I saw how he
clutched his cane when the shaking began inside
him. The expression of his hands became so severe
and relentless then that I placed all my hope in his
willpower, which was bound to be strong. But what
could mere willpower do? The moment had to come
when his strength would be exhausted; it couldn't be
long now. And I, who followed him with my heart
pounding, I gathered my little strength together like

money and, gazing at his hands, I begged him to take it if it could be of any use.

I think he took it; is it my fault that it wasn't enough?

At the Place Saint-Michel there were many vehicles, and pedestrians hurrying here and there; several times we were caught between two carriages, and then he would take a breath and relax a bit, and there would be a bit of hopping and nodding. Perhaps that was the trick by which the imprisoned illness hoped to subdue him. His willpower had cracked in two places, and the damage had left in his possessed muscles a gentle, alluring stimulation and this compelling two-beat rhythm. But the cane was still in its place, and the hands looked annoyed and angry. As we stepped onto the bridge, it was all right. It was still all right. But now his walk became noticeably uncertain; first he ran two steps, then he stopped. Stopped. His left hand gently let go of the cane, and rose so slowly that I could see it tremble in the air. He pushed his hat back slightly and drew his hand across his brow. He turned his head slightly, and his gaze wobbled over sky, houses, and water, without grasping a thing. And then he gave in. The cane was gone, he stretched out his arms as if he were trying to fly, and some kind of elemental force exploded from him and bent him forward and dragged him back and made him keep nodding and bowing and flung a horrible dance out of him into the midst of the crowd. For he was already surrounded by people, and I could no longer see him.

What sense would there have been in going anywhere now; I was empty. Like a blank piece of paper, I drifted along past the houses, up the boulevard again.

— ••• —

* I am attempting to write to you, although there is really nothing to say after a necessary parting. I am attempting it nevertheless; I think I must, because I have seen the saint in the Panthéon, the solitary, holy woman and the roof and the door and the lamp inside with its modest circle of light and, beyond, the sleeping city and the river and the far-away, moonlit landscape. The saint watches over the sleeping city. I cried. Because as I looked, it was all so immediately and unexpectedly there; I couldn't help crying.

I am in Paris. People who hear this are glad; most of them envy me. They're right. It is a great city, great and filled with strange temptations. For myself, I must admit that I have, in a certain sense, succumbed to them. I don't think there is any other way to express it. I have succumbed to these temptations, and this has brought about certain changes, if not in

* A draft of a letter.

71

my character, at least in my point of view and, in any case, in my life. An entirely different conception of all things has developed in me under these influences; I have had certain experiences that separate me from other people, more than anything I have ever felt in the past. A different world. A new world filled with new meanings. For the moment I am finding it a bit difficult, because everything is too new. I am a beginner in my own life.

Wouldn't it be possible for once to get a glimpse of the sea?

Yes, but just think, I was imagining that you'd be able to come. Could you perhaps have told me if there was a doctor? I forgot to find out about that. Anyway, I no longer need to know.

Do you remember Baudelaire's incredible poem "Une Charogne"? Perhaps I understand it now. Except for the last stanza, he was in the right. What should he have done after that happened to him? It was his task to see, in this terrifying and apparently repulsive object, the Being that underlies all individual beings. There is no choice, no refusal. Do you think it was by chance that Flaubert wrote his "Saint Julien l'Hospitalier"? This, it seems to me, is the test: whether you can bring yourself to lie beside a leper and warm him with the warmth of your own heart—such an action could only have good results.

But don't think I am suffering from disenchant-

ment here—on the contrary. I am sometimes astonished by how readily I have given up everything I
expected, in exchange for what is real, even when
that is awful.

My God, if only something of this could be shared.
But would it *be* then; would it *be*? No, it *is* only at
the price of solitude.

— ••• —

The existence of the horrible in every atom of air.
You breathe it in as something transparent; but inside
you it condenses, hardens, takes on pointed, geo-
metric shapes between your organs; for all the tor-
ments and agonies suffered on scaffolds, in torture-
chambers, madhouses, operating rooms, under bridges
in late autumn: all this has a stubborn permanence,
all this endures in itself and, jealous of everything
that is, clings to its own dreadful reality. People
would like to forget much of it; sleep gently files
down these grooves in the brain, but dreams drive it
away and trace the designs again. And they wake up
gasping and let the gleam of a candle dissolve in the
darkness and drink the half-bright solace as if it were
sugared water. But alas, what a narrow ledge this
security is standing on. The slightest movement, and
once again vision plunges beyond what is known
and friendly, and the outline that was so comforting
just a moment ago comes into focus as the edge of

terror. Beware of the light that makes space more hollow; don't turn around to see whether, behind you as you sat up, a shadow has arisen as your master. It would have been better, perhaps, if you had stayed in the darkness, and your heart, without any limits, had tried to be the heavy heart of everything indistinguishable. Now you have pulled yourself together; you see yourself end in your own hands; from time to time, with an imprecise movement, you re-draw the outline of your face. And inside you there is hardly any room; and it almost calms you to think that nothing very large can enter this narrowness; that even the tremendous must become an inner thing and shrink to fit its surroundings. But outside—outside there is no limit to it; and when it rises out there, it fills up inside you as well, not in the vessels that are partly in your control or in the phlegm of your most impassive organs: it rises in your capillaries, sucked up into the outermost branches of your infinitely ramified being. There it mounts, there it overflows you, rising higher than your breath, where you have fled as if to your last refuge. And where will you go from there? Your heart drives you out of yourself, your heart pursues you, and you are already almost outside yourself and can't get back in. Like a beetle that someone has stepped on, you gush out of yourself, and your little bit of surface hardness and adaptability have lost all meaning.

O night without objects. Dim outward-facing window; doors that were carefully shut; arrangements from long ago, transmitted, believed in, never quite understood. Silence on the staircase, silence from adjoining rooms, silence high up on the ceiling. O mother: you who are without an equal, who stood before all this silence, long ago in childhood. Who took it upon yourself to say: Don't be afraid; I'm here. Who in the night had the courage to *be* this silence for the child who was frightened, who was dying of fear. You strike a match, and already the noise is you. And you hold the lamp in front of you and say: I'm here; don't be afraid. And you put it down, slowly, and there is no doubt: you are there, you are the light around the familiar, intimate Things, which are there without afterthought, good and simple and sure. And when something moves restlessly in the wall, or creaks on the floor: you just smile, smile transparently against a bright background into the terrified face that looks at you, searching, as if you knew the secret of every half-sound, and everything were agreed and understood between you. Does any power equal your power among the lords of the earth? Look: kings lie and stare, and the teller of tales cannot distract them. Though they lie in the blissful arms of their favorite mistress, horror creeps over them and makes them palsied and impotent. But you come and keep the monstrosity behind you and are entirely in front of it; not like a curtain it can lift up here or there. No: as if you had caught up with it as soon as the child cried out for you. As if you had arrived far ahead of anything that might still happen, and had behind you only your hurrying-in, your eternal path, the flight of your love.

— ••• —

The mouleur, whose shop I pass every day, has hung two plaster masks beside his door. The face of the young drowned woman, which they took a cast of in the morgue, because it was beautiful, because it smiled, because it smiled so deceptively, as if it knew. And beneath it, *his* face, which knows. That hard knot of senses drawn tightly together. That inexorable self-condensing of a music continually trying to evaporate. The countenance of a man whose hearing a god had closed up, so that there might be no sounds but his own; so that he might not be led astray by what is turbid and ephemeral in noises—he who knew in himself their clarity and permanence. So that only the soundless senses might carry the world in to him, silently, a world in suspense, waiting, unfinished, before the creation of sound.

World-consummator: as that which comes down as rain over the earth and upon the waters, falling carelessly, at random,—inevitably rises again, invisible and joyous, out of all things, and ascends and floats and forms the heavens: so our precipitations rose out of you, and vaulted the world with music.

Your music: it could have encircled the whole universe; not merely us. A grand-piano could have been built for you in the Theban desert, and an angel would have led you to that solitary instrument, through mountain-ranges in the wilderness, where kings are buried and courtesans and anchorites. And he would have flung himself up and away, for fear that you would begin.

And then you would have streamed forth, unheard, giving back to the universe what only the universe can endure. Bedouins in the distance would have galloped by, superstitiously; but merchants would have flung themselves to the ground at the edges of your music, as if you were a storm. Only a few solitary lions would have prowled around you at night, in wide circles, afraid of themselves, menaced by their own excited blood.

For who will now take you out of ears that are lascivious? Who will drive them from the concert halls, these corrupted ears whose sterile hearing fornicates and never conceives, as the semen spurts out onto them and they lie beneath it like whores, playing with it; or it falls onto the ground like Onan's, while they writhe in their abortive pleasures.

But, Master, if some pure spirit with a virgin ear were to lie down beside your music: he would die of bliss; or he would become pregnant with infinity, and his fertilized brain would explode with so much birth.

— ••• —

I don't underestimate it. I know it takes courage. But let us suppose for a moment that someone had it, this *courage de luxe* to follow them, in order to know forever (for who could forget it again or confuse it with anything else?) where they creep off to afterward and what they do with the rest of the long day and whether they sleep at night. That especially should be ascertained: whether they sleep. But it will take more than courage. For they don't come and go like other people, whom it would be child's play to follow. They are here and then gone, put down and snatched away like toy soldiers. The places where they can be found are somewhat out-of-the-way, but by no means hidden. The bushes recede, the path curves slightly around the lawn: there they are, with a large transparent space around them, as if they were standing under a glass dome. You might think they were pausing, absorbed in their thoughts, these inconspicuous men, with such small, in every way unassuming bodies. But you are wrong. Do you see the left hand, how it is grasping for something in the slanted pocket of the old coat? how it finds it and takes it out and holds the small object in the air, awkwardly, attracting attention? In less than a minute, two or three birds appear, sparrows, which come hopping up inquisitively. And if the man succeeds in conforming to their very exact idea of immobility, there is no reason why they shouldn't come even closer. Finally one of them flies up, and flutters nervously for a while at the level of that hand, which is holding out God knows what crumbs of used-up bread in its unpretentious, explicitly renunciatory fingers. And the more people gather around him—at a suitable distance, of course—the less he has in common with them. He stands there like a candle that is almost consumed and burns with the small remnant of its wick and is all warm with it and has never moved. And all those small, foolish birds can't understand how he attracts, how he tempts them. If there were no onlookers and he were allowed to stand there long enough, I'm certain that an angel would suddenly appear and, overcoming his disgust, would eat the stale, sweetish breadcrumbs from that stunted hand. But now, as always, people keep that from happening. They make sure that only birds come; they find this quite sufficient and assert that he expects nothing else. What else could it expect, this old, weather-beaten doll, stuck into the ground at a slight angle, like a painted figurehead in an old sea-captain's garden? Does it stand like that because it too had once been placed somewhere on the forward tip of its life, at the point where motion is greatest?

7 9

Is it now so washed out because it was once so bright? Will you go ask it?

Only don't ask the women anything when you see them feeding the birds. You could even follow them; they do it just in passing; it would be easy. But leave them alone. They don't know how it happens. All at once they have a whole purseful of bread, and they hold out large pieces from under their flimsy shawls, pieces that are a bit chewed and soggy. It does them good to think that their saliva is getting out into the world a little, that the small birds will fly off with the taste of it in their mouths, even though a moment later they naturally forget it again.

— ••• —

There I sat before your books, obstinate man, trying to understand them as the others do, who don't leave you in one piece but chip off their little portion and go away satisfied. For I still didn't understand fame, that public demolition of someone who is in the process of becoming, whose building-site the mob breaks into, knocking down his stones.

Young man anywhere, in whom something is welling up that makes you shiver, be grateful that no one knows you. And if those who think you are worthless contradict you, and if those whom you call your friends abandon you, and if they want to destroy you because of your precious ideas: what is this obvious danger, which concentrates you inside yourself, compared to the cunning enmity of fame, later, which makes you innocuous by scattering you all around?

Don't ask anyone to speak about you, not even contemptuously. And when time passes and you notice that your name is circulating among men, don't take this more seriously than anything else you might find in their mouths. Think rather that it has become cheapened, and throw it away. Take another name, *any* other, so that God can call you in the night. And hide it from everyone.

Loneliest of men, holding aloof from them all, how quickly they have caught up with you because of your fame. A little while ago they were against you body and soul; and now they treat you as their equal. And they pull your words around with them in the cages of their presumption, and exhibit them in the streets, and tease them a little, from a safe distance. All your terrifying wild beasts.

When I first read you, these words broke loose and fell upon me in my wilderness, in all their desperation. As desperate as you yourself became in the end, you whose course is drawn incorrectly on every chart. Like a crack it crosses the heavens, this hopeless hyperbola of your path, which curves toward us only once, then recedes again in terror. What did you care if a woman stayed or left, if this man was seized by vertigo and that one by madness, if the dead were alive and the living seemed dead: what did you care? It was all so natural for you; you passed through it the way someone might walk through a vestibule, and didn't stop. But you lingered, bent over, where our life boils and precipitates and changes color: inside. Farther in than anyone has ever been; a door had sprung open before you, and now you were among the alembics in the firelight. In there, where, mistrustful, you wouldn't take anyone with you, in there you sat and discerned transitions. And there, since your blood drove you not to form or to speak, but to reveal, there you made the enormous decision to so magnify these tiny events, which you yourself first perceived only in test tubes, that they would be seen by thousands of people, immense before them all. Your theater came into being. You couldn't wait until this life almost without spatial reality, this life which had been condensed by the weight of the centuries into a few small drops, could be discovered by the other arts: until it could gradually be made visible to a few connoisseurs who, little by little, acquire insight and finally demand to see these august rumors confirmed in the parable of the scene opened in front of them. You couldn't wait for that; you were there, and everything that is barely measurable—an emotion that rises by half a degree, the angle of deflection, read off from up close, of a will burdened by an almost infinitesimal weight, the slight cloudiness in a drop of longing, and that barely perceptible color-change in an atom of confidence—all this you had to determine and record. For it is in such reactions that life existed, *our* life, which had slipped into us, had drawn back inside us so deeply that it was hardly possible even to make conjectures about it any more.

Because you were a revealer, a timelessly tragic poet, you had to transform this capillary action all at once into the most convincing gestures, into the most available forms. So you began that unprecedented act of violence in your work, which, more and more impatiently, desperately, sought equivalents in the visible world for what you had seen inside. There was a rabbit there, an attic, a room where someone was pacing back and forth; there was a clatter of glass in a nearby bedroom, a fire outside the windows; there was the sun. There was a church, and a rock-strewn valley that was like a church. But this wasn't enough: finally towers had to come in and whole mountainranges; and the avalanches that bury landscapes spilled onto a stage overwhelmed with what is tangible, for the sake of what cannot be grasped. Then you could do no more. The two ends, which you had bent together until they touched, sprang apart; your demented strength escaped from the flexible wand, and your work was as if it had never existed.

If this hadn't happened, who could understand why in the end you refused to go away from the window, obstinate as you always were? You wanted to see the people passing by; for the thought had occurred to you that someday you might make something out of them, if you decided to begin.

— ❖ —

Then, for the first time, I realized that nothing can be said about a woman; I noticed when they spoke about her, how much they left blank, how they named and described other people, surroundings, objects, up to a certain point where it all stopped, gently and as it were cautiously stopped at the light never-retraced outline that enclosed her. "What was she like?" I would ask then. "Blonde, more or less like you," they would say, and they would add all kinds of further details; but as they did, she would again grow quite indistinct, and I could no longer form her image in my mind. I was able to really *see* her only when Maman told me the story, which I asked for again and again—.

—And every time she came to the scene with the dog, she would close her eyes and, with a kind of fervor, would hold her face, hidden yet everywhere visible and shining, between her hands, the touch of her fingertips cold against her temples. "I saw it, Malte," she would declare: "I saw it." It was during the last years of her life that I heard her tell this story. She no longer wanted to see anyone, and always, even while traveling, had the little, fine silver strainer in her purse, through which she would filter everything she drank. She no longer ate solid food, except for some biscuits or bread which, when she was alone, she would break into little pieces and eat bit by bit, the way a child would. She was already dominated by her fear of needles. By way of apology, she would tell people: "I really can't digest anything any more, but don't let that upset you; I feel very well indeed." But to me, she would sometimes turn, suddenly, (for I was already a little bit grown up) and, with a smile that was a great effort for her, she would say: "What a lot of needles there are, Malte; they are lying around everywhere, and when you think how easily they could fall . . ." She meant to say this in a playful tone of voice; but horror shook her at the thought of all the poorly fastened needles, which could fall down anywhere, at any moment.

— ••• —

But when she was speaking about Ingeborg, nothing could harm her; she didn't spare herself; she spoke louder, she laughed as she remembered Ingeborg's laugh, and you could see how beautiful Ingeborg had been.

"She made us happy," she said, "your father too, Malte, literally happy. But afterward, when we were told she was going to die, though she seemed just slightly ill, and we all went around hiding the truth from her, she sat up in bed one day and said to herself, like someone who wants to hear how a thought sounds out loud: 'You mustn't make such a great effort; we all know it, and I can assure you that things are all right as they are; there is nothing more that I want.' Just imagine; she said: 'There is nothing more that I want'; she, who made us all happy. Will you understand that, someday when you are grown up, Malte? Think about it later on; perhaps you'll see what it means. It would be good if there were someone who understood such matters."

"Such matters" occupied Maman when she was alone, and she was always alone during those last years.

"I will never arrive at it, Malte," she would sometimes say with her strangely bold smile, which wasn't meant to be seen by anyone and fulfilled its whole purpose when it was smiled. "But to think that no one is tempted to understand! If I were a man—yes, certainly, if I were a man—I would meditate on it in the proper order and sequence, and right from the beginning. For there has to be a beginning, and if one could only grasp it, that would already be something. Ah Malte, we pass away like that, and it seems to me that people are all distracted and preoccupied and don't really pay attention when we pass away. As if a shooting star fell and no one saw it and no one made a wish. Never forget to make a wish, Malte. One should never give up wishing. I don't think there is such a thing as fulfillment, but there are wishes that endure, that last a whole lifetime, so that anyhow one couldn't wait for their fulfillment."

Maman had had Ingeborg's little secretary-desk brought up and put into her own room. I often found her in front of it, for I was allowed to go in whenever I wanted to. My steps completely disappeared in the carpet, but she felt my presence and held out one of her hands to me over the other shoulder. This hand was entirely weightless, and kissing it was almost like kissing the ivory crucifix that was held out to me before I went to sleep. At this low desk, with its drop-leaf open in front of her, she would sit as if at a harpsichord. "There is so much sunlight in it," she said, and indeed the interior was remarkably bright, with its old yellow lacquer, on which flowers were painted, always a red one with a blue one beside it. And where there were three together, a violet flower appeared in the middle, separating the other two. These colors, and the green of the narrow horizontal border of arabesques, were as dim as the background was luminous (though it wasn't really distinct). This resulted in a strangely muted harmony of tones, which stood in intimate relation to one another, without stating it explicitly.

Maman pulled out the little drawers, which were all empty.

"Ah, roses," she said, bending forward a little into the faint smell that had not quite disappeared. She always imagined that something might suddenly turn up in a secret compartment which no one had thought of and which wouldn't open until some hidden mechanism was pressed. "All at once it will pop open—you'll see," she said, her voice solemn and anxious, and she hurriedly pulled at all the drawers. But any papers that had in fact been left in the compartments, she had carefully folded and locked away, without reading them. "I wouldn't understand anyway, Malte; I'm sure it would be too hard for me." She was convinced that everything was too complicated for her. "There are no classes in life for beginners; right away you are always asked to deal with what is most difficult." People assured me that she had only been like this since the horrible accident that had happened to her sister, Countess Øllegaard Skeel, who had been burnt to death one evening before a ball, as she stood in front of a candle-lit mirror trying to rearrange the flowers in her hair. But more recently it was Ingeborg who seemed to her the most difficult of all to comprehend.

And now I will write down the story, just as Maman told it when I asked her to.

"It was in the middle of summer, on the Thursday after Ingeborg's funeral. From the place on the terrace where we were having tea, one could see through the giant elms to the roof of the family vault. The table had been set as if there had never been one more person sitting at it, and we had also spread ourselves out around it. And we had each brought something along, a book or a basket of needlework, so that we were even a little crowded. Abelone" (Maman's youngest sister) "was pouring the tea, and we were all busy passing the dishes around, except for your grandfather, who was looking from his armchair toward the house. It was the hour when the mail was expected, and it usually happened that Ingeborg brought it, since she had to stay in the house longer making the arrangements for dinner. During the weeks of her illness we had had ample time to get accustomed to her not coming; for we knew only too well that she couldn't come. But that afternoon, Malte, when truly she could no longer come—: she came. Perhaps it was our fault; perhaps we called her. For I remember that all at once I was sitting there trying to think what it was that was so different now. Suddenly it became impossible to say what it was; I had completely forgotten. I looked up and saw all the others turned toward the house, not in any special or conspicuous way, but very calmly, as if they were waiting for some simple, everyday occurrence. And I was about to (I feel quite cold, Malte, when I think of it), but, God help me, I was just about to say, 'Where is . . .'— when Cavalier shot out from under the table, as he always did, and ran to meet her. I saw it, Malte; I saw it. He ran toward her, although she wasn't coming; for him she *was* coming. We understood that he was running to meet her. Twice he looked around at us, as if he were asking a question. Then he rushed at her, as he always did, Malte, just as he always did, and he reached her; for he began to jump around and around, Malte, around something that wasn't there, and then he jumped up at her, he jumped up again and again to lick her. We heard him whimpering with joy, and from the way he was leaping into the air, several times in quick succession, you might really have thought it was his body that was hiding her from us. But suddenly there was a howl, and whirling around in midair from his own momentum, he pitched back with incredible clumsiness, and lay stretched out before us, strange and flat on the ground, not moving a muscle. From the other wing of the house a servant came out with the letters. He hesitated for a moment; apparently it wasn't very easy to walk toward our faces. Besides, your father had already motioned to him that he should stop. Your father, Malte, didn't like animals; but now, in spite of that, he went up, slowly, it seemed to me, and bent down over the dog. He said something to the servant, something brief, monosyllabic. I saw the servant jump forward to pick Cavalier up. But your father himself took the animal in his arms and carried it, as if he knew exactly where to take it, into the house."

— ••• —

On one occasion, when it had grown almost dark during her recitation, I was about to tell Maman the story of "the hand": at that moment I could have done it. I had taken a long breath before beginning; but then it occurred to me how well I had understood the servant's hesitation at approaching their faces. And, in spite of the growing darkness, I was afraid of what Maman's face would look like when it saw what I had seen. Quickly I took another breath, to make it look like that was all I had meant to do. A few years later, after the strange night in the gallery at Urnekloster, I went around for days intending to tell Erik my secret. But after our nocturnal conversation he had once more completely shut off from me; he avoided me; I think he even despised me. And just because of this I wanted to tell him about "the hand." I imagined I would win his respect (which for some reason I urgently desired) if I could make him understand that I had really had that experience. But Erik was so skillful in eluding me that I never had the chance. And then we left shortly afterward. So, strangely enough, this is the first time I am telling (and after all only for myself) about an event that now lies far back in my childhood.

How small I must have been at that time, I see from the fact that I was kneeling on the armchair so I could comfortably reach up to the table I was drawing on. It was a winter evening, in our apartment in town, if I'm not mistaken. The table stood in my room, between the windows, and there was no lamp in the room except for the one that shone on my pages and on Mademoiselle's book; for Mademoiselle was sitting beside me, her chair pushed back a little, reading. She was far away when she read, and I don't know whether she was in her book; she could read for hours, she seldom turned a page, and I had the impression that the pages kept growing fuller beneath her gaze, as if she looked words onto them, certain words that she needed and that weren't there. That's how it seemed to me as I went on drawing. I drew slowly, without any very definite intention, and when I got stuck, I would look at my drawing with my head bent a little to the right; in that position I could always figure out soonest what was missing. They were officers on horseback, who were riding into battle, or they were already in the midst of it—which was much easier, since then almost all you needed to draw was the smoke that covered everything. Maman, it's true, claimed that I only painted islands—islands with large trees and a castle and a staircase and flowers along the edge that were supposed to be reflected in the water. But I think she was making that up, or it must have been at a later time. /

It is certain that on that particular evening I was drawing a knight, a solitary, easily recognizable knight, on a strikingly caparisoned horse. He grew so brightly colored that I often had to change crayons; but the red one was most in demand, and I reached for it again and again. Once more I was going to use it, when it rolled (I can see it now) right across the lighted page to the edge of the table and, before I could stop it, fell past me and was gone. I needed it quite urgently, and felt very annoyed that I had to climb down after it. Awkward as I was, this involved all sorts of preparations; my legs seemed much too long, I couldn't pull them out from under me; the too-prolonged kneeling position had made my limbs numb; I didn't know what belonged to me and what was the chair's. At last I did get down, somewhat bewildered, and found myself on a fur rug that stretched under the table as far as the wall. But then a new difficulty arose. My eyes, accustomed to the brightness above and still quite dazzled by the colors on the white paper, could not perceive anything at all under the table, where the blackness seemed so dense that I was afraid I would knock against it. I was thus forced to rely on my sense of touch and, kneeling, propped up on my left hand, I combed around with my other hand through the cool, long-haired rug, which felt quite familiar; but there was no crayon. I imagined I must be losing a good deal of time and was about to call Mademoiselle and ask her to bring over the lamp for me, when I noticed that to my involuntarily adapted eyes the darkness was gradually growing more transparent. I could already distinguish the wall in back, which ended in a light-colored molding; I saw where I was in relation to the table legs; above all I recognized my own out-spread hand moving down there all alone, like some strange crab, exploring the ground. I watched it, I remember, almost with curiosity; it seemed to know things I had never taught it, as it groped down there so completely on its own, with movements I had never noticed in it before. I followed it as it crept forward; it interested me; I was ready for all kinds of adventures. But how could I have been prepared to see, all at once, out of the wall, another hand coming to meet it—a larger, extraordinarily thin hand, such as I had never seen before. It came groping in a similar fashion from the other side, and the two outspread hands blindly moved toward each other. My curiosity was not yet satisfied, but suddenly it was gone and there was only horror. I felt that one of the hands belonged to me and that it was about to enter into something it could never return from. With all the authority I had over it, I stopped it, held it flat, and slowly pulled it back to me, without taking my eyes off the other one, which kept on groping. I realized that it wouldn't stop, and I don't know how I got up again. I sank deep into the armchair, my teeth were chattering, and my face was so drained of blood that I felt there couldn't be any more blue in my eyes. "Mademoiselle—," I wanted to say, and couldn't. But then she took fright on her own, she flung her book aside and knelt beside my chair and called out my name; I think she may have shaken me. But I was quite conscious. I swallowed once or twice; for now I wanted to tell her.

But how? I made an indescribable effort to pull myself together, but there was no way it could be expressed so that someone else could understand. If there were words for this occurrence, I was too small to find them. And suddenly the fear seized me that nevertheless, beyond my years, these words would all at once be there, and what seemed to me the most horrible thing of all was that I would then have to say them. To once again live through the reality down there, differently, conjugated, from the beginning; to hear myself admitting it—no, I didn't have any strength left for that.

It is of course imagination on my part to say now that at that time I already felt something had entered my life which I alone would have to walk around with, forever and ever. I see myself lying in my little bed, unable to sleep, and somehow vaguely foreseeing that life would be like that: full of truly strange experiences that are meant for one person alone and can never be spoken. What is certain is that gradually a sad and heavy pride arose in me. I pictured to myself how a person could walk around full of inner happenings and silent. I felt a passionate sympathy for grownups; I admired them, and made up my mind to tell them that I admired them. I made up my mind to tell it to Mademoiselle at the next opportunity.

— ••• —

And then came one of those illnesses which aimed at proving to me that this wasn't my first private adventure. The fever dug into me and out of the depths it pulled experiences, images, facts, which I had known nothing about; I lay there, overloaded with myself, and waited for the moment when I would be told to pile all this back into myself, neatly and in the right order. I began, but it grew in my hands, it resisted, it was much too much. Then rage took hold of me, and I threw everything into myself pell-mell and squeezed it together; but I couldn't close myself back over it. And then I screamed, half open as I was, I screamed and screamed. And when I began to look outside myself, they had been standing around my bed for a long time and were holding my hands, and a candle was there, and their large shadows were moving behind them. And my father ordered me to say what was the matter. It was a friendly, softened order, but it was an order nevertheless. And he got impatient when I didn't answer.

Maman never came at night—, or rather, she did come once. I had been screaming and screaming, and Mademoiselle had come, and Sieversen the housekeeper, and Georg the coachman; but it had done no good. And finally they had sent the carriage for my parents, who were at a great ball, at the Crown Prince's, I think. And all at once I heard it drive in to the courtyard and I stopped screaming, sat up and looked over to the door. And then there was a faint rustling in the adjoining rooms, and Maman came in, in her magnificent court gown—she was hardly aware she had it on—and almost ran in and let her white fur fall behind her and took me in her bare arms. And I, astonished and enchanted as I had never been before, touched her hair and her little smooth face and the cold jewels in her ears and the silk at the edge of her shoulders, which smelled of flowers. And we stayed like that and cried tenderly and kissed each other, until we felt that Father was there and that we had to separate. "He has a high fever," I heard Maman say timidly, and Father reached for my hand and took my pulse. He was wearing the uniform of the Master of the Hunt, with its beautiful, broad, watered blue ribbon of the Order of the Elephant. "What nonsense to send for us," he said, speaking into the room without looking at me. They had promised to go back if it was nothing serious. And certainly it was nothing serious. But on my blanket I found Maman's dance-card, and white camellias, which I had never seen before and which I placed on my eyes when I felt how cool they were.

— ••• —

But it was the afternoons that were endless during such illnesses. In the morning after a bad night you always fell asleep, and when you woke up and thought

that now it was morning again, it was really afternoon and remained afternoon and never stopped being
afternoon. So you lay there in the freshly made bed
and you grew a little in your joints perhaps and were
much too tired to imagine anything at all. The taste
of applesauce lasted for a long time and it was even
a great achievement to somehow interpret it, involuntarily, and let the clean tartness circulate through
you instead of thoughts. Later, as your strength returned, the pillows were propped up behind you, and
you could sit there and play with soldiers; but they
fell over so easily on the slanting bed-tray and always
the whole row at once; and you were not yet so completely back inside life that you could always begin
all over again. Suddenly it was too much, and you
begged them to take everything away, quickly, and
it felt good to see just your two hands again, a little
further off on the empty blanket.

When Maman sometimes came for a half hour and
read me fairy tales (the real readings, the long ones,
Sieversen did), it wasn't for the sake of the stories.
For we agreed that we didn't like fairy tales. We had
a different conception of the marvelous. We found
that things which happened in a totally natural
manner were always the most marvelous of all. We
didn't think much of flying through the air; fairies
disappointed us; and when we read about magical
transformations we didn't expect anything but a very

superficial change. But we did read a little, so that we would look occupied; it was unpleasant for us, when anyone came in, to have to explain what we were doing; especially toward Father, we were exaggeratedly explicit.

Only when we were quite sure we wouldn't be disturbed, and it was growing dark outside, it might happen that we abandoned ourselves to memories, memories we had in common, which seemed ancient to us both and which we smiled over; for we had both grown up since then. We remembered that there had been a time when Maman wished I had been a little girl and not the boy that I undeniably was. I had somehow guessed this, and the idea had occurred to me of sometimes knocking in the afternoon at Maman's door. Then, when she asked who was there, I would delightedly answer "Sophie," making my voice so dainty that it tickled my throat. And when I entered (in the little, girlish house-dress that I wore anyway, with its sleeves rolled all the way up), I really was Sophie, Maman's little Sophie, busy with her household chores, whose hair Maman had to braid, so that she wouldn't be mistaken for that naughty Malte, if he should ever come back. This was not at all desirable; Maman was as pleased at his absence as Sophie was, and their conversations (which Sophie always carried on in the same high-pitched voice) consisted mainly in enumerating Malte's misdeeds and complaining about him. "Oh dear, that Malte," Maman would sigh. And Sophie could go on and on about the naughtiness of boys in general, as if she knew a great number of them.

"I wish I knew what has become of Sophie," Maman would suddenly say in the midst of these reminiscences. Of course Malte couldn't give her any information about that. But when Maman suggested that she must certainly be dead, he would stubbornly contradict her and beg her not to believe that, however little he could prove it wasn't true.

— ••• —

When I think about it now, I can't help being astonished that I always managed to completely return from the world of these fevers and was able to adjust to that social existence where everyone wanted to be reassured that they were among familiar objects and people, where they all conspired to remain in the realm of the intelligible. If you looked forward to something, it either came or didn't come, there was no third possibility. There were Things that were sad, once and for all, and there were pleasant Things, and a great number of incidental ones. And if a joy was arranged for you, it was in fact a joy, and you had to behave accordingly. All this was basically very simple, and once you got the knack of it, it took care of itself. For everything entered into these appointed boundaries: the long, monotonous school hours, when it was summer outside; the walks that afterward you had to describe in French; the visitors into whose presence you were summoned and who thought you were amusing, just when you were feeling sad, and laughed at you the way people laugh at the melancholy expression of certain birds, who don't have any other face. And of course the birthday parties, to which children were invited whom you hardly knew, embarrassed little girls who made *you* embarrassed, or rude little boys who scratched your face, and broke the presents you had just received, and then suddenly left when all the toys had been pulled out of their boxes and wrappings and were lying piled up on the floor. But when you played by yourself, as always, it could happen that you inadvertently stepped out of this agreed-upon, generally harmless world, and found yourself in circumstances that were completely different, and unimaginable.

At times Mademoiselle had her migraine, which was extremely violent, and these were the days when I was hard to find. I know that on these occasions the coachman was sent to look for me in the park when Father happened to ask for me and I wasn't there. From one of the upper guest-rooms I could see him running out and calling my name at the entrance to the long tree-lined driveway. These rooms were situated, side by side, in the gable of Ulsgaard and, since we very seldom had house-guests in those days, were almost always empty. But adjoining them was that large corner room that attracted me to it so powerfully. There was nothing in it except an old bust of Admiral Juel, I think, but all around, the walls were paneled with deep, gray wardrobes, so that the window had had to be installed in the bare, whitewashed space above them. In one of the wardrobe doors I had found a key, and it opened all the others. So in a short time I had examined everything: eighteenth-century chamberlains' coats, cold with their inwoven silver threads, and the beautiful embroidered vests that went with them; official costumes of the Order of Danneborg and the Order of the Elephant, so rich and ceremonious, with linings so soft when you touched them, that at first you thought they were women's dresses. Then real gowns which, held out by their panniers, hung stiffly like marionettes from some too-large puppet show, now so completely outmoded that their heads had been taken off and used for some other purpose. But alongside these, there were wardrobes that were dark when you opened them, dark with high-buttoned uniforms that seemed much more worn than all the others and that wished they had never been preserved.

No one will find it surprising that I pulled all these clothes out and took them into the light; that I held one of them up to my chest or wrapped another one around me; that I hastily tried on some costume that might fit me and, curious and excited, ran to the nearest guest-room, in front of the tall, narrow mirror, which was made up of irregular pieces of green glass. Ah, how I trembled to be there, and how thrilling when I was: when something approached out of the cloudy depths, more slowly than myself, for the mirror hardly believed it and, sleepy as it was, didn't want to promptly repeat what I had recited to it. But in the end it had to, of course. And now it was something very astonishing, strange, totally different from what I had expected, something sudden, independent, which I glanced over quickly, only to recognize myself a moment later, not without a certain irony, which came within a hairsbreadth of spoiling all the fun. But if I immediately began to talk, to bow, to nod at myself, if I walked away, looking around at the mirror all the while, and walked back, brisk and determined, I had imagination on my side, as long as I wanted.

It was then that I first came to know the influence that can emanate from a particular costume. Hardly had I put on one of them when I had to admit to myself that it had me in its power; that it dictated my movements, my facial expression, even my thoughts. My hand, over which the lace cuff fell and fell again, was in no way my ordinary hand; it moved like an actor; I might even say that it watched itself move, however exaggerated that sounds. These disguises, though, never went so far as to make me feel a stranger to myself; on the contrary, the more complete my transformation, the more convinced I was of my own identity. I grew bolder and bolder; flung myself higher and higher; for my skill at catching myself again was beyond all doubt. I didn't notice the temptation in this quickly growing security. My undoing came when the last wardrobe, which I hadn't been able to open before, yielded one day, furnishing me with, not specific costumes, but all kinds of random paraphernalia for masquerades, whose fantastic possibilities made my head spin. There is no way to describe everything I found there. In addition to a *bautta* that I remember, there were dominos in various colors, women's skirts which tinkled brightly with the coins that were sewn into them; there were Pierrot costumes, which I thought looked ridiculous, and pleated Turkish pants, and Persian fezzes, from which little sacks of camphor slipped out, and coronets with stupid, expressionless stones. All these I rather despised; they were so shabbily unreal, and hung there so stripped and wretched, and collapsed so helplessly when they were dragged out into the light. But what transported me into a kind of intoxication were the spacious cloaks, the scarves, the shawls, the veils, all those yielding, wide, unused fabrics that were so soft and caressing, or so smooth that I could hardly keep hold of them, or so light that they flew by me like a wind, or simply heavy with all their own weight. It was in them that I first saw possibilities that were free and infinitely varied: I could be a slave-girl who was about to be sold, or Joan of Arc or an old king or a wizard; all this was possible now, especially since there were also masks, enormous menacing or astonished faces with real beards and thick or up-raised eyebrows. I had never seen any masks before, but I immediately understood that masks ought to exist. I had to laugh when it occurred to me that we had a dog who looked as if he wore one. I remembered his affectionate eyes, which always seemed to be looking out from behind two holes in his hairy face. I was still laughing as I put on the clothes, and in the process I completely forgot what I had intended to dress up as. All right, it was new and exciting not to decide until I was in front of the mirror. The face I tied on had a peculiarly hollow smell; it fitted closely over my own face, but I was able to see through it comfortably, and only after the mask was on did I choose all kinds of materials, which I wound around my head like a turban, in such a way that the edge of the mask, which extended downward into a gigan-tic yellow cloak, was almost completely hidden on top also and on the sides. Finally, when there was nothing more to add, I considered myself adequately disguised. To complete the costume, I picked up a large staff and walked it along beside me at arm's length, and in this way, not without difficulty but, as it seemed to me, full of dignity, I trailed into the guest-room toward the mirror.

It was really magnificent, beyond all expectation. And the mirror repeated it instantly: it was too convincing. It wouldn't have been at all necessary to move; this apparition was perfect, even though it didn't do a thing. But I wanted to find out what I actually was, so I turned around slightly and lifted both arms: large gestures, as if I were a sorcerer, were (as I saw immediately) the only appropriate ones. But just at this solemn moment I heard quite near me, muffled by my disguise, a multiple, complicated noise. Very frightened, I lost sight of the creature in the mirror and, to my great dismay, saw that I had knocked over a small round table with heaven knows what on it, probably very fragile objects. I bent down as well as I could and found my worst fears confirmed: everything seemed to be in pieces. The two useless, green-violet porcelain parrots were of course shattered, each in a different, malign way. A small bowl had spilled out its pieces of candy, which looked like insects in their silk cocoons, and had tossed its cover far away—only half of it was visible, the other half had completely disappeared. But the most annoying sight of all was a perfume bottle that had broken into a thousand tiny fragments, from which the remnant of some ancient essence had spurted out, that now formed a stain with a very repulsive physiognomy on the light rug. I quickly tried to wipe it up with some of the material that was hanging all over me, but it only got darker and more unpleasant. I was truly desperate now. I got up and looked for some object I could repair the damage with. But there was nothing. Besides, I was so hampered, in my vision and in every movement, that a violent rage flared up against my absurd situation, which I no longer understood. I began to pull at the knots of my costume, but that only made them tighter. The strings of the cloak were strangling me, and the material on my head was pressing down as if more and more were being added to it. In addition, the air had grown thick and misty with the vapor of the spilled liquid.

Hot and furious, I rushed to the mirror and with difficulty watched, through the mask, the frantic movements of my hands. But the mirror had been waiting for just this. Its moment of revenge had come. While I, with a boundlessly growing anguish, kept trying to somehow squeeze out of my disguise, it forced me, I don't know how, to look up, and dictated to me an image, no, a reality, a strange, incomprehensible, monstrous reality that permeated me against my will: for now it was the stronger one, and I was the mirror. I stared at this large, terrifying stranger in front of me, and felt appalled to be alone with him. But at the very moment I thought this, the worst thing happened: I lost all sense of myself, I simply ceased to exist. For one second, I felt an indescribable, piercing, futile longing for myself, then only *he* remained: there was nothing except him.

I began to run, but now it was he that was running.

He knocked against everything, he didn't know the house, had no idea where to go; he stumbled down a flight of stairs, he tripped over someone who screamed and struggled free. A door opened, people came out: Ah, what a relief it was to recognize them. Sieversen was there, with her kind face, and the chambermaid and the butler: now everything would be decided. But they didn't rush forward to rescue me. They stood there, with infinite cruelty, and laughed; my God, they just stood there and laughed. I was crying, but the mask didn't let the tears escape, they fell inside it, onto my face, and dried immediately, and fell again and dried. And finally I kneeled in front of them, as no one had ever kneeled before; I kneeled and lifted my hands toward them and begged: "Take me out, if you still can, save me," but they didn't hear; there was no voice left in me.

To the day of her death, Sieversen used to tell how I had collapsed onto the floor and how they had kept on laughing, thinking this was part of the game. They were used to that from me. But then I had continued to lie there and hadn't answered. And the fright when they had finally discovered that I was unconscious and lay there like a piece of cloth among all those wrappings, yes, just like a piece of cloth.

— ••• —

Time went by incalculably fast, and all at once it had again come around to the point when the minister, Dr. Jespersen, had to be invited over. This meant a luncheon, painful and tedious for everyone concerned. Accustomed to the very pious country-people who were always overwhelmed in his presence, Dr. Jespersen was entirely out of his element in our house; he was left, as it were, lying on dry land and gasping for breath. The gills he had developed in himself hardly worked; bubbles formed; and it all became rather dangerous. Materials of conversation were, to be exact, nonexistent; remainders were on sale at unbelievable prices, it was a liquidation of all assets. In our house, Dr. Jespersen had to be satisfied with being a kind of private person; but that was precisely what he had never been. He was, as far back as he could remember, employed in the soul business. For him the soul was a public institution, of which he was a representative, and he saw to it that he was never off duty, not even in his relations with his wife, "his modest, faithful Rebecca, sanctified by the bearing of children," as Lavater expressed it on another occasion.

* [As for my father, his attitude toward God was perfectly correct and irreproachably courteous. In church it sometimes seemed to me as if he were Master of the Hunt to God himself, when he stood there and waited and bowed his head. Maman, on the other hand, thought it almost offensive that anyone's

* Written on the margin of the MS.

relationship with God could be merely polite. If she had been born into a religion with expressive, complicated observances, it would have been bliss for her to remain kneeling for hours, to prostrate herself and make the sign of the cross with broad, emphatic gestures on her breast and shoulders. She didn't actually teach me to pray, but it was a comfort to her that I liked to kneel and hold my palms together, with fingers sometimes interlaced and sometimes straight, whichever seemed to me more expressive. Left a good deal to myself, I early on went through a series of developments which I didn't connect with God until much later, during a period of despair; and then, indeed, with such violence that God formed and shattered almost at the same moment. After this I obviously had to begin all over again from the beginning. And for that beginning I sometimes thought I needed Maman, though naturally it was better to go through it alone. And of course by that time she had been dead for many years.]

Sitting next to Dr. Jespersen, Maman could speak with a vivacity that was almost boisterous. She would begin conversations with him which he took seriously, and then, as soon as he heard himself talking, she judged that she had done enough and completely forgot him, as if he had already gone. "How can he," she sometimes said, "drive around and walk in to people, just when they are dying."

He came to her also on that occasion, but she certainly was no longer able to see him. Her senses were fading, one after another, and her sight was the first to go. It was in the autumn; we were supposed to be leaving for the city, but just then she got sick, or rather, she immediately began to die, slowly and hopelessly, over the whole surface of her body. The doctors came, and on one particular day they were all there together and took over the whole house. For a few hours it seemed to belong to the specialist and his assistants, as if we no longer had any say. But right after that, they lost all interest and came only one at a time, as though out of pure politeness, to smoke a cigar and drink a glass of port. And meanwhile Maman died.

We were just waiting for Maman's only brother, Count Christian Brahe, who, as will be remembered, had served for a while in the Turkish army, where we had always heard he had gained great distinction. He arrived one morning accompanied by a strange-looking foreign servant, and I was surprised to see that he was taller than Father and apparently older as well. The two gentlemen exchanged a few words which, as I guessed, had to do with Maman. There was a pause. Then my father said, "She is very much disfigured." I didn't understand this expression, but I shivered when I heard it. I had the impression that my father too had had to master himself before he could utter it. But it was probably his pride that suffered most in making this admission.

— ••• —

Not until several years later did I hear further mention of Count Christian. That was at Urnekloster; and it was Mathilde Brahe who liked to talk about him. I am sure, though, that she elaborated upon the various episodes of his career in a rather arbitrary way; for my uncle's life, which the public and even our family knew about only through rumors that he never took the trouble to contradict, offered infinite possibilities for embellishment. Urnekloster belongs to him now. But no one knows whether he is actually living there. Perhaps he is still traveling, as he used to; perhaps the news of his death is on its way from some remote continent, written by his foreign servant in bad English or in some unknown language. Or perhaps this man will give no sign of life when he is left alone one day. Perhaps they have both long since disappeared and remain only on the passenger list of some lost ship under names that weren't their own.

I must confess that in those days, whenever a carriage drove into the courtyard at Urnekloster, I always expected to see *him* step out, and my heart began pounding in a peculiar way. Mathilde Brahe declared that that was how he would come, that was one of his strange habits, to suddenly turn up when you thought it least possible. He never did come, but my imagination was occupied with him for weeks at a time. I felt as if we owed each other some kind of relationship, and I would have loved to know something real about him.

When, shortly after this, however, my interest shifted and as a result of certain events fastened entirely on Christine Brahe, I did not, strangely enough, make any attempt to learn about the circumstances of her life. On the other hand, I was troubled by the question of whether her portrait was among the paintings in the gallery. And the desire to find out grew so insistent and tormenting that for several nights I couldn't sleep; until, quite unexpectedly, the night came when, God help me, I got out of bed and went upstairs with my candle, which seemed to be afraid.

For my own part, I wasn't thinking of fear. I wasn't thinking at all: I was just walking. The high doors yielded so playfully before me and above me; the rooms I walked through kept very quiet. And finally I noticed, from the depth which brushed my face like a wind, that I had entered the gallery. On my right I felt the windows, filled with night, and the pictures had to be on my left. I lifted my candle as high as I could. Yes: there were the pictures.

At first I intended to look at the women only, but I soon recognized one man and then another, whose portraits were also at Ulsgaard, and when I shined my candlelight on them from below, they moved and wanted to come into the light, and it seemed heartless not to give them time at least for that. There was Christian IV, again and again, with his beautiful braided hair along his broad, gradually rounded cheek. There were presumably his wives, of whom I recognized only Kirstine Munk; and suddenly Mrs. Ellen Marsvin was looking at me, suspicious in her widow's weeds and with the same string of pearls on the brim of her tall hat. There were King Christian's children: always new ones by more recent wives, the "incomparable" Eleonore on a white palfrey, in her most radiant period, before the ordeal. The Gyldenløves: Hans Ulrik, of whom the women in Spain thought that he painted his face, so full-blooded was he; and Ulrik Christian, whom people, once they saw him, never forgot. And nearly all the Ulfelds. And that one over there, with one eye painted black, might well be Henrik Holck, who at the age of thirty-three became Count of the Empire and Field Marshal, and it happened like this: on his way to the damsel Hilleborg Krafse, he dreamed that instead of a bride he was given a naked sword; and he took this dream to heart and turned back and began his short, impetuous career, which the plague put an end to. I knew them all. We also had at Ulsgaard the ambassadors to the Congress of Nimwegen, who slightly resembled one another, because they had all been painted at the same time, each with the same narrow, eyebrow-like mustache over the sensual, almost seeing mouth. That

I recognized Duke Ulrik goes without saying, and Otte Brahe and Claus Daa and Sten Rosensparre, the last of his race; for I had seen paintings of them all in the dining room at Ulsgaard or had found, in old albums, copper-plate engravings that portrayed them.

But then there were many others I had never seen; few women, but there were children. My arm had long since grown tired and was shaking, yet again and again I held up the candle in order to see the children. I understood them, those little girls who carried a bird on their hand and forgot all about it. Sometimes a little dog sat at their feet, a ball lay on the floor, and on the nearby table there were fruits and flowers; and on a pillar behind them, small and provisional, hung the coat-of-arms of the Grubbes or the Billes or the Rosenkrantzes. So much had been collected around them, as if a lot had to be made up for. But they stood there, simply, in their dresses, and waited; you could see they were waiting. And that made me think about the women again and about Christine Brahe, and I wondered if I would recognize her.

I was deciding whether I should quickly run to the end of the gallery and look as I walked back, when I knocked against something. I turned around so abruptly that Erik jumped back, whispering: "Be careful with your light!"

"Are *you* here?" I said breathlessly, and I wasn't sure whether this was a good or a very bad omen. He just laughed. I had no idea what would happen next.

My candle was flickering, and I could barely see the expression on his face. Probably it was a bad omen that he was there. But then, coming nearer, he said: "*Her* picture isn't here; we're still looking for it upstairs." With his hushed voice and the one movable eye he made a kind of upward gesture. And I realized that he meant the attic. But all at once a strange thought occurred to me.

"We?" I asked. "Is she upstairs too?"

"Yes," he nodded, standing very close to me.

"Is she looking for it herself?"

"Yes, we're both looking."

"You mean the picture has been put away?"

"Yes, just imagine!" he said indignantly. But I didn't quite understand what she wanted it for.

"She wants to see herself," he whispered into my ear.

"Oh," I said, as if I understood. At this, he blew out the candle. I saw him straining forward, into the light, with his eyebrows raised high. Then it was dark. I involuntarily stepped back.

"What are you doing?" I called out in a stifled voice, quite dry in the throat. He leapt toward me and grabbed my arm, giggling.

"What!" I hissed at him, trying to shake him off; but he held on. I couldn't stop him from putting his arm around my neck.

"Should I tell you?" he whispered, and a little saliva sprayed my ear.

"Yes, yes, quick."

I didn't know what I was saying. He had gotten his arms completely around me now.

"I've brought her a mirror," he said and giggled again.

"A mirror?"

"Yes, because her picture isn't there."

"No, no," I murmured.

He suddenly pulled me closer to the window and pinched my arm so sharply that I screamed.

"She's not inside," he breathed into my ear.

Involuntarily I pushed him away; something in him cracked; I thought I had broken him.

"Come on . . . ," and now I had to laugh myself. "Not inside? What do you mean, not inside?"

"You're stupid," he answered angrily, no longer whispering. His voice had changed register, as if he were beginning a new, still-unused part of it. "Either someone is inside," he pronounced with a severity beyond his years, "and in that case he isn't here; or when he is here, he can't be inside."

"Of course," I answered, quickly, without thinking. I was frightened that if I didn't agree he would go away and leave me alone. I even grabbed at him.

"Let's be friends," I proposed. He wanted to be begged. "It's all the same to me," he said curtly.

I tried to inaugurate our friendship, but I didn't dare to embrace him. "Dear Erik" was all I could manage, touching him lightly. I was all at once very tired. I looked around; I no longer understood how I had come here or how it was that I hadn't been afraid. I didn't really know where the windows and where the pictures were. And as we left, he had to lead me.

"They won't hurt you," he magnanimously assured me, and giggled again.

— ••• —

Dear, dear Erik; perhaps you were after all my only friend. For I've never had one. It's a pity you didn't care about friendship. I would have liked to tell you so many things. Perhaps we would have gotten along together. One can never know. I remember that your portrait was being painted at that time. Grandfather had hired someone to come and paint you. An hour every morning. I can't recall what the painter looked like; his name escapes me, though Mathilde Brahe used to repeat it every moment.

Did he see you as I see you? You were wearing a suit of heliotrope-colored velvet. Mathilde Brahe adored that suit. But that doesn't matter now. I would just like to know whether he saw you. Let's assume he was a real painter. Let's assume it didn't occur to him that you might die before he was finished; that he didn't look at the matter at all sentimentally; that he simply worked. That the difference between your two brown eyes enchanted him; that he was not for one moment ashamed of the immovable one; that he had the tact not to place anything on the table by your hand, which perhaps was lightly resting on it—. Let's assume whatever else is necessary and approve it: we then have a portrait, your portrait, the last one in the gallery at Urnekloster.

(And when people are on the way out, having seen them all, there is still a little boy there. Just a moment: who's that? A Brahe. Do you see the silver pole on the black field and the peacock feathers? There's the name too: Erik Brahe. Wasn't it an Erik Brahe who was executed? Yes, of course, everyone knows that. But this can't be the same one. This boy died when he was quite young, it doesn't matter when. Can't you see that?)

— ••• —

When visitors came and Erik was called in, Miss Mathilde Brahe always asserted that it was simply amazing how much he resembled the old Countess Brahe, my grandmother. People say that she was a very great lady. I didn't know her. But I have a very vivid memory of my father's mother, the real mistress of Ulsgaard. For she had always remained that, however strongly she resented Maman for entering the house of the Master of the Hunt's wife. Afterward, she continually acted in a self-effacing manner, and referred the servants to Maman for even the most trivial detail; while in important matters she calmly made decisions herself and carried them out without accounting to anyone. I don't think Maman wanted it to be otherwise. She was so poorly fitted to manage a large house; she was completely without the capacity to distinguish what was important from what wasn't. As soon as someone spoke to her about anything at all, that became the whole, and she forgot everything else; though of course other things didn't cease to exist. She never complained about her mother-in-law. And whom could she have complained to? Father was an extremely respectful son, and Grandfather had little to say.

Mrs. Margarete Brigge had always been, as far back as I can remember, a tall, unapproachable old woman. I can't picture her except as much older than the Chamberlain. She lived her life in our midst, without caring for anyone. She wasn't dependent on any of us, and always had with her a kind of lady-companion, the aging Countess Oxe, whom through some favor or other she had placed under a boundless obligation. This must have been an extraordinary exception in her life; she wasn't known for her favors. She didn't like children, and animals weren't allowed near her. I don't know whether there was anything she did like. It was said that as a very young girl she had been engaged to the handsome Felix Lichnowsky, who came to so cruel an end at Frankfurt. And indeed, after her death, among her belongings a portrait of the prince was found, which, if I am not mistaken, was returned to his family. I now think that perhaps, through this retired country existence, which living at Ulsgaard more and more became over the years, she had missed another, brilliant life, the one that nature had intended her for. It's hard to say whether she regretted this. Perhaps she despised it for not coming, for missing the opportunity of being lived with skill and talent. She had taken all this so deeply inside herself and had covered it with shells, many hard, brilliant, slightly metallic shells, and the layer that was for the moment on top always looked cool and new. Now and then, though, by her naive impatience she betrayed a feeling that people weren't paying enough attention to her. I can remember her at table suddenly choking, in some obvious and complicated way that assured her of everyone's concern and made her appear, for a few moments at least, as sensational and fascinating as she would have liked to be in general. But I suspect that my father was the only one who took these much-too-frequent accidents seriously. He would watch her, politely bending forward, and you could see how, in thought, he was offering her his own, normally-functioning windpipe, placing it completely at her disposal. Of course the Chamberlain too had stopped eating; he took a little sip of wine and refrained from making a comment.

Only once had he, during dinner, upheld his own opinion against his wife. That had been long ago; yet the story was still repeated, maliciously and in secret; almost everywhere there was someone who had never heard it. It seemed that there had been a time when the Chamberlain's wife would fly into a rage about wine stains on the tablecloth; any such stain, whatever the occasion, was noted by her and, you might say, exposed, under the severest rebuke. This had even happened once when several distinguished guests were present. A few innocent stains, which she made far too much of, were the subject of her sarcastic accusations, and though Grandfather tried his best to warn her by little signs and facetious interruptions, she obstinately kept on with her reproaches, which, a moment later, she was forced to cut short in the middle of a sentence. For something unprecedented and absolutely incomprehensible happened. The Chamberlain had called for the red wine, which had just been passed around the table, and was now most attentively filling his glass himself. Except that, strangely enough, he didn't stop pouring although the glass had been full for a long time, but amid the growing silence slowly and carefully continued to pour; until Maman, who could never hold herself back, burst out laughing and thus set the whole affair right by turning it to laughter. For now everyone joined in, relieved, and the Chamberlain looked up and handed the bottle to the servant.

Later on, another peculiarity took possession of my grandmother. She wouldn't permit anyone in the house to get sick. Once, when the cook had cut herself and she happened to see her with her bandaged hand, she maintained that the whole house reeked of iodoform, and it was difficult to convince her that the woman couldn't be fired for that reason. She didn't want to be reminded of the possibility that she herself could get sick. If anyone was imprudent enough to manifest even the slightest discomfort in her presence, she considered it to be nothing less than a personal insult, and resented it for a long time afterward.

That autumn, when Maman died, the Chamberlain's wife shut herself off completely, stayed in her rooms with Sophie Oxe, and broke off all relations with us. Even her son was no longer admitted. It is true that this death came at a most inconvenient time. The rooms were cold, the stoves were smoky, and the mice had thronged into the house; no place was safe from them. But it was more than that: Mrs. Margarete Brigge was indignant that Maman was dying; that there was a subject on the agenda which she refused to talk about; that the young wife presumed to take precedence over her, when she herself intended to die sometime, at a date that was still not definitely set. For she often thought about the fact that she would have to die. But she didn't want to be hurried. She would die, of course, when she chose to, and then they could all go ahead and die themselves, after her, if they were in such a hurry.

Maman's death was something she never quite forgave us for. Besides, she aged very quickly during the following winter. When she walked she was as tall as ever, but she drooped in her armchair, and grew more and more hard of hearing. You could sit and stare at her for hours, and she wouldn't feel it. She was somewhere inside herself; only seldom and for just a few moments at a time did she come back into her senses, which were empty, which she no longer inhabited. Then she would say something to the Countess, who adjusted her shawl and, with her large, freshly washed hands, tucked in her dress, as if water had been spilled or as if we weren't quite clean.

She died as spring was approaching, in the city, one night. Sophie Oxe, whose door was open, hadn't heard a thing. When they found *her* in the morning, she was cold as glass.

Immediately after that the Chamberlain's great and terrifying illness began. It was as if he had waited for her end, so that he could die as pitilessly as he had to.

— ••• —

It was in the year after Maman's death that I first really noticed Abelone. Abelone was always there. This did her great harm. And then Abelone wasn't likeable, as I had decided a long time before, on some occasion or other, and I had never seriously reviewed that opinion. Until now it would have seemed to me almost ludicrous to ask what Abelone was like or what purpose she served. She was simply there, and people used her however they could. But all at once I asked myself: *Why* is Abelone there? Each of us had a reason for being there, even if it wasn't always as obvious as, for example, the utility of Sophie Oxe. But why was Abelone there? For a short time people used to say that she needed a little entertainment. But that was quickly forgotten. No one contributed anything to Abelone's entertainment, and she certainly didn't give you the impression that she felt entertained.

Besides, Abelone had one good quality: she sang. That is to say, there were times when she sang. There was a strong, imperturbable music in her. If it is true that angels are male, you could say that there was something male in her voice: a radiant, celestial maleness. I, who even as a child had been distrustful of music (not because it lifted me out of myself more powerfully than anything else, but because I had noticed that it never put me back where it had found me, but lower down, somewhere deep in the uncompleted), I endured this music, on which you could ascend upright, higher and higher, until you thought you must have been more or less in heaven for a little while. I didn't suspect then that Abelone was to open still other heavens for me.

At first our relationship consisted in her telling me stories about when Maman was a girl. She wanted very much to convince me how brave and youthful Maman had been. There was no one at that time, she assured me, who could compare with Maman in dancing or riding. "She was the most daring of all the girls and was quite tireless; and then all of a sudden she got married," Abelone said, still astonished after so many years. "It happened so unexpectedly; no one could really understand it."

I was curious to know why Abelone hadn't gotten married. She seemed relatively old, and it never occurred to me that she might still be able to.

"There just wasn't anyone," she answered simply, and as she said these words she became truly beautiful. Is Abelone beautiful? I asked myself, surprised. Then I left home to go to the Academy for Young Noblemen, and an odious and painful period of my life began. But there at Sorø, when I stood at a window, apart from the others, and they left me in peace for a while, I would look out into the trees; and in such moments, and at night, the certainty grew in me that Abelone was beautiful. And I began to write her all those letters, long ones and short ones, many secret letters, in which I thought I was talking about Ulsgaard and my unhappiness. But, as I can see now, they really must have been love letters. For when summer vacation finally came, though at first it seemed it never would, it was as if by prearrangement that we didn't meet in the presence of the others.

Nothing at all had been agreed upon between us, but when the carriage turned into the park, I couldn't help getting out, perhaps just because I didn't want to drive up to the house as any stranger would. Summer was already there in its full glory. I took one of the side paths and ran toward a laburnum tree. And there was Abelone. Beautiful, beautiful Abelone.

I will never forget how you looked at me then. How you wore your look, holding it up on your back-tilted face like something that could never be defined.

Ah, didn't the climate change at all, didn't it grow milder around Ulsgaard, from all our warmth? Aren't there certain roses in the park that bloom for a longer time now, right into December?

I won't tell anything about you, Abelone. Not because we deceived each other—since even then you loved someone whom you have never forgotten, and I loved all women—but because only wrong is done in the saying.

— ••• —

There are tapestries here, Abelone. I am imagining that you are with me; there are six tapestries; come, let's walk slowly in front of them. But first step back and look at them all together. How peaceful they are, aren't they? There is little variety in them. Look, there is always that oval, blue island, floating on the subdued red background, which is covered with flowers and inhabited by little animals busy with their own affairs. Only there, in the last tapestry, the island rises a little, as if it has grown lighter. It always has one figure on it, a woman, in various costumes, but always the same one. Sometimes there is a smaller form beside her, a handmaid, and the heraldic animals are always there, large, also on the island, also involved in the action. On the left a lion, and on the right, pure white, the unicorn; they are carrying the same pennants, which show high above them: three silver moons, rising, in a blue band on a red field.—Have you looked? Shall we begin with the first?

She is feeding a falcon. How magnificent her clothing is! The bird is on her gloved hand and is moving. She is looking at it and at the same time reaching into the bowl that the handmaid brings her, in order to give it something. Below, on the right, a little silken-haired dog is lying on the train of her dress; it is looking up and hoping that they will remember it. And— have you noticed?—a low rose-trellis closes off the island at the back. The lion and unicorn are standing on their hind legs with heraldic arrogance. The coat-of-arms is repeated as a cloak around their shoulders. A beautiful clasp holds it together. It is floating.

Don't we involuntarily walk toward the next tapestry more softly, as soon as we see how deeply absorbed she is? She is weaving a garland, a small, round floral crown. Thoughtfully she chooses the color of the next carnation in the flat basin which the handmaid holds out for her, while she strings the one she chose a few moments ago. Behind her on a bench, unused, stands a basket full of roses, which a monkey has discovered. But this time she needs carnations.

The lion is no longer participating; but on the right the unicorn understands.

Shouldn't music come into this silence? Isn't it already secretly there? Gravely and silently adorned, she has walked (how slowly—do you see?) to the portable organ and is standing there, playing it, separated by the row of pipes from the handmaid, who is working the bellows on the other side. She has never been so beautiful. Her hair has been strangely pulled forward in two plaits and fastened together over the headdress in such a way that its ends rise out of the knot like a short helmet-plume. The lion, in a bad mood, endures the sounds unwillingly, holding back a howl behind clenched teeth. But the unicorn is beautiful, as if floating on waves.

The island grows wider. A tent has been put up. Of blue damask and shot with golden flames. The animals hold it open and, almost plain in her regal dress, she steps forth. What are her pearls, compared with herself? The handmaid has opened a small casket, and now she takes out a necklace, a heavy, magnificent treasure, which has always been locked away. The little dog sits beside her, on a high place prepared for it, and looks on. And have you discovered the motto up on the rim of the tent? There it is: 'À mon seul désir.'

What has happened? Why is the little rabbit running, down there, why can you immediately see that it's running? Everything is so restrained. The lion has nothing to do. She herself is holding the pennant. Or is she clinging to it? With her other hand she has grasped the unicorn's horn. Is this mourning? Can mourning stand up so straight, can a mourning-dress be so mute as this velvet, green-black and faded in some places?

But here is still another festival; no one is invited to it. Expectation plays no role in it. Everything is here. Everything forever. The lion looks around almost menacingly: no one is allowed to come. We have never before seen her tired; is she tired? Or has she only sat down because she is holding something heavy? A monstrance, you might think. But she bends her other arm toward the unicorn, and the animal rears up, flattered, and rises and leans onto her lap. What she is holding is a mirror. Do you see: she is showing the unicorn its image——.

Abelone, I am imagining that you are here. Do you understand, Abelone? I think you must understand.

Now even the tapestries of the Dame à la Licorne are no longer in the old château of Boussac. The time has come when everything is leaving the houses; they can no longer keep anything. Danger has become more safe than safety. No one from the family of the Delle Viste walks beside us with these Things in his blood. They are all gone. No one speaks your name, Pierre d'Aubusson, grandest Grand-master from an ancient house, by whose command perhaps these pictures were woven, which give praise to everything and give nothing up. (Ah, why have the poets ever written differently about women, more literally, as they thought? It is certain that we were supposed to know nothing but this.) Now we come in front of them by chance among chance spectators and are almost afraid to be here uninvited. But there are others who pass by, though they are never many. The young people hardly stop to look, unless their schoolwork somehow obliges them to have seen these Things once, with regard to this or that quality.

But occasionally you do find young girls in front of them. For there are a lot of young girls in the museums, who have here or there left their houses, which no longer keep anything. They find themselves in front of these tapestries and forget themselves a little. They have always felt that this existed —a quiet life like this, of slow, never quite clarified gestures, and they dimly remember that for a time they even thought this life would be their own. But then they suddenly take out a sketchbook and begin to draw, anything at all: one of the flowers, or a small, happy animal. It doesn't matter, someone has told them, what exactly it is. And it really doesn't matter. The main thing is just to keep drawing; for that is the reason they left home one day, rather violently. They come from good families. But when they lift their arms as they draw, it appears that their dress isn't buttoned in back, or at any rate not completely. There are a few buttons that they couldn't reach. For when the dress was made, no one had imagined that they would suddenly go away, alone. In the family there is always someone to help with such buttons. But here, dear God, who is going to bother with it in such a big city? Unless you have a friend; but friends are in the same predicament, and you would end up buttoning each other's dresses. That would be ridiculous, and would remind you of your family, which you don't want to be reminded of.

But inevitably you sometimes wonder, as you draw, whether it wouldn't have been possible to stay home after all. If only you could have been religious, sincerely religious, in tune with the others. But it seemed so absurd to try doing that in common. The path has somehow grown narrower: families can no longer come to God. So there remained only various other things that you could, if necessary, share. But if you shared them equally, each person received so shamefully little. And if you cheated in the sharing, all sorts of disputes arose. No, it is really better to draw, anything at all. In time the resemblance will appear. And art, when you acquire it this way, little by little, is after all something truly enviable.

And in their intense absorption with their work, these young girls no longer think of looking up. They don't notice how in everything they draw they are merely suppressing inside themselves the unalterable life that in these woven pictures has radiantly opened in front of them, infinite and unsayable. They don't want to believe it. Now that so much is changing, they too want to change. They are on the verge of abandoning themselves and thinking about themselves as men might speak of them when *they* aren't there. This seems to them like progress. They are already almost convinced that you search out one pleasure and then another and then an even stronger one: that life consists in this, if you don't want to stupidly lose it. They have already begun to look around, to search; they, whose strength has always consisted in being found.

That comes, I think, from their tiredness. Over the centuries they have taken upon themselves the entire task of love; they have always played the whole dialogue—both parts. For man has only repeated their words, and done it badly. And has made their learning difficult with his distractedness, his negligence, his jealousy, which was itself a kind of negligence. And despite that, they have persevered day and night, and have increased in love and misery. And from among them, under the pressure of endless sorrows, those powerful examples of women in love have come forth, who, even while they called him, surpassed the man they loved; who grew above him and beyond him when he didn't return, like Gaspara Stampa or the Portuguese nun, who didn't cease until their torment suddenly turned into a bitter, icy magnificence, which nothing could confine. We know about these women because there are letters that have, as if by a miracle, been preserved, or books of poems written in accusation and lament, or portraits in some gallery that look at us through an almost irresistible desire to cry, which the painter caught because he didn't know what it was. But there have been innumerably more of them—those who burned their letters, and others who no longer had the strength to write them. Old women who had become hardened, with a kernel of tenderness inside them, which they kept hidden. Shapeless women who, grown fat through exhaustion, let themselves become like their husbands and who nevertheless were entirely different inside, where their love had been working, in the dark. Child-bearing women who never wanted to bear children and who, when they finally died during their eighth delivery, still had the gestures and the lightness of girls looking forward to love. And those who remained with bullies and drunkards, because they had found the means to be farther away from them inside themselves than anywhere else; and when they came among people, they couldn't suppress this and were radiant as if they lived with saints. Impossible to know how many or who they were. It is as if they had in advance destroyed all the words by which they might be grasped.

— ••• —

But now that so much is changing, isn't it time for us to change? Couldn't we try to gradually develop and slowly take upon ourselves, little by little, our part in the great task of love? We have been spared all its trouble, and that is why it has slipped in among our distractions, as a piece of real lace will sometimes fall into a child's toy-box and please him and no longer please him, and finally it lies there among the broken and dismembered toys, more wretched than any of them. We have been spoiled by superficial pleasures like all dilettantes, and are looked upon as masters. But what if we despised our successes? What if we started from the very outset to learn the task of love, which has always been done for us? What if we went ahead and became beginners, now that much is changing?

— ••• —

Now I know too what happened when Maman unrolled the little pieces of lace. For she had taken only one of the drawers in Ingeborg's secretary for her own use.

"Shall we look at them, Malte?" she would say, and was as happy as if everything in the small yellow-lacquered drawer were about to be given to her as a present. And then she got so overwhelmed with anticipation that she couldn't even unfold the tissue paper. I had to do that every time. But I too was filled with excitement when the laces appeared. They were wound on a wooden spindle, which couldn't be seen because of all the laces. Then we would slowly turn it and watch the designs unroll, and we were a little frightened every time one of them came to an end. They stopped so suddenly.

First came strips of Italian work, tough pieces with drawn threads, in which everything was repeated over and over, as clearly as in a peasant's garden. Then, all at once, a whole series of our glances was latticed with Venetian needlepoint, as if we were cloisters or prisons. But the view was freed again, and we saw deep into gardens that became more and more artificial, until everything was as dense and warm to the eyes as in a greenhouse: luxuriant plants, which we didn't recognize, spread out their enormous leaves, tendrils groped for one another as if they were dizzy, and the large open blossoms of the Points d'Alençon scattered their pollen over everything. Suddenly, tired and dazed, we stepped outside into the long track of the Valenciennes, and it was an early morning in winter, the ground was covered with frost. And we pushed through the snowy thicket of the Binche and came to places where no one had ever been; the branches hung downward so strangely, perhaps there was a grave beneath them, but we hid that from each other. The cold pressed more and more closely upon us, and at last, when the tiny pillow lace came, Maman said, "Oh, now we'll get frostflowers on our eyes," and it was true, for inside us it was very warm.

When the time came to roll up the laces again, we both sighed; it took so long; but we weren't willing to entrust it to anyone else.

"Just think, if we had had to make them," Maman said, looking really frightened. I couldn't imagine that at all. I caught myself thinking about little animals incessantly spinning these Things and which for that reason are left in peace. No, of course they were women.

"The women who made these have certainly gone to heaven," I said, filled with awe. I remember it occurred to me that I hadn't asked about heaven for a long time. Maman took a deep breath; the laces once again lay rolled up together.

After a while, when I had already forgotten my last words, she said, quite slowly, "To heaven? I think they are completely in these laces. Each one,

looked at in the right way, can become an eternal
bliss. We know so little about it."

— ••• —

Often, when visitors came, it was said that the Schulins were economizing. Their large, old manor-house
had burned down a few years before, and they were
now living in the two narrow wings and were economizing. But having guests was in their blood. They
couldn't give it up. If someone arrived at our house
unexpectedly, he probably came from the Schulins';
and if someone suddenly looked at the clock and
rushed off with a frightened look on his face, he was
certainly expected at Lystager.

By this time, Maman really didn't go out any more,
but the Schulins couldn't understand that; there was
nothing to be done, we had to drive over and visit
them one day. It was in December, after a few early
snowfalls; the sleigh was ordered for three o'clock;
I was to come along. But we never left the house on
time. Maman, who didn't like having the carriage
announced, usually came down much too early, and
when she found no one there, she always remembered
something that should have been done a long time
ago, and she would begin searching or arranging
somewhere upstairs, so that she could hardly be found
again. Finally we would all stand there and wait. And
when she was at last seated in the sleigh and bundled
up, it appeared that something had been forgotten,

and Sieversen would have to be called; for only Sieversen knew where it was. But then we would suddenly drive off, before Sieversen returned.

It had never really cleared up that day. The trees stood as if they had lost their way in the mist, and there was something presumptuous about driving into it. At intervals it began to quietly snow again, and now it was as if even the last line had been erased and we were driving into a blank page. There was nothing but the sound of the sleighbells, and you couldn't really tell where it was coming from. At one moment it stopped, as if the last bell had been spent; but then it gathered itself up again and was all together and again poured forth in all its abundance. We might have imagined we saw the church steeple on the left. But the outline of the park wall suddenly appeared, high up, nearly on top of us, and we found ourselves in the long driveway. The sound of the sleighbells no longer fell away completely; it seemed to hang, in clusters, right and left on the trees. Then we swung in and drove around something, past something else on the right, and came to a halt in the middle.

Georg had completely forgotten that the house wasn't there, and for us all it *was* there at that moment. We walked up the front steps that led to the old terrace, and were amazed that it was so dark. All at once a door opened, below and behind us to the left, and someone called out, "Over here!", lifting and swinging a hazy lamp. My father laughed: "We are climbing around like ghosts," and he helped us back down the stairs.

"But there was a house here just now," Maman said, and couldn't get used to Viera Schulin right away, who had come running out, warm and laughing. Now, of course, we had to quickly go in, and there was no more time to think of the house. Coats were taken off in a small vestibule, and then we were suddenly among the lamps and opposite the warmth.

These Schulins were a powerful family of independent women. I don't know if there were any sons. I only remember three sisters. The eldest had been married to a marchese in Naples, from whom she was now being slowly divorced, amid many lawsuits. Then came Zoë, about whom it was said that there was nothing she didn't know. And above all there was Viera, this warm Viera; God knows what has become of her. The Countess, a Narishkin, was really the fourth sister and in certain respects the youngest. She didn't know about anything and continually had to be educated by her children. And the good Count Schulin felt as if he were married to all these women and went around kissing them somewhat at random.

Just as we entered he was laughing loudly, and he greeted us with meticulous courtesy. I was passed around among the women and touched and questioned. But I had firmly decided to somehow slip out, as soon as that was over, and look around for the house. I was convinced that it was there. Leaving the room was not very hard; down among all the dresses you could creep along like a dog, and the door to the vestibule had been left ajar. But the front door wouldn't yield. There were a number of mechanisms on it, chains and bolts, which I couldn't undo in my hurry. Suddenly it did open after all, but with a loud noise, and before I could get outside, I was seized and pulled back.

"Halt! You can't sneak out on us like that," said Viera Schulin, her voice bright with amusement. She bent down to me, and I was determined not to reveal anything to this warm, laughing person. But since I didn't say a word, she took it for granted that nature's call had driven me to the door; she grasped my hand and had already begun to walk, intending, half confidential, half domineering, to take me to the bathroom. This intimate misunderstanding mortified me beyond all measure. I tore myself loose and shot her an angry look. "What I want to see is the house," I said with dignity. She didn't understand.

"The big house outside near the stairs."

"You silly goose," she said, snatching at me; "there's no house there any more."

I insisted that there was.

"We'll go look sometime in the daylight," she proposed, in a conciliating manner. "You can't crawl around there at this hour. There are holes there, and right behind are Papa's fishponds, which aren't allowed to freeze over. You'll fall in and turn into a fish."

With that, she pushed me in front of her, back into the lighted rooms. They were all sitting there and talking, and I looked at them one after another: of course they only go when it isn't there, I thought with contempt; if Maman and I lived here, it would always be there. Maman looked distracted, while the others were all speaking at the same time. She was undoubtedly thinking of the house.

Zoë sat down next to me and began to ask questions. She had a well-regulated face, in which insight kept being renewed from time to time, as if she were continually understanding something. My father sat leaning a little to the right and listened to the Marchesa, who was laughing. Count Schulin stood between Maman and his wife and was telling a story. But the Countess, I saw, interrupted him in the middle of a sentence.

"No, child, you're imagining that," said the Count good-naturedly, but all at once he had the same troubled look on his face, which he stretched forward above the two ladies. The Countess could not be diverted from what she had supposedly imagined. She had a very strained expression, like someone who doesn't wish to be disturbed. She was making little gestures of self-defense with her soft, ring-filled hands;

someone said "Sst!" and suddenly there was complete silence.

Behind the people in the room, the enormous objects from the old house were crowding in, much too close. The massive family silver glittered and bulged as if it were being seen through a magnifying glass. My father looked around in surprise.

"Mamma smells something," said Viera Schulin behind him, "and then we always have to be quiet; she smells with her ears." But she herself stood there with raised eyebrows, attentive and all nose.

The Schulins, in this respect, had grown a little peculiar since the fire. In the small, overheated rooms an odor might rise at any moment, and then everyone would analyze it and give their opinion. Zoë did something at the stove, practical and conscientious; the Count walked around, stopped for a moment at each corner and waited; and then said, "It isn't here." The Countess had stood up and didn't know where she ought to look. My father slowly turned around in a circle, as if he had the smell behind him. The Marchesa, who had immediately assumed that it was an offensive smell, held her handkerchief over her mouth and looked from one person to the next to see if it had gone. "Here, here," Viera called from time to time, as if she had found it. And around each word there was a strange silence. As for me, I had diligently sniffed along with the others. But all at once (was it the heat of the room or the closeness of so many lights?) I was overcome, for the first time in my life, by something very like the fear of ghosts. I realized that all these well-defined grownups, who just a few minutes before had been talking and laughing, were going around stooped over and occupied with something invisible; that they admitted there was something here that they couldn't see. And it was terrifying to know that it was stronger than all of them.

My fear intensified. It seemed to me as if what they were looking for might suddenly break out of me like a rash; and then they would see it and point their fingers at me. In desperation I looked over at Maman. She was sitting strangely upright in her chair; I felt she was waiting for me. I had hardly sat down beside her and sensed that she was trembling inwardly, when I knew that the house had just now started to vanish again.

"Malte, you fraidy-cat," someone laughed. It was Viera's voice. But we didn't let go of each other, and endured it together; and we stayed like that, Maman and I, until the house had completely vanished.

— ••• —

Richest in nearly incomprehensible experiences, though, were the birthdays. You already knew, of course, that life took pleasure in not making distinctions; but on this day you got up with a right to joy that couldn't be doubted. Probably the feeling that you had such a right had developed in you at a very early age, the age when you grasp at everything and really get everything; when, with the unerring power of the imagination, you take the Things you happen to have and raise them to the primary-color intensity of the desire that just then happens to possess you.

But then, all at once, come those strange birthdays when, fully established in the consciousness of this right, you see the others becoming uncertain. You would still like to have someone dress you as in earlier years, and then take to yourself everything that follows. But you are hardly awake when someone outside your door shouts that the cake hasn't arrived yet; or you hear something break as the presents are being laid out on the table in the next room; or someone comes in and leaves the door open, and you see everything before you should see it. That is the moment when something like an operation is performed on you. A brief, atrociously painful incision. But the hand that does it is experienced and steady. Everything is finished before you know it. And a moment later you no longer think about yourself; you just want to save the birthday, watch the others, anticipate their mistakes, and confirm them in their illusion that they are taking care of everything admirably. They don't make it easy for you. They seem to be extraordinarily inept, almost stupid. They manage to come in with presents that are meant for other people; you run to meet them and then you have to pretend you were just running around the room for exercise, not toward anything in particular. They want to surprise you and, with a very superficial pretense of expectation, they lift the bottom layer of the toy-carton, where there is nothing but cotton padding; then you have to relieve them of their embarrassment. Or if it's a mechanical toy they're giving you, they break the spring the first time they wind it up. So it's a good idea to practice beforehand by surreptitiously reaching out with your foot and pushing along an overwound mouse or some such toy: in this way you can often deceive them and help them over their shame.

In the end, you did everything you had to do; it didn't require any great skill. Talent was really necessary only when someone had taken pains and, filled with importance and good humor, brought you a joy, and even at a distance you saw that it was a joy for someone quite different from you, a completely alien joy; you didn't even know anyone it would have been right for: that's how alien it was.

— ••• —

The days when people knew, really knew, how to tell stories must have been before my time. I never heard one. When Abelone used to speak to me about Maman's youth, it became obvious that she couldn't tell a story. Count Brahe could still do that, she said. I want to write down what she knew about it.

As a very young girl, Abelone must have had a special and far-reaching sensitivity. In those days, the Brahes lived in town, on the Bredgade, and entertained quite often. When she went up to her room late in the evening, she would think she was tired like the others. But then all at once she would feel the window and, if I understood her correctly, she could stand in front of the night, for hours, thinking: that is my true life. "I stood there like a prisoner," she said, "and the stars were freedom." In those days, she was able to go to sleep without making herself heavy. The expression "to fall asleep" doesn't apply to this year of her girlhood. Sleep was something that ascended with you, and from time to time your eyes were open and you lay on a new surface that was still far from being the highest. And then you were up before daybreak; even in winter, when the others came sleepy and late to the late breakfast. In the evenings, when it grew dark, there were of course only lights for the entire household, communal lights. But those two candles quite early in the new darkness, with which everything began again—those you had to yourself. They stood in their low two-branched candlestick and shone peacefully through the small oval lampshades of tulle painted with roses, which had to be moved farther down from time to time. There was nothing bothersome in that; for one thing, you were in no hurry at all, and then you would sometimes have to look up and think, when you were writing a letter or in the diary that had once been begun, long ago, in a completely different hand-writing, timid and beautiful.

Count Brahe lived entirely apart from his daughters. He considered it a mere figment of imagination when anyone asserted that they were sharing their life with others. ("Hmm, sharing—," he would say.) But he wasn't displeased when people spoke to him about his daughters; he would listen attentively, as if they were living in another town.

It was therefore something quite extraordinary when one day after breakfast he gestured for Abelone to approach him. "We have the same habits, it seems; I too write very early in the morning. You can help me." Abelone still remembered it as if it were yesterday.

The very next morning she was led into her father's study, which had always been considered a forbidden area. She didn't have time to observe what was there, for she was immediately sat down facing the Count at his desk, which seemed to her like a vast plain with books and piles of paper as villages.

The Count dictated. Those who asserted that Count Brahe was writing his memoirs weren't completely wrong. Only these weren't the political and military reminiscences that everyone was looking forward to so eagerly. "I forget those," the old gentleman would say curtly, when anyone questioned him about such matters. But what he didn't want to forget was his childhood. That was what he clung to. And it was quite natural, according to him, that this very distant time had taken control of him now; that when he turned his gaze inward, it lay there as in a brilliant northern summer night, intensified and unsleeping.

Sometimes he would jump up and speak into the candles so passionately that they flickered. Or whole sentences had to be crossed out, and then he would pace violently back and forth, and his Nile-green silk dressing gown would billow out behind him. During all this there was one other person present: Sten, the Count's old valet, a Jutlander, whose job it was, when Grandfather jumped up, to quickly put his hands over the single loose pages, covered with notes, which lay around on the desk. His Lordship thought that modern paper was worthless, that it was much too light and flew away at the slightest breath. And Sten, whose long upper half was the only visible part of him, shared this distrust and seemed to squat on his hands, blind in the daylight and solemn as an owl.

This Sten spent his Sunday afternoons reading Swedenborg, and none of the servants would have dared to enter his room, because he was supposed to be summoning the dead. His family had always trafficked with spirits, and Sten was especially pre-destined for this kind of commerce. His mother had seen an apparition the night she gave birth to him. Sten had large, round eyes, and the other end of his glance seemed to lie somewhere behind the person he was looking at. Abelone's father often asked him how the spirits were, the way you might ask someone about the health of his relatives. "Are they coming, Sten?" he would say benevolently. "It is good if they come."

The dictation went its way for a few mornings. But then Abelone couldn't spell "Eckernførde." It was a proper noun, and she had never heard it before. The Count, who for quite some time had been looking for an excuse to give up the writing, pretended to be annoyed.

"She isn't able to write it," he said sharply, "and others won't be able to read it. And will they really *see* what I am saying?" he continued angrily, keeping his eyes fixed on Abelone. "Will they see him, this Saint-Germain?" he shouted at her. "Did we say Saint-Germain? Cross that out. Write: the Marquis de Belmare."

Abelone crossed out and wrote. But the Count went on speaking so fast that it was impossible to keep up with him.

"He couldn't stand children, this admirable Belmare; but he took me in his lap, small as I was, and for some reason I started to bite his diamond buttons. That delighted him. He laughed and tilted my chin until we were looking into each other's eyes. 'You have excellent teeth,' he said, 'teeth that are willing to attempt something . . .' But I was looking at his eyes. I have traveled around quite a bit since then. I have seen all sorts of eyes; but believe me, I never again saw any like his. For those eyes a thing didn't need to be present; they contained it inside them. You have heard of Venice? Well, let me assure you, those eyes could have looked Venice right into this room, so that it would have appeared before you as clearly as this desk. I once sat in a corner listening as he told my father a story about Persia: sometimes I think that my hands still smell of it. My father had the greatest respect for him, and His Highness the Landgrave was in a way his disciple. But there were of course quite a few people who reproached him with believing in the past only when it was *inside* him. They couldn't understand that the whole business has no meaning unless you were born with it.

"Books are empty," the Count shouted, turning toward the walls with a furious gesture; "it is blood that matters, it is blood that we must learn to read. He had strange stories and remarkable images in his blood, this Belmare; he could open it wherever he wanted, there was always something written there; not a page had been left blank. And when he locked himself in from time to time and skimmed through it in solitude, he came to the passages about alchemy and precious stones and colors. Why shouldn't all those things have been there? They must certainly be somewhere.

"He would easily have been able to live with a Truth, this man, if he had been alone. But it was no small matter to be alone with a Truth like his. And he was not so indelicate as to invite people to visit him when he was with her; he didn't want her to be gossiped about: he was far too much of an Easterner for that. 'Adieu, madame,' he said to her in all truthfulness, 'until we meet again. Perhaps in another thousand years we will be somewhat stronger and more undisturbed. Your beauty is just beginning to blossom, madame,' he said, and this was not merely a polite compliment. With that, he went off and laid out his zoo for the people, a kind of Jardin d'Acclimatation for the larger kinds of lies, which had never been seen in our country, and a palm-house of exaggerations, and a small, well-tended fig garden of false mysteries. Then people came from all sides, and he walked around with diamond buckles on his shoes and was entirely at the disposal of his guests.

"A superficial existence, you think? Yet it expressed a basic chivalry toward his lady, and in the process he managed to conserve his years very well."

For some time now the old man had no longer been speaking to Abelone, whom he had forgotten. He paced back and forth like a madman and threw challenging glances at Sten, as if Sten, at a given moment, were supposed to change into the man he was thinking about. But Sten was not yet changing.

"He had to be *seen*," Count Brahe continued relentlessly. "There was a time when he was perfectly visible, although in many cities the letters he received weren't addressed to anyone: they just had the name of the city on them, nothing else. But I saw him.

"He wasn't handsome." The Count burst out in a strangely hurried laugh. "He wasn't even what people call important-looking or distinguished: there were always more distinguished men around him. He was rich: but with him that was just a kind of caprice, which you couldn't rely on. He was well-formed, though other men carried themselves better. Of course in those days I couldn't judge whether he was witty, whether he had this or that quality that people value—: but he *was*."

The Count, trembling, stood still and made a movement as if he were positioning in space some object that would remain there.

At that instant he became aware of Abelone.

"Do you see him?" he bellowed at her. And suddenly he seized one of the silver candlesticks and held the light blindingly into her face.

Abelone remembered that she had seen him.

During the next few days Abelone was summoned regularly, and after this incident the dictation proceeded much more calmly. The Count was collecting from all kinds of manuscripts his earliest memories of the Bernstorff circle, in which his father had played a certain role. Abelone now felt so well adjusted to the peculiarities of her work that anyone who saw the two together might easily have mistaken their purposeful collaboration for true intimacy.

One day, as Abelone was about to retire, the old gentleman walked up to her with his hands behind his back, as if he were holding a surprise there. "Tomorrow we shall write about Julie Reventlow," he said; and then, savoring his words: "She was a saint."

Probably Abelone looked at him incredulously.

"Yes, yes, such things are still possible," he insisted in a tone of authority; "all things are possible, Countess Abel."

He took Abelone's hands and opened them like a book.

"She had the stigmata," he said; "here and here." And he tapped on both her palms, hard and sharp, with his cold finger.

Abelone didn't know what "stigmata" meant. I'll understand later, she thought; she was very impatient to hear about the saint whom her father had actually seen. But she was not summoned again, neither the next morning nor afterward.—

"Countess Reventlow has often been spoken about in your family since then," Abelone concluded briefly, when I asked her to tell me more. She looked tired; she also maintained that she had forgotten most of these events. "But sometimes I still feel the two marks," she said, smiling, and she couldn't stop smiling, and looked, almost with curiosity, into her empty hands.

— •••—

Even before my father's death everything had changed. Ulsgaard no longer belonged to us. My father died in town, in an apartment house that seemed to me utterly hostile and alien. I was already living abroad and returned too late.

They had laid him on a bier, between two rows of tall candles, in a room that looked out on the court-yard. The smell of the flowers was unintelligible, like many voices speaking at the same time. His hand-some face, in which they had closed the eyes, wore the expression of a man who out of politeness is trying to remember something. He was dressed in the uniform of the Master of the Hunt, but for some reason or other the white ribbon had been put on instead of the blue one. His hands weren't folded; they lay obliquely crossed and looked artificial and meaningless. Someone had hurriedly told me that he had suffered enormously: nothing of that could be seen. His features had been tidied up like the furni-ture in a guest-room after a visitor has moved out. I felt as if I had seen him dead several times before: so familiar did all this seem.

Only the surroundings were new; unpleasantly so. This oppressive room was new, with windows oppo-site it, probably the windows of other people. It was new that Sieversen came in from time to time and did nothing. Sieversen had grown old. Then I was supposed to have breakfast. Several times breakfast was announced. But I absolutely didn't feel like having breakfast that day. I didn't notice that they wanted to get me out of the room; finally, since I still hadn't gone, Sieversen somehow managed to communicate to me that the doctors were there. I had no idea why. There was still something left to do, Sieversen said, and looked at me intently with her reddened eyes. Then two gentlemen walked in, so hastily that they seemed in danger of tripping over themselves: these were the doctors. The first one, with an abrupt movement, lowered his head (as if he had horns and were getting ready to butt) so that he could look at us over his pince-nez: first at Sieversen, then at me.

He bowed with the stiff formality of a cadet. "His Excellency the Master of the Hunt had one last wish," he said in a voice exactly like the way he had entered the room; I again had the feeling that his haste would make him trip. I somehow forced him to direct his gaze through his pince-nez. His colleague was a chubby, thin-skinned, blond man; it occurred to me that it would be easy to make him blush. There was a long pause. It seemed strange that the Master of the Hunt still had wishes.

I involuntarily glanced again at the handsome, well-proportioned face. And then I knew that he wanted certainty. This was what, fundamentally, he had always wanted. Now he would have it.

"You are here for the perforation of the heart: please go ahead."

I bowed and stepped back. The two doctors returned my bow simultaneously and immediately began to confer about their work. Someone was already pushing the candles aside. But the elder of the two once again took a few steps toward me. At a certain point he stretched forward, in order to spare himself the last part of the way, and looked at me angrily.

"It is not necessary," he said, "that is, I think it would perhaps be better if you . . ."

He seemed to me neglected and shabby in his frugal, hurried attitude. I bowed once more; the circumstances dictated that I should already be bowing again.

"Thanks," I said curtly. "I won't disturb you."

I knew that I could endure this and that there was no reason for avoiding it. It had to happen this way. It was perhaps the meaning of all the rest. Besides, I had never seen what it is like when someone's breast is perforated. It seemed appropriate not to reject such a rare experience when it presented itself so freely and naturally. Even then I no longer really believed in disappointments; so there was nothing to be afraid of.

No, no, there is nothing in the world that can be imagined in advance, not the slightest thing. Everything is made up of so many unique particulars that are impossible to foresee. In imagination, we pass over them in our haste and don't notice that they're missing. But realities are slow and indescribably detailed.

Who would have thought, for example, of that resistance? Hardly had the wide, high breast been laid bare when the hurried little man had already located the right spot. But the quickly applied instrument didn't penetrate. I felt as if all time had suddenly left the room. We were like a group in a picture. But then time rejoined us with a faint, gliding sound, and there was more of it than we could use up. All at once there was a knocking somewhere. I had never heard that kind of knocking before: a warm, closed, double knocking. My ear transmitted it, and at the same time I saw that the doctor had pushed through to the bottom. But it took a few moments for the two impressions to combine inside me. So, I thought, now it is through. The knocking, as to its tempo, sounded almost sadistically happy.

I looked at the man I had now known for such a long time. No, he was in complete command of himself: a gentleman working quickly and objectively, who had to leave right away. There wasn't a trace of pleasure or satisfaction in his work. Only on his left temple a few hairs had stood on end, out of some ancient instinct. He carefully withdrew the instrument, and in that spot something like a mouth appeared, from which, twice in succession, blood spurted out, as if the mouth were uttering a two-syllable word. The young, blond doctor, with an elegant movement, quickly soaked it up in his piece of cotton. And now the wound stayed motionless, like a closed eye.

I assume that I bowed once more, without really paying attention this time. At any rate, I was astonished to find myself alone. Someone had buttoned up the uniform again, and the white ribbon lay across it as before. But now the Master of the Hunt was dead, and not only he. Now the heart had been perforated, our heart, the heart of our family. Now it was all over. This, then, was the shattering of the helmet: "Today Brigge and nevermore," said something inside me.

I wasn't thinking of my own heart. But when it occurred to me later, I knew for the first time with total certainty that it didn't come into consideration for this purpose. It was an individual heart. It was already at its work of beginning from the beginning.

— ••• —

I know that I imagined I wouldn't be able to go abroad again right away. First everything has to be put in order, I repeated to myself. *What* needed to be put in order wasn't clear to me. There was practically nothing to do. I walked around in the city and noticed that it had changed. It was pleasant to step out of the hotel where I was staying, and to see that it was now a city for grownups, on its best behavior for me, almost as if I were a stranger. Everything had shrunk a little, and I walked down the Langelinie to the lighthouse and back again. As I approached the Amaliengade, it wasn't surprising that from somewhere an influence emanated which I had acknowledged for years and which was trying to assert its old power again. In that part of the city there were certain corner-windows or porches or lanterns that knew a great deal about me and threatened me with that knowledge. I looked them in the face and let them feel that I was staying at the Hotel Phoenix and could leave the country again at any moment. But my conscience wasn't happy in doing that. The suspicion arose in me that none of these influences and associations had really been overcome yet. I had secretly abandoned them one day, unfinished as they were. So my childhood too would still, so to speak, have to be achieved, if I didn't want to give it up as forever lost. And while I understood how I had lost it, at the same time I felt that I would never have anything else I could appeal to.

Every day I spent a few hours in the Dronningens Tvaergade, in those small rooms, which had the insulted look of all apartments in which someone has died. I walked back and forth between the desk and the large white porcelain stove, burning the Master of the Hunt's papers. I had begun by throwing the letters into the fire in bundles, just as I had found them; but they were tied together too firmly, and only charred at the edges. I had to exercise a good deal of self-control before I could loosen them. Most of them had a strong, convincing fragrance, which penetrated me as if it wanted to stir up memories in me as well. I didn't have any. Then some photographs, heavier than the rest, happened to slip out; these photographs took an unbelievably long time to burn. I don't know why, but suddenly I imagined that Ingeborg's picture might be among them. Each time I looked, though, I saw mature, splendid, obviously beautiful women, who suggested a different train of thought to me. For it turned out that I wasn't entirely without memories after all. In exactly such eyes as these I had sometimes seen myself when, as a growing boy, I used to walk down the avenues with my father. Then, from inside a passing carriage, they might surround me with a look that I could hardly find my way out of. I knew now that in those days they had been comparing me with him and that the comparison hadn't turned out in my favor. Certainly not; the Master of the Hunt had no need to be afraid of comparisons.

It may be that I now know something he *was* afraid of. Let me explain how I arrived at this supposition. Deep inside his wallet there was a piece of paper that had been folded up for a long time, crumbling, broken at the folds. I read it before putting it in the fire. It was in his most careful handwriting, firmly and regularly written; but I immediately noticed that it was just a copy.

"Three hours before his death," it began, and it referred to Christian IV. I can't of course reproduce the contents word for word. Three hours before his death he desired to get up. The doctor and Wormius, his valet, helped him to his feet. He stood a bit unsteadily, but he stood, and they put on his quilted dressing-gown. Then he suddenly sat down on the front end of the bed and said something. It was incomprehensible. The doctor kept constant hold of his left hand to prevent him from falling back on the bed. They sat like this, and from time to time the king said, thickly and painfully, this unintelligible word. Finally the doctor began to speak encouragingly to him; he hoped to gradually figure out what the king was trying to say. After a little while, the king interrupted him and said, all at once quite distinctly, "O doctor, doctor, what is your name?" The doctor had some difficulty in remembering.

"Sperling, Your Majesty."

But this was really not the important point. The king, as soon as he heard that they understood him, stared out of his wide-open right eye (the one he could still use) and said with his whole face the single word that his tongue had been forming for hours, the only word that still existed: "Døden," he said, "Døden."*

* Death, death.

There was nothing more on the page. I read it several times before putting it into the fire. And I remembered that my father had suffered enormously at the end. That is what they had told me.

— ••• —

Since then I have thought a great deal about the fear of death, not without taking into consideration certain of my own experiences. I think I can honestly say that I have felt it. It has overtaken me in cities, in the midst of people, often for no reason at all. But often there have been abundant reasons; when, for example, someone on a bench gave way, and the others all stood around and looked at him, and he was already far beyond fear: then I had his fear. Or that time in Naples, when the young girl sat opposite me in the electric trolley and died. At first it seemed that she had fainted; we even drove on for a while. But then there was no doubt that we had to stop. And behind us the carriages halted and piled up, as if nothing would ever move again in that direction. The pale, fat girl might have died peacefully like that, leaning against the woman beside her. But her mother wouldn't allow that. She created all possible difficulties for her. She disheveled her clothes and poured some kind of liquid into the mouth that could no longer keep anything in. She rubbed her forehead with a salve someone had brought, and when the eyes rolled back a little, she began to shake her, to make them come forward again. She screamed into those eyes, which couldn't hear, she pushed and pulled the whole thing back and forth like a doll, and finally she hauled off and slapped the fat face with all her might, so that it wouldn't die. That time I was afraid.

But I had already been afraid before. For example, when my dog died. The one who blamed me once and for all. He was very sick. I had been kneeling beside him all day long, when suddenly he looked up and barked, quickly and abruptly, as he used to do when a stranger entered the room. A bark like that was a kind of signal that we had arranged between us for such occasions, and I involuntarily glanced toward the door. But it was already inside him. Alarmed, I turned back and looked into his eyes, and he looked into mine; but not to say goodbye. He looked at me with an expression of harshness and surprise. He reproached me for allowing it to enter. He was convinced that I could have prevented it. It was obvious now that he had always overestimated me. And there was no time left to explain. He continued to look at me out of an infinite surprise and solitude until it was over.

Or I was afraid when in autumn, after the first nights of frost, the flies came into the rooms and revived once again in the warmth. They were strangely dried up and were terrified at their own buzzing; I could see that they no longer really knew what they were doing. They stayed motionless for hours and let themselves be, until it occurred to them that they were still alive; then they flung themselves blindly in every direction and didn't know what to do when they got there, and I could hear them falling down again in this, that, or the other place. And finally they crawled around everywhere and slowly covered the whole room with their death.

But even when I was alone I could be afraid. Why should I pretend that those nights never existed, when the fear of death made me sit up in bed, clinging to the thought that sitting up was at any rate something only a living person could do: that the dead didn't sit up. This always happened in one of those chance rooms which immediately abandoned me when things went wrong, as if they were afraid of being cross-examined and implicated in my troubles. There I sat, and I probably looked so frightening that nothing had the courage to approach me; even the candle, which I had just obliged by lighting it, wouldn't have anything to do with me. It burned there for itself, as in an empty room. My last hope was always the window. I imagined that outside there might still be something that belonged to me, even now, even in this sudden poverty of dying. But hardly had I looked toward it when I wished that the window had been barricaded, closed like the wall. For now I knew that everything was happening out there with the same indifference, that outside too there was nothing but my solitude. The solitude which I had brought upon myself and which had become too vast for my heart to take in. I remembered people I had once left, and I didn't understand how someone could ever abandon another person.

My God, my God, if such nights still lie in wait for me, allow me at least one of those thoughts that I have occasionally been able to think. What I am asking is not so unreasonable; for I know that they were born of fear itself, because my fear was so vast. When I was a boy, they hit me in the face and told me I was a coward. That was because I still didn't know how to be completely afraid. But since then I have learned to be afraid with real fear, which only increases when the energy that engenders it increases. We have no conception of this energy, except in our fear. For it is so utterly inconceivable, so entirely opposed to us, that our brain disintegrates at the point where we force ourselves to think about it. And yet for some time now I have believed that it is *our* energy, all our energy, which is still too strong for us. It is true that we don't know it, but aren't we most ignorant about what is most our own? Sometimes I think about how the sky came to be, and death: because we moved outside ourselves what is most precious to us, since there was still so much else to do first and it wasn't safe with us in all our busyness. Now much time has passed over this, and we have grown accustomed to smaller things. We no longer recognize what belongs to us and are terrified by its extreme vastness. May this not be so?

— ••• —

Besides, I now understand quite well how someone could carry, all those years, deep inside his wallet, the description of a death hour. It wouldn't even have to be a specially selected one; they all have something unusual about them. I can imagine, for example, someone copying out how Félix Arvers died. It was in a hospital. He was dying gently and serenely, and the nun perhaps thought that he was further along in it than he really was. She shouted out some instructions, in a very loud voice, indicating where something or other could be found. She was a rather uneducated nun; she had never seen in writing the word "corridor," which at that moment she couldn't avoid using. Thus it happened that she said "collidor," thinking that this was the proper way to pronounce it. Thereupon Arvers postponed dying. He felt it was necessary to clear up this matter first. He became perfectly lucid and explained to her that it should be "corridor." Then he died. He was a poet and hated the approximate; or perhaps he was concerned only with the truth; or it annoyed him to be taking along as his last impression the thought that the world would continue to go on so carelessly. Whatever the reason was can no longer be determined. But let no one think it was pedantry. Otherwise, the same reproach would fall on the saintly Jean de Dieu, who in the midst of his dying jumped up and ran out to the garden, just in time to cut down the man who had hanged himself there, tidings of whom had in some miraculous way penetrated the hidden tension of his agony. He too was concerned only with the truth.

— ••• —

There exists a creature that is perfectly harmless; when it passes before your eyes, you hardly notice it and immediately forget it again. But as soon as it somehow, invisibly, gets into your ears, it begins to develop, it hatches, and cases have been known where it has penetrated into the brain and flourished there devastatingly, like the pneumococci in dogs which gain entrance through the nose.

This creature is Your Neighbor.

Now ever since I have been drifting about on my own like this, I have had innumerable neighbors; neighbors above me and below me, neighbors on my right and on my left, sometimes all four kinds at once. I could simply write the history of my neighbors; that would take up a whole lifetime. Actually, it would be more of a history of the symptoms they have generated in me; because they share with all creatures of a similar nature the characteristic that their presence can be detected only through the disturbances they cause in certain tissues.

I have had unpredictable neighbors and others whose habits were extremely regular. I have sat for hours trying to discover the law of the former type; for I was convinced that even they were acting in accordance with some law. And when my punctual neighbors failed to come home at their usual time one evening, I have imagined the disasters that might have happened to them, and have kept my candle burning, and have been as anxious as a young wife. I have had neighbors who felt nothing but hatred, and neighbors who were involved in a passionate love affair; or I experienced the moment when one emotion abruptly turned into the other, in the middle of the night, and then, of course, sleep was unthinkable. In fact, this led me to observe that sleep is much less frequent than people generally suppose. My two neighbors in St. Petersburg, for example, attached very little importance to sleep. One of them stood and played the violin, and I'm sure that as he played he looked across into the too-awake houses that never stopped being brightly lit during those improbable August nights. As to my neighbor on the right, I know at least that he lay in bed; in my time, indeed, he no longer got up at all. He even kept his eyes closed; but you couldn't say that he slept. He lay there and recited long poems, poems by Pushkin and Nekrasov, in the singsong tone that children use when they are asked to recite a poem. And despite the music of my neighbor on the left, it was this fellow with his poems who wove a cocoon inside my head, and God knows what would have hatched out of it if the student who occasionally visited him hadn't knocked on the wrong door one day. He told me the story of his friend, and it turned out to be more or less reassuring. At any rate, it was a simple, unambiguous story, which put an end to the swarming maggots of my conjectures.

This petty bureaucrat next door had one Sunday decided to solve a strange problem. He assumed that he would live for quite a long time, say another fifty years. The generosity he thus showed toward himself put him in a radiantly good mood. But now he wanted to outdo himself. It occurred to him that these years could be changed into days, hours, minutes, even (if you could stand it) into seconds; and he multiplied and multiplied, and a grand total appeared such as he had never seen before. It made him giddy. He had to recover for a while. Time was valuable, he had always heard, and he was astonished that a man who possessed such a vast quantity of time didn't have a guard beside him at every moment. How easy it would be to rob him! But then his good, almost exuberant humor came back again; he put on his fur coat, to appear a little broader and more imposing, and gave himself the whole of this fabulous capital, addressing himself in a slightly condescending manner:

"Nikolai Kuzmitch," he said benevolently, and imagined himself also sitting without the fur coat, thin and shabby on the horsehair sofa; "I do hope, Nikolai Kuzmitch," he said, "that you won't get a swelled head from your new fortune. You must always bear in mind that wealth isn't the main thing; there are poor people who are thoroughly respectable; there are even impoverished noblemen and generals' daughters who go around peddling things on the sidewalk." And the benefactor cited a few more examples that were well known throughout the city.

The other Nikolai Kuzmitch, the one on the horsehair sofa, the recipient of this gift, didn't look the slightest bit puffed up; you might safely assume that he was going to be reasonable. In fact he didn't make any changes in his modest, regular way of life, and he now spent his Sundays putting his accounts in order. But after a few weeks it became obvious that he was spending an incredible amount. I will have to economize, he thought. He got up earlier, he washed his face less thoroughly, he drank his tea standing up, he ran to the office and arrived much too early. He saved a little time everywhere. But when Sunday came around, there was nothing left of all this saving. Then he realized that he had been duped. I should never have gotten change, he said to himself. How long a fine, unbroken year would have lasted! But these damned small coins—they keep disappearing, God knows how. And one ugly afternoon, he sat down in a corner of the sofa, waiting for the gentleman in the fur coat, from whom he meant to demand his time back. He would bolt the door and not let him out until he had forked over the whole amount. "In bills," he would say, "of ten years, if you don't mind." Four bills of ten and one of five, and the rest he could keep and go to hell with. Yes, he was prepared to give him the rest, as long as there were no difficulties. Exasperated, he sat on the horsehair sofa and waited; but the gentleman never came. And he, Nikolai Kuzmitch, who just a few weeks before had so easily seen himself sitting there, was unable, now that he really sat there, to picture the other Nikolai Kuzmitch, the one in the fur coat, the benefactor. What had become of him, only heaven knew; probably his embezzlements had been traced, and he was behind bars somewhere. Certainly there must have been many others whose lives he had ruined. Swindlers like that always work on a large scale.

It occurred to him that there had to be some public agency, a kind of Time Bank, where he could change at least some part of his miserable seconds. After all, they *were* genuine. He had never heard of an institution like this, but he would certainly be able to find something of the sort in the directory, under T, or perhaps it was called "Bank of Time"; he could easily look under B. If necessary he might also check under the letter I, for presumably it was an imperial institution; that would be in keeping with its importance.

Later, Nikolai Kuzmitch always used to give his word of honor that, although he was understandably in a very depressed mood that Sunday evening, he hadn't had a thing to drink. He was therefore perfectly sober when the following incident occurred, as far as one can tell what actually happened. Perhaps he had dozed off for a few minutes in the corner of the sofa; he might easily have done that. At first this little nap gave him the greatest relief. I have been meddling with numbers, he said to himself. All right, I don't understand the first thing about numbers. But it's obvious that they shouldn't be granted too much importance; they are, after all, just a kind of arrangement created by the government for the sake of public order. No one had ever seen them anywhere but on paper. It was impossible, for instance, to meet a Seven or a Twenty-five at a party. There simply weren't any there. And so this slight confusion had taken place, out of pure absent-mindedness: time and money, as if there were no difference between the two. Nikolai Kuzmitch almost laughed. It was really wonderful to have found the mistake, and in good time, that was the important thing, in good time. Now it would be different. Time was certainly a great embarrassment. But was he the only one this had happened to? Didn't time pass for other people, just as he had discovered, in seconds, even if they weren't aware of it?

Nikolai Kuzmitch was not entirely free from enjoying other people's misfortune. "Let it nevertheless . . . ," he was just about to think, when something bizarre happened. He suddenly felt a breath on his face; it moved past his ears; it was on his hands now. He opened his eyes wide. The window was definitely closed. And as he sat there in the dark room, with eyes wide open, he began to realize that what he was feeling now was *real* time, as it passed by. He recognized, with absolute clarity, all these tiny seconds, all equally tepid, each one exactly like the others, but fast, but fast. What else they were planning, only God knew. Why was this happening to him, of all people, who experienced every kind of draft as an insult? Now he would sit there, and the breeze would go past him like this, ceaselessly, his whole life long. He foresaw all the attacks of neuralgia that would result from this; he was beside himself with rage. He jumped up, but the surprises were not yet over. Beneath his feet too there was something moving; not just one motion, but several, which strangely shook in and against one another. He stiffened with terror: could that be the earth? Of course it was. The earth did, after all, move. He had heard about that in school; but it was passed over rather quickly, and later on was completely hushed up; it was considered not a proper subject for discussion. But now that he had become more sensitive, he was able to feel this too. Did the others feel it? Perhaps, but you couldn't really tell. Probably it didn't bother them, good sailers as they were. But it was in precisely this respect that Nikolai Kuz-

174

mitch was so delicate; he avoided even the streetcars. He staggered around in his room as if he were on the deck of a ship and had to reach out left and right for support. Unfortunately he then remembered something else, about the oblique position of the earth's axis. No, he couldn't endure all these motions. He felt sick. Lying down and keeping quiet were the best remedy, he had once read somewhere. And since that day Nikolai Kuzmitch had been lying in bed.

He lay there and kept his eyes closed. And there were times, during the less shaken days, so to speak, when it was quite bearable. And then he had devised this routine with the poems. It was unbelievable how much that helped. When you recited a poem slowly, with a regular emphasis on the rhyme words, then something more or less stable existed, which you could keep a steady gaze on, inwardly of course. It was lucky that he knew all these poems by heart. But he had always been particularly interested in literature. He didn't complain about his situation, said the student, who had known him for many years. But in the course of time an exaggerated admiration had developed in him for those who, like the student, managed to walk around and endured the motion of the earth.

I remember this story in such detail because it was extraordinarily reassuring to me. I can even say that I have never again had such a pleasant neighbor as this Nikolai Kuzmitch, who certainly would also have admired me.

— ••• —

After this experience I decided that in similar cases I would go straight to the facts. I noticed how simple they were and what a relief, as opposed to conjectures. As if I hadn't known that all our insights are added on later, that they are balance-sheets, nothing more. Right afterward a new page begins, with a completely different account, and no total carried forward. What help in the present case were the few facts, which it was child's play to establish? I will enumerate them in a moment, as soon as I have told my immediate concern: that these facts tended rather to make my situation, which (as I now admit) was already difficult, even more oppressive.

Let it be said, in my honor, that I wrote a great deal in those days; I wrote with compulsive fervor. True, when I had gone out I didn't look forward to coming home again. I even made slight detours and in this way lost a half hour during which I could have been writing. I admit that this was a weakness. But once I was in my room, I had no reason to reproach myself. I wrote; I had *my* life, and the one next door was a completely different life, that I shared nothing with: the life of a medical student who was studying for his exam. I had nothing like that awaiting me; this was already an essential difference. And in other respects as well, our circumstances were as different as they possibly could be. All this seemed crystal clear. Until the moment when I knew *it* would come; then I forgot that we had nothing in common. I listened so intently that my heart began to beat out loud. I stopped whatever I was doing, and listened. And then it came: I was never wrong about that.

Everyone knows the sound made by any round, tin object—the lid of a can, for instance—when it falls out of your hand. Usually it doesn't even make a very loud noise as it hits the floor; there is a sharp clang, then it rolls along on its edge; it becomes really jarring only when its momentum runs down and it bumps around on all sides, clattering, before it finally comes to rest. Well, that is the whole story: some such tin object fell in the next room, rolled, lay motionless, and as this was going on, at certain intervals, someone stamped on the floor. Like all noises formed by repetition, this one too had its internal organization; it went through a whole gamut of inflections and was never exactly the same. But this was precisely what confirmed its regularity. It could be violent or gentle or melancholy; it could furiously rush to its conclusion, or glide along for what seemed like an eternity. And the final vibration was always a surprise. In contrast, the stamping that accompanied it seemed almost mechanical. But it punctuated the sound differently each time; that appeared to be its function. I can review these details much more accurately now; the room next to me is empty. He has gone home, somewhere in the country. He needed to recuperate. I live on the top floor. On my right there is another house; no one has moved into the room below me: I have no neighbors.

In this condition it almost surprises me that I took the matter so seriously. Although each time I was warned in advance by some intuitive sense. I should have taken advantage of that. Don't be frightened, I should have told myself, now *it* is coming. For I knew I was never mistaken. But my fear may have arisen from the very facts I had learned about him; after I knew them, I was even more easily scared. There was a thought which kept making my hair stand on end, as if I had been tapped on the shoulder by a ghost: the thought that what caused this sound was the small, slow, silent movement with which his eyelid would, of its own accord, sink down and close over his right eye while he read. This was the essential thing in his story: a mere trifle. He had already had to let the exams go by a few times; his ambition had become sensitive, and probably his people at home were pressuring him every time they wrote. So what could he do except pull himself together for one final attempt? But a few months before the decisive date, this weakness had appeared; this small, impossible fatigue, which seemed so ridiculous, as when a venetian blind refuses to stay up. I'm sure that for weeks he felt he should be strong enough to master it. Otherwise I would never have hit upon the idea of offering him my will. Because one day I realized that he had come to the end of his. And after that, whenever I felt *it* coming, I stood on my side of the wall and begged him to help himself to mine. And after a while I understood that he was accepting it. Perhaps he shouldn't have; especially since it didn't really help. Even supposing that we delayed matters a bit, it's still questionable whether he was actually in a position to make use of the moments that we gained. And in the meantime my expenditures were beginning to make themselves felt. I know I was wondering how much longer things could go on this way, on the very afternoon when someone walked up to our floor. Because the staircase was so narrow, this always caused a good deal of disturbance in the small hotel. After a while it seemed to me that someone was entering my neighbor's room. Our doors were the last ones in the hallway; his was at an angle to mine and right next to it. But I knew that he occasionally had friends over and, as I have said, I wasn't at all interested in his affairs. Possibly his door opened several times more, and people came and went. I was really not responsible for that.

Well, on this same evening it was worse than ever. It was not yet very late, but I already felt so tired that I had gone to bed; I thought I would probably be able to sleep. Suddenly I leaped up as if someone had touched me. Right afterward, *it* began. It jumped and rolled and slammed against something and rocked and clattered. The stamping was horrible. As this was going on, someone downstairs began banging, distinctly and angrily, on the ceiling. The new tenant was naturally upset. Now: that had to be his door. I was so wide awake that I thought I heard his door, though he was astonishingly careful in opening it. It seemed to me that he was approaching. He would certainly try to find out what room the noise was coming from. But I thought it was strange that he was being so exaggeratedly considerate. He must have noticed, after all, that silence didn't exactly have first priority in this house. Why in the world was he softening his footsteps? For a moment I thought he was standing at my door; and then I heard him—there was no doubt about it—walking into the next room. He walked in without knocking.

And now (how can I describe this?), now everything was absolutely silent. Silent as after a severe pain stops. A strangely feelable, prickling silence, as if a wound were healing. I could have fallen asleep instantly; I could have taken a deep breath and gone off. It was only my amazement that kept me awake. Someone was speaking in the next room, but this too belonged as part of the silence. You had to experience that silence to know what it was like; it's impossible to describe it. Outside, too, everything seemed to have been smoothed out. I sat up, I listened, it was like being in the country. Good God, I thought, his mother is here. She was sitting beside the lamp, she was talking to him, perhaps he had leaned his head so that it was resting against her shoulder. In a minute or two she would be putting him to bed. Now I understood why the steps out in the hallway had been so soft. Ah, that this could exist. A creature like this, before whom doors give way as they never do for us. Yes, now we could sleep.

— ••• —

I have already almost forgotten my neighbor. I realize that it wasn't genuine sympathy that I felt for him. Downstairs I do occasionally ask, as I pass by, what news, if any, there is of him. And I'm happy when it is good news. But I am exaggerating. In reality, I don't need to know. It no longer has any connection with him if I sometimes feel myself suddenly tempted to enter the next room. It's just a step from my door to his, and the room isn't locked. It would interest me to know what that room really looks like. It's easy to imagine any particular room, and often that image more or less corresponds to the reality. The room next door is the only one that is always completely different from what you think.

I tell myself that this is what really tempts me. But I know perfectly well that what is awaiting me in there is a certain tin object. I have assumed that it is really the lid of a can, though of course I may be wrong. That doesn't bother me. It simply accords with my personality to attribute the whole affair to the lid of a can. There was no reason that he should have taken it with him. Probably they cleaned up the room, they put the lid back onto its can, where it belonged. And now both of them together form the concept "can," or more accurately, "round can," a simple, very familiar concept. I seem to remember them standing on the mantelpiece, these two parts that make up the can. Yes, they are even standing in front of the mirror, so that behind it a second can appears, an imaginary one that is indistinguishable from the first. A can which we consider absolutely worthless, but which a monkey, for example, would try to grab. In fact, there would even be two monkeys grabbing for it, since the monkey itself would be doubled as soon as it got to the edge of the mantelpiece. At any rate, it was the lid of this can that had it in for me.

Let us agree on one point: the lid of a can—or let us say, of a can that is in good condition, whose edge curves in the same way as its own—a lid like this should have no other wish than to find itself on top of its can; this would be the utmost that it could imagine for itself; an unsurpassable satisfaction, the fulfillment of all its desires. Indeed, there is something almost ideal about being patiently and gently turned and coming to rest evenly on the small projecting rim, and feeling its interlocking edge inside you, elastic and just as sharp as your own edge is when you are lying alone. Ah, but there are hardly any lids now that can still appreciate this. Here it is very evident how much confusion has been caused among Things by their association with humans. For humans—if it is permissible to compare them, just in passing, with tin lids—humans sit upon their occupations ungracefully and with extreme unwillingness. Some because in their haste they haven't found the right one; some because they have been put on in anger, crooked; some because the corresponding rims have been dented, each in a different way. Let us admit in all sincerity that basically they have just one thought: as soon as they get a chance, to jump down and roll around and clatter. Otherwise, where do all these so-called amusements come from, and the noise they make?

For centuries now, Things have been looking on at this. It's no wonder that they are corrupted, that they lose their taste for their natural, silent functions and want to take advantage of existence, the way they see it being taken advantage of all around them. They make attempts to evade their duties; they grow listless and negligent, and people are not at all surprised when they catch Things red-handed in some scandalous situation. People know that so well from their own experience. They get annoyed because they are the stronger ones, because they think they have more of a right to change, because they feel they are being aped; but they let the matter go, as they let themselves go. But wherever there is someone who gathers himself together, some solitary person, for example, who wants to rest roundly upon his whole circumference, day and night, he immediately provokes the opposition, the contempt, the hatred of those degenerate objects which, in their own bad consciences, can no longer endure the knowledge that something can actually hold itself together and strive according to its own nature. Then they combine to harass and frighten and confuse him, and they know they can do that. Winking to one another, they begin the seduction, which then grows on into the infinite and sweeps along all creatures, even God himself, against the solitary one, who will perhaps endure: the saint.

— ••• —

How well I now understand those strange pictures in which Things meant for limited and ordinary uses stretch out and stroke one another, lewd and curious, quivering in the random lechery of distraction. Those kettles that walk around steaming, those pistons that start to think, and the indolent funnel that squeezes into a hole for its pleasure. And already, tossed up by the jealous void, and among them, there are arms and legs, and faces that warmly vomit onto them, and windy buttocks that offer them satisfaction.

And the saint writhes and pulls back into himself; yet in his eyes there was still a look which thought this was possible: he had glimpsed it. And already his senses are precipitating out of the clear solution of his soul. His prayer is already losing its leaves and stands up out of his mouth like a withered shrub. His heart has fallen over and poured out into the muck. His whip strikes him as weakly as a tail flicking away flies. His sex is once again in one place only, and when a woman comes toward him, upright through the huddle, with her naked bosom full of breasts, it points at her like a finger.

There was a time when I considered these pictures obsolete. Not that I doubted their reality. I could imagine that long ago such things had happened to saints, those overhasty zealots, who wanted to begin with God, right away, whatever the cost. We no longer make such demands on ourselves. We suspect that he is too difficult for us, that we must postpone him, so that we can slowly do the long work that separates us from him. Now, however, I know that this work leads to combats just as dangerous as the combats of the saint; that such difficulties appear around everyone who is solitary for the sake of that work, as they took form around God's solitaries in their caves and empty shelters, long ago.

— ••• —

When we speak of solitaries, we always take too much for granted. We think people know what we are talking about. But they know absolutely nothing.

They have never seen someone like that; they have just hated him. They have been his neighbors who used him up, and the voices in the next room that tempted him. They have incited Things against him, to make noise and drown him out. Children combined to oppose him, when he was tender and was himself a child, and with every growth he grew up against the grownups. They tracked him to his hiding-place like a hunted animal, and his long youth never had an off-season. And when he wasn't worn out, when he got away, they decried what came forth from him and called it ugly and cast suspicion on it. And when he refused to listen, they became more visible and ate away his food and breathed up his air and spat into his poverty so that it disgusted him. They denounced him as if he had a contagious disease, and threw stones at him to make him go away more quickly. And they were right in their ancient instinct: for he was indeed their enemy.

But then, when he didn't look up, they began to think. They suspected that in all this they had been acting as he had wanted them to; that they had been strengthening him in his solitude and helping him to separate from them for ever. And now they changed their tactics and picked up their final weapon, the other form of resistance, the deadliest of all: fame. And at this noise, there was hardly a single one who didn't look up and let himself be distracted.

— ❖❖❖ —

Last night I thought again of the little green book
that I once must have possessed when I was a boy; and
I don't know why I imagine that it was originally
Mathilde Brahe's. I wasn't interested in it when it
was given to me, and several years went by before I
read it, I think during one summer vacation at Ulsgaard. But from the very first moment it was enormously important to me. It was filled with significance,
through and through—even its exterior. The green
of its binding meant something, and you immediately
understood that what was written inside had to be as
it was. As if it had been agreed upon in advance,
first came that smooth endpaper, watered white on
white, and then the title page, which seemed so mysterious. It looked as if there might well have been
illustrations inside; but there weren't any, and you
had to admit, almost in spite of yourself, that this too
was just as it ought to be. It was a kind of compen-
sation to find, tucked in at a slight angle, the narrow
bookmark—so old that a touch could make it crumble,
and pathetic in its confidence that it was still pink—
which had lain between the same two pages since God
knows when. Perhaps it had never been used, and the
bookbinder had hastily stuck it in, without looking
where. But possibly its position wasn't accidental.
Someone may have stopped reading at that point,

187

who never read in it again; fate may have knocked on his door at that moment, calling him out on some business that took him far away from books, which after all are not life. It was impossible to tell whether the book had been read any further. But it might simply have been that the reader had opened to this passage again and again, and that this had happened often, sometimes even very late at night. At any rate, I felt an immense shyness about these two pages, as you might feel about a mirror that someone is standing in front of. I never read them. I don't even know if I read the whole book. It wasn't very thick, but there were a lot of stories in it, especially during the afternoon; then there was always one that I didn't know yet.

I remember only two of them: the End of Grishka Otrepyov and Charles the Bold's Downfall.

God knows whether it made any real impression on me at the time. But now, after so many years, I still remember the description of how the corpse of the false Tsar was thrown among the mob and lay there for three days, mutilated and riddled with stab-wounds, with a mask on its face. Of course, there isn't the slightest prospect that the little book will ever come into my hands again. But this passage must have been remarkable. I would also like to re-read the part about the meeting with his mother. He must have felt very confident, since he had her come to Moscow; I am even convinced that at that time he believed in himself so strongly that he actually thought he was summoning his mother. And this Maria Nagoi, who arrived from her impoverished convent in just a few days of hurried travel, had everything to gain, after all, by assenting. But didn't his uncertainty begin with the very fact that she acknowledged him? I am not disinclined to believe that the strength of his transformation lay in his no longer being anybody's son.

* [This, in the end, is the strength of all young people who have left home.]

The fact that the nation desired him, without imagining anyone in particular, only made him even freer and more unlimited in his possibilities. But the mother's declaration, even if it was a conscious deception, still had the power to diminish him; it lifted him out of this magnificent self that he had invented; it confined him to a tired imitation; it reduced him to the individual he wasn't: it made him an impostor. And now there also came, more gently dissolving him, this Marina Mniszech, who in her own way disavowed him, since, as it later turned out, she believed not in him but in anyone. I can't of course guarantee how far all this was dealt with in the little green book. But it seems to me that it should have been part of the story.

But even aside from that, this incident is not in the

* Written on the margin of the MS.

least out of date. It is possible even now to imagine a storyteller who would devote a great deal of attention to these last moments; and he wouldn't be wrong in doing so. They are crowded with action: how, shaken from the depths of sleep, he leaps to the window and out over the window, down into the courtyard among the guards. He can't get up by himself; they have to help him. Probably he has broken his foot. Leaning on two of the men, he senses that they believe in him. He looks around: the others believe in him too. He almost feels pity for them, these gigantic *streltsy*; what a sorry state of affairs: they have known Ivan Grozny in all his reality, and still they believe in *him*. He would like to enlighten them; but opening his mouth would mean screaming. The pain in his foot is agonizing, and he thinks so little of himself at this moment that he isn't aware of anything but the pain. And then there is no time. They are crowding in; he sees Shuisky, and behind him all the others. Soon it will be over. But now his guards close around him. They aren't giving him up. And a miracle happens. The faith of these old men spreads; all at once no one is willing to step forward. Shuisky, right in front of him, calls up in desperation to an upper window. *He* doesn't look around. He knows who is standing there; he realizes that everything has become silent, without any transition: absolute silence. Now the voice will come that he recognizes from long ago;

the high, false voice that overstrains itself. And then he hears the Tsarina Mother disavowing him.

Up to this point the whole incident proceeds on its own momentum; but now we need someone who knows how to tell a story: because from the few lines that still remain to be written, a force has to emerge which will transcend every contradiction. Whether or not it is actually stated, you must be ready to swear that between voice and pistol-shot, infinitely compressed, there was once again inside him the will and the power to be everything. Otherwise people won't understand what magnificent sense it made that they pierced his night-shirt and stabbed him all over his body, to see if they would strike the hard core of a personality. And that for three days after he died, he still wore the mask which already he had almost renounced.

—◆◆◆—

When I think about it now, it seems strange to me that in this same book there was a story about the last days of a man who remained, his whole life long, one and the same, hard and unchangeable as granite, and weighing more and more heavily on those who supported him. There is a portrait of him in Dijon. But even without that, we know that he was short, thickset, headstrong, and desperate. His hands are the only part of him that we might not have thought of. They are excessively warm hands, which are continually trying to cool themselves and involuntarily come to rest on any cold object, outspread, with air between the fingers. The blood could shoot into these hands as it might rush to someone else's head; and when clenched into fists, they did seem like the heads of madmen, raging with fantasies.

It required unbelievable caution to live with this blood. The Duke was locked in with it, inside himself, and at times he was afraid of it, when it moved around in him, dark and cringing. Even to him it could seem terrifyingly foreign, this nimble, half-Portuguese blood, which he hardly knew. He was often frightened that it would attack him as he slept, and tear him to pieces. He pretended that it had been mastered, but he always stood in terror of it. He never dared to love a woman, for fear that it would be jealous, and so ravening was it that he never let wine pass his lips; instead of drinking, he appeased it with a jam made from rose-leaves. One time he did drink, in the camp at Lausanne, when Granson had been lost; he was sick then and alone and drank a great deal of undiluted wine. But that time his blood slept. During his frenzied last years it would sometimes fall into this heavy, bestial sleep. Then it became apparent how completely he was in its power; for when it slept, he was nothing. Then none of his entourage was allowed to enter; he didn't understand what they were saying. Nor could he show himself to the foreign envoys, desolate as he was. Then he sat and waited for it to awaken. And usually it would leap up and burst out of his heart, bellowing.

For the sake of this blood he dragged around with him all these objects that he cared so little about. The three large diamonds and all the precious stones; the Flemish laces and the Arras tapestries, in piles. His silk pavilion with its cords of twisted gold and the four hundred tents for his retinue. And pictures painted on wood, and the twelve disciples in massive silver. And the Prince of Taranto and the Duke of Clèves and Philip of Baden and the Lord of Château-Guyon. For he wanted to persuade his blood that he was emperor and there was nothing above him: so that it would fear him. But his blood didn't believe it, in spite of all the proofs; it was a distrustful blood. Perhaps he kept it in doubt for a while. But the horns of Uri betrayed him. After that, his blood knew that it was circulating in a lost man: and it wanted to escape.

That is how I see it now; but when I was a boy, what used to make the strongest impression of all was the story of how they searched for him on the day of the Epiphany.

The young Duke of Lorraine, who the day before had ridden into his wretched city of Nancy after the remarkably short battle, had awakened his entourage very early in the morning and asked for the Duke of Burgundy. Messenger after messenger was dispatched, and he himself appeared at the window from time to time, restless and worried. He didn't always recognize the men they were carrying in on their carts and stretchers; he saw only that it wasn't the Duke. Nor was he among the wounded, and none of the prisoners who were continually being brought in had seen him. But the fugitives carried different reports in every direction and were confused and frightened, as if they were afraid of running into him. It was already growing dark, and nothing had been heard of the Duke. The news that he had disappeared had had time to spread during the long winter evening. And wherever it spread, it produced in everyone a sudden, exaggerated certainty that he was still alive. Never perhaps had the Duke been so real in every imagination as on that night. There was no house where people weren't sitting up and waiting for him and imagining his knock on their door. And if he didn't come, it was because he had already gone by.

It froze that night, and it was as if the idea that he still existed had also frozen; so solid did it become. And years and years passed before it dissolved. All these people, without really knowing it, depended on his being alive. The fate he had brought upon them was bearable only through his presence. It had been hard for them to learn that he existed; but now that they knew him by heart, they found that he was easy to retain and they could no longer forget him.

But the next morning, the seventh of January, a Tuesday, the search nevertheless began again. And this time there was a guide. He was one of the Duke's pageboys, and it was said that from a distance he had seen his master fall; now he was going to point out the spot. He himself hadn't said a word; the Count of Campobasso had brought him in and had spoken for him. Now he walked in front, the others following close behind him. Anyone who saw him now, bundled up and strangely unsure of himself, would have found it hard to believe that this really was Gian-Battista Colonna, who had the beauty and the slender limbs of a young girl. It was so cold that he was shivering; the air was stiff with the night frost; the snow crunched underfoot like the grinding of teeth. They were *all* freezing, for that matter. The Duke's fool, nicknamed Louis-Onze, kept in constant motion. He pretended he was a dog, ran ahead, came back, trotted for a while on all fours beside the boy; but whenever he saw a corpse in the distance, he ran over to it, bent down, and exhorted it to make a great effort and be the one they were searching for. He gave it a little time to consider, but then returned to the others, grumbling, and threatened and swore and complained about the obstinacy and laziness of the dead. And they walked on and on, and there was no end to it. The city was hardly visible now; for in the meantime the air had closed, in spite of the cold, and had become gray and impenetrable. The countryside lay there flat and indifferent, and the little, compact group looked more and more lost the farther it went.

No one spoke; only an old woman who had been running behind them muttered a few words and shook her head; perhaps she was praying.

All at once the boy stood still and looked around. Then he turned abruptly toward Lupi, the Duke's Portuguese doctor, and pointed to something in front of them. A few steps farther on, there was a stretch of ice, a kind of pond or mash, and in it lay ten or twelve corpses, half immersed. They were almost completely stripped and plundered. Lupi walked from one to the next, bent over and examining them carefully. And now you could recognize Olivier de la Marche and the chaplain as they walked separately among the bodies. But the old woman was already kneeling in the snow, whimpering as she bent over a large hand, whose outspread fingers pointed stiffly toward her. They all came running. Lupi with some of the servants tried to turn over the corpse, for it was lying on its belly. But the face was frozen into the ice, and as they pulled it out, one of the cheeks peeled off, thin and brittle, and you could see that the other cheek had been ripped out by dogs or wolves; and the whole thing had been split by a large wound that began at the ear, so that you could hardly speak of a face at all.

One man after the other looked around; each thought he would find the Roman behind him. But they saw only the fool, who was running toward them, angry and bloodstained. He was holding out a cloak at arm's length, shaking it as if something were supposed to fall out; but the cloak was empty. Next they began to look for identifying marks, and they found a few. A fire had been made, and the body was washed with warm water and wine. The scar on the throat appeared, and the traces of the two large abscesses. The doctor no longer had any doubt. But there was further evidence. Louis-Onze had discovered, a few steps farther on, the dead body of Moreau, the large black stallion the Duke had ridden at the battle of Nancy. He was sitting astride it, letting his short legs hang down. The blood was still running from his nose into his mouth, and you could see him tasting it. One of the servants on the other side remembered that the Duke had an ingrown toenail on his left foot; now they all began to search for it. But the fool squirmed as if someone were tickling him, and called out, "Ah, monseigneur, forgive these idiots for uncovering your gross defects, when they could have recognized you from my long face, in which all your virtues are written."

* [The Duke's fool was also the first to enter when the corpse was laid out. It was in the house of a certain Georges Marquis, no one could tell why. The pall had not yet been spread, and so he received the full impression. The white of the doublet and the crimson of the cloak stood in harsh, unfriendly con-

* Written on the margin of the MS.

trast between the two blacks of baldaquin and couch. Scarlet long-boots stood in front, pointing toward him with their large gilded spurs. And that thing up there was a head: you didn't dispute that as soon as you saw the crown. It was a large ducal crown set with precious stones of some kind. Louis-Onze walked around and inspected everything carefully. He even felt the satin, though he didn't know much about materials. It was probably good satin, perhaps a bit too cheap for the house of Burgundy. He stepped back one last time to take in the whole scene. The colors seemed incredibly unrelated in the light reflected from the snow. He filed each one separately in his memory. "Well-dressed," he acknowledged finally: "perhaps a little too obviously." Death seemed to him like a puppet-master who suddenly needs a duke.]

— ••• —

It is good to recognize certain facts that simply will not change, without regretting that they are as they are and without judging them. Thus it became obvious to me that I never was a real reader. As a child, I thought that reading was a profession which would have to be taken on at some future time, when all the professions came around, one by one, for consideration. To tell the truth, I didn't have a clear idea of when that would be. I believed that I would be able to tell when life turned around, as it were, and came only from outside, as it had until then come from inside. I imagined it would then become intelligible and unambiguous and never liable to misunderstanding. Not simple, by any means; on the contrary, very exacting; intricate and difficult, perhaps, but always visible. Childhood's strangely unbounded world, its unconditionality and elusiveness, would then have been surmounted; though of course I didn't know how. In reality, that world kept increasing, closing together on all sides; and the more I looked outside, the more I stirred up what was inside me: God knows where it came from. But probably it grew to its utmost limits and then suddenly broke off. It was easy to observe that grownups were hardly disturbed by it at all; they went around judging and doing, and if they ever got into difficulties, they blamed that on external circumstances.

So I postponed reading, along with other such matters, until the beginning of these changes. Then I would act toward books as I acted toward friends; there would be time for them, a definite time that would pass regularly and pleasantly, just as much of it as I felt like. Naturally, certain of them would be closer to me than others, and this is not to say that I would be certain of not wasting a half-hour over them every once in a while, when I might have been enjoying a walk, a conversation, the first act of a play, or an urgent letter. But that a person's hair could get mussed up and tangled, as if he had been lying on it; that his ears could grow flaming red and his hands feel as cold as metal; that the long candle beside him could burn down right into the candlestick—all this was, thank God, not within the realm of possibility.

I mention these symptoms because I myself experienced them, quite vividly, during the vacation at Ulsgaard when I so suddenly discovered reading. It became immediately obvious that I didn't know how. I had, of course, begun my reading before the future time I had assigned it to. But the year I spent at Sorø, among so many boys of about my own age, had made me distrustful of such calculations. There were a number of sudden, astonishing experiences that had overtaken me there; and it was obvious that they treated me like a grownup. These experiences were as large as life, and made themselves as heavy as they actually were. But to the degree that I grasped their actuality, my eyes also opened to the infinite reality of my childhood. I knew that it wouldn't cease, any more than the other period was just beginning. I said to myself that everyone was, of course, free to make divisions between the two, but these were completely artificial. And it appeared that I wasn't clever enough to think out any for myself. Every time I tried, life taught me that it didn't know the first thing about them. And if I insisted on believing that my childhood was past, then at that same moment the whole future had vanished too, and I was left with exactly as much to stand on as a tin soldier has beneath his feet.

Of course, this discovery isolated me even more. It preoccupied me with myself and filled me with a kind of ultimate joy, which I mistook for sadness, because it was far beyond my age. I was also disturbed, I remember, by the thought that since nothing was predetermined for any particular period of my life, many worthwhile experiences might be entirely missed. And so when I returned to Ulsgaard and saw all the books, I flung myself upon them; in a great hurry, almost with a bad conscience. I somehow had a premonition of what I so often felt later on: that you didn't have the right to open one book unless you were prepared to read them all. With every line, you broke off a piece of the world. Before books came it was whole, and perhaps it would again be that way afterward. But how could I, who didn't know how to read, cope with them all? There they stood, even in that modest library, in such hopeless abundance and solidarity. Headstrong and desperate, I plunged from book to book and fought through the pages like someone who has to perform a task far beyond his strength. At that time I read Schiller and Baggesen, Oehlenschläger and Schack-Staffeldt, whatever I could find of Walter Scott and Calderón. Many of them came into my hands which probably should have been read before then, while for others it was much too soon; there was almost nothing that really fitted my needs at that time. And nevertheless I read.

In later years it occasionally happened that I woke

up at night, and the stars stood out with such reality and moved forward so meaningfully, and I couldn't understand how people managed to miss so much world. I had a similar feeling, I think, whenever I looked up from the books and glanced outside, where the summer was, where Abelone was calling me. It seemed quite surprising to us that she had to call and that I didn't even answer. This was in the midst of our happiest time. But since the fever had now taken hold of me, I convulsively clung to my reading and hid, self-important and obstinate, from our daily holidays. Unskilled as I was at taking advantage of the many (though often inconspicuous) opportunities of enjoying a natural happiness, I accepted our growing dissension and saw in it a promise of future reconciliations, which became more delightful the longer they were postponed.

Furthermore, my reader's trance ended one day, as suddenly as it had begun; and then we made each other thoroughly angry. For Abelone didn't spare me any kind of ridicule or condescension, and when I met her in the arbor she would declare that she was reading. On this particular Sunday morning, the book was indeed lying beside her, unopened, but she seemed a bit too obviously busy with the red currants, which with the help of a fork she was stripping out of their small clusters.

It must have been one of those early mornings that

sometimes appear in July—fresh, rested hours in which joyful and spontaneous events are happening everywhere. Out of a million small irrepressible movements a mosaic of life is created, utterly convincing in its reality; Things vibrate into one another and out into the air, and their coolness makes the shadows vivid and gives the sun a light, spiritual clarity. In the garden nothing stands out above the rest; every flower is everywhere, and you would have to be inside each leaf and each petal not to miss anything.

And in Abelone's small occupation the whole scene reappeared. It was such a happy discovery to be doing just that and exactly the way she was doing it. Her hands, bright in the shade, worked together so lightly and harmoniously, and from the fork the round berries leaped playfully into the bowl, which was lined with dew-moistened grape leaves, to join the others piled up there, red and blond ones, glistening, with unbroken grains inside the tart pulp. All I wanted was to stand there and look on; but since I would probably be rebuked for doing that, and in order to seem more at ease, I picked up the book, sat down on the other side of the table, and, after leafing through it for a moment or two, started in at random.

"At least you could read out loud, bookworm," Abelone said after a while. This didn't sound very hostile at all, and since I thought it was high time for us to make up, I started to read out loud, going right on to the end of the section, and then on to the next heading: "To Bettina."

"No, not the answers," Abelone said, interrupting me, and all at once, as if she were exhausted, she put down the little fork. Then she laughed at the way I was looking at her.

"My God, what a bad reader you are, Malte."

I had to admit that I hadn't been paying the slightest bit of attention to the meaning. "I was just reading so that you'd interrupt me," I confessed, and grew hot and turned back to the title page. Only then did I know what it was. "And why not the answers?" I asked with curiosity.

Abelone seemed as if she hadn't heard me. She sat there in her bright dress, as if she were growing dark everywhere inside her: as dark as her eyes were growing.

"Give it to me," she said suddenly, as if in anger, taking the book out of my hand and opening it right to the page she wanted. And then she read one of Bettina's letters.

I don't know how much of it I took in, but it was as if a solemn promise had been made to me that one day I would understand it all. And while her voice rose and at last was nearly the same voice that I knew from her singing, I felt ashamed that I had had such a trivial idea of our reconciliation. For I understood quite well that this was it. But now it was happening on a larger scale, somewhere high above me, in a place I couldn't reach.

— ••• —

The promise is still being fulfilled; at some time or other that same book appeared among my books, among the few books that I always have with me. It opens now, for me too, at the passages I happen to be thinking of, and when I read them, I'm not sure whether I think of Bettina or Abelone. No, Bettina has become more real in me; Abelone, whom I knew in the flesh, was like a preparation for her, and now she has completely merged into Bettina as if into her own instinctive being. For this strange Bettina created space with all her letters, a world of vastly enlarged dimensions. From the beginning she spread herself out through everything, as if she had already passed beyond her death. Everywhere, she deeply entered into existence, became part of it, and whatever happened to her had from all eternity been contained in nature; in it she recognized herself, and she detached herself from it almost painfully, laboriously guessed herself back, as if out of the past, conjured herself like a ghost and endured it.

A short time ago you still *were*, Bettina; I understand you. Isn't the earth still warm with you, and don't the birds still leave room for your voice? The dew is different, but the stars are still the stars of your nights. And isn't the whole world yours? For how often you set it on fire with your love and saw it blaze and burn up and secretly replaced it with another world while everyone slept. You felt in such complete harmony with God, when every morning you asked him for a new earth, so that all the ones he had made could have their turn. You thought it would be shabby to save them and repair them; you used them up and held out your hands, again and again, for more world. For your love was equal to everything.

How is it possible that everyone isn't still telling of your love? What has happened since then that is more important? What are they so concerned with? You yourself knew the value of your love; you said it aloud to your greatest poet, so that he would make it human; for it was still elemental. But in writing to you, he dissuaded people from believing in it. They have all read his answers and believe them more, because the poet is more intelligible to them than nature is. But perhaps someday it will be apparent that here was the outer limit of his greatness. This woman in love was imposed upon him, and he couldn't stand up to her. What does it mean that he wasn't able to respond? Such love doesn't need any response; it contains both call-note and answer in itself; it is its own fulfillment. But he should have humbled himself before her in all his splendor and written what she dictated, with both hands, like John on Patmos, kneeling. There was no choice for him in the presence of this voice which "performed the angels' function," which had come to enwrap him and carry him off into eternity. Here was the chariot of his fiery ascension. Here was, prepared against his death, the dark myth that he left empty.

— ••• —

Fate loves to invent designs and patterns. Its difficulty lies in complexity. But life itself is difficult because of its simplicity. It has just a few elements, of a grandeur that we can never fathom. The saint, rejecting fate, chooses these and comes face to face with God. But the fact that woman, in accordance with her nature, must make the same choice in relation to man —this is what calls forth the doomed quality of all love relationships: resolute and fateless, like an eternal being, she stands beside the one who is transformed. The woman who loves always surpasses the man she loves, because life is larger than fate. Her self-surrender wants to be infinite: this is her happiness. But the nameless suffering of her love has always been that she is required to limit this self-surrender.

There is no other lament that has ever been lamented by women. The first two letters of Héloïse contain only this, and five hundred years later it rises from the letters of the Portuguese nun; it is as recognizable as a bird-call. And suddenly through the bright space of this insight, the so-distant form of

Sappho passes, whom the centuries have never found, because they looked for her not in life but in fate.

— ••• —

I have never dared to buy a newspaper from him. I'm not really sure that he always has copies with him, as he slowly shuffles back and forth outside the Jardin du Luxembourg, all evening long. He turns his back to the railings, and his hand rubs along the stone ledge from which the bars rise. He presses himself so flat that every day many people go past who have never seen him. True, he still has a shred of a voice that calls attention to his existence; but it isn't any different from a noise in a lamp or a stove or the sound water makes when it drips at irregular intervals in a cave. And the world is arranged in such a way that there are people who, all their lives, pass by during the pauses, when he, more soundless than anything that moves, goes forward like the hand of a clock, like the shadow of that hand, like time itself.

How wrong I was to look at him so reluctantly. I am ashamed to write that often when I approached him I walked by, the way the others did, as if I didn't know he was there. Then I heard something inside him say "La Presse" and a moment later a second time and then a third, with hardly a breath in between. And the people near me turned around and looked for the voice. I was the only one who hurried on, faster than any of them, as if I hadn't noticed anything, as if I were extremely busy with some idea.

And in fact I was. I was busy picturing him to myself; I had undertaken the task of imagining him, and was sweating from the effort. For I had to make him as you make a dead man, who has lost all the proofs and all the constituent parts of his existence, who has to be achieved entirely within you. I know now that it helped me a little to think of those many demounted Christs made of striated ivory that lie around in every antique shop. The thought of some Pietà came and went—: all this probably just to evoke a particular angle at which his long face was held, and the desolate stubble in the shadows of his cheeks, and the definitively painful blindness of his sealed-up expression, which was turned obliquely upward. But there was so much in addition that belonged to him; for even then I understood that nothing about him was insignificant: not the way that his jacket or coat, gaping at the back, let his collar be seen all the way around—that low collar, which curved in a wide arc around the stretched and pitted neck, without touching it; not the greenish black tie loosely fastened around him; and especially not the hat, an old, high-crowned, stiff felt hat, which he wore the way all blind men wear their hats: without any relation to the lines of the face, without the possibility of adding this feature to themselves and forming a new external unity: but merely as an arbitrary, extraneous object. In my cowardly refusal to look at him, I went so far that finally the image of this man, often for no reason at all, intensely and painfully contracted inside me to such a harsh wretchedness that, no longer able to bear it, I decided to intimidate and neutralize the increasingly precise picture in my imagination by confronting it with the external reality. It was toward evening. I told myself to walk by and look at him closely.

Now it is important to know that spring was approaching. The wind had died down; the streets were long and satisfied; at the end of each one, houses gleamed, as fresh as new cuts in some white metal. But it was a metal that surprised you by its lightness. In the wide boulevards many people were out walking, almost without fear of the carriages, which were infrequent. It must have been a Sunday. The towers of Saint-Sulpice stood out serene and unexpectedly high in the still air, and through the narrow, almost Roman streets you found yourself involuntarily looking out into the season. Inside the Luxembourg and in front of it so many people were milling around that I didn't see him right away. Or was it that I didn't recognize him at first through the crowd?

Immediately I knew that my picture of him was worthless. His absolute abandonment and wretchedness, unlimited by any precaution or disguise, went far beyond what I had been able to imagine. I had understood neither the angle of his face nor the terror which the inside of his eyelids seemed to keep radiating into him. I had never thought of his mouth, which was contracted like the spout of a gutter. He may possibly have had memories; but now no experience was ever added to his soul except the amorphous feeling of the stone ledge behind him, on which his hand was being gradually worn away. I had stood still, and as I saw all this almost simultaneously, I realized that he was wearing a different hat and a necktie that was undoubtedly reserved for Sundays; it had a pattern of diagonal yellow and violet checks; and as for the hat, it was a cheap new straw hat with a green band. The colors are meaningless, of course, and it's petty of me to remember them. I just want to say that on him they were like the softest down on a bird's breast. He himself didn't get any pleasure from them, and who among all these people (I looked around me) could have thought that this finery was meant for them?

My God, I thought with sudden vehemence, so you really *are*. There are proofs of your existence. I have forgotten them all and never even wanted any, for what a huge obligation would lie in the certainty of you. And yet that is what has just been shown to me. This, then, is what tastes good to you; this is what gives you pleasure. That we should learn to endure everything and never judge. What things are filled with gravity? What things with grace? Only you know.

When winter comes again and I need a new coat—grant that I may wear it like that, for as long as it is new.

— ••• —

It's not that I want to distinguish myself from them, when I walk around in better clothes that have always belonged to me, and when I insist on having somewhere to live. It's just that I haven't gotten as far as they have. I don't have the courage to live that kind of life. If my arm were to wither, I think I would hide it. But she (beyond this I don't know who she was), she appeared every day in front of the café terraces, and though it was very difficult for her to take off her coat and disentangle herself from her confused clothes and underclothes, she didn't shrink from the trouble and spent such a long time taking off one piece of clothing after another that the waiting was almost unbearable. And then she stood in front of us, modestly, with her dried-out, shriveled stump, and you could see that it was something rare.

No, it's not that I want to distinguish myself from them; but I would be overvaluing myself if I tried to be like them. I'm not. I have neither their strength nor their proportions. I eat three meals a day, and in between, my life doesn't need any miracle to sustain it; but they exist on their own, almost like eternal beings. They stand on their daily corners, even in November, and don't cry out when winter comes.

The fog envelops them and makes them indistinct and uncertain: they exist nevertheless. I went on a long journey, I got sick, many things went wrong in my life: but they didn't die.

* [I don't even know how it is possible for children to get up in the morning, in their bedrooms full of gray-smelling cold, and go to school; who strengthens them, these little hurried skeletons, so that they can run out into the grown-up city, into the gloomy dregs of the night, into the eternal schoolday, always small, always full of foreboding, always late. I have no conception of the amount of help that is constantly being used up.]

This city is full of people who are slowly sliding down to their level. Most of them resist at first; but then there are these faded, aging girls who constantly let themselves slip over without a struggle, strong girls, still unused in their innermost selves, who have never been loved.

Perhaps you want me, Lord, to leave everything behind and love them. Otherwise why do I find it so difficult not to follow them when they pass me in the street? Why do I all at once invent the sweetest, most nocturnal words, while my voice tenderly stays between my throat and my heart? Why do I imagine how I would hold them to my breath, with unutterable caution, these dolls that life has played with, flinging their arms open, springtime after springtime,

* Written on the margin of the MS.

for nothing, and again for nothing, until they grow loose in the shoulders. They have never fallen from a very high hope, so they aren't broken; but they are badly chipped and already in too poor a condition for life to care about. Only stray cats come to them in the evening, into their rooms, and scratch them up in secret, and fall asleep on top of them. Sometimes I follow one of them for a couple of blocks. They walk along past the houses; people keep coming who hide them from view; they vanish behind them and are nothing.

And yet I know that if someone tried to love them, they would weigh upon him, like people who have been walking too long and have to stop. I think only Jesus could endure them, who still has resurrection in all his limbs; but he can't be bothered with them. Only women in love can seduce him, not those who wait with a small talent for loving, as if with a lamp that has grown cold.

— ••• —

I know that if I am destined for the worst, it won't help me at all to disguise myself in my better clothes. Didn't he, even though he was a king, slide down among the lowest of men? He, who instead of rising sank to the very bottom. It's true that at times I have believed in the other kings, although their magnificent parks no longer prove anything. But it is night; it is winter; I am freezing; I believe in him. For glory stays just for a moment, and we have never seen anything more lasting than wretchedness. But the King shall endure.

Isn't he the only one who held up under his madness like wax flowers under a bell-jar? They prayed for the others, in the churches, that they would have long lives; but of him Chancellor Jean Charlier de Gerson asked that he be eternal, and this was when he was already the neediest of all, wretched and in the most abject poverty, in spite of his crown.

It was in the days when strangers with blackened faces would from time to time attack him in his bed, in order to tear from him the shirt which had rotted into his ulcers, and which for a long time now he had considered part of himself. It was dark in the room, and they ripped off the foul rags from under his rigid arms. One of them brought a light, and only then did they discover the purulent sore on his chest, where the iron amulet had sunk in, because every night he pressed it to him with all the strength of his ardor; now it lay deep in his flesh, horribly precious, in a pearly border of pus, like some miracle-working bone in the hollow of a reliquary. Hardened men had been chosen for the job, but they weren't immune from nausea when the worms, disturbed, stood up and reached toward them from the Flemish fustian and, falling out of the folds, began to creep up their sleeves. His condition had undoubtedly grown worse since the days of the *parva regina*; for she had still been willing to lie beside him, young and radiant as she was. Then she died. And since that time, no one had dared to bed another concubine beside this rotting flesh. She hadn't left behind her the words and caresses that had given the King such comfort. No one now could penetrate the wilderness of this mind; no one helped him out of the ravines of his soul; no one understood, when he suddenly walked out of them himself, with the round gaze of an animal that is going to pasture. And when he recognized the preoccupied face of Juvénal, he remembered the kingdom as it had been the last time he was aware of it. And he wanted to catch up with what he had missed.

But it was characteristic of the events of these times that nothing could be held back in describing them. When something happened, it happened with all its weight, and seemed to be all of a piece when you told it. How could you have hidden the fact that his brother had been murdered; that yesterday Valentina Visconti, whom he had always called his dear sister, had kneeled in front of him, lifting her widow's veil from the lament and accusation of her disfigured face? And today a persistent, talkative lawyer had stood for hours and proved that the princely murderer was justified, until the crime became transparent and seemed as if it would rise, blazing, to heaven. And justice meant admitting that everyone was right; for Valentina of Orleans died of grief, although vengeance had been promised her. And what good was it to pardon the Duke of Burgundy, and pardon him again; the dark passion of despair had taken hold of him, so that for weeks now he had been living in a tent deep in the forest of Argilly and declared that the only thing that gave him relief was the sound of the stags belling in the night.

When you had given thought to all that, over and over, to the end, brief as it was, the populace demanded to see you, and they saw you: bewildered. But they rejoiced at the sight; they realized that this was the King: this silent, patient man, who was only there in order to let God act above him in his tardy impatience. In these lucid moments on the balcony of his palace at Saint-Pol, the King perhaps intuited his own secret progress; he remembered the day of Roosebeke, when his uncle the Duke of Berry had taken him by the hand and led him to the site of his first ready-made victory; there, in the strangely prolonged light of that November day, he had surveyed the masses of the men of Ghent, suffocated by their own density when the cavalry had attacked them from all sides. Intertwined with one another like a huge brain, they remained there in the knots that they had tied themselves into in order to stand solid. You began to gasp for breath when you saw their smothered faces; you couldn't help imagining that the air had been driven out far above these corpses—which were still packed together, standing erect—by the sudden flight of so many despairing souls.

They had impressed this upon him as the beginning of his glory. And he remembered it. But if that had been the triumph of death, this moment, as he stood here on his trembling legs, upright in the sight of all: this was the mystery of love. He had seen in the eyes of others that you could understand that battlefield, immense though it was. But this moment refused to be understood; it was just as marvelous as the stag with the golden collar that had appeared to him in the forest of Senlis, long ago. Except that now he himself was the vision, and others were rapt in contemplation. And he didn't doubt that they were breathless and filled with the same vast expectation which had overtaken him that time (he was fourteen, out hunting for the day), when that quiet face, staring, had stepped out from among the branches. The miracle of his visibility spread over all his gentle form; he didn't stir, for fear of vanishing; the thin smile on his broad, simple face took on a natural permanence, as if it were carved into the statue of a saint, and required no effort. That is how he offered himself, and it was one of those moments that are eternity, seen in foreshortened form. The crowd was hardly able to endure it. Strengthened, fed with an inexhaustibly multiplied solace, it broke through the silence with a loud cry of joy. But above, on the balcony, only Juvénal des Ursins was left, and in the next interval of calm he shouted that the King would be coming to the Brotherhood of the Passion on the rue Saint-Denis, to see the Mysteries.

On such days the King was filled with benign awareness. Had a painter of that time been looking for some hint about what heaven was like, he couldn't have found a more perfect model than the calmed figure of the King, as it stood, in one of the high windows of the Louvre, under the cascade of its shoulders. He was turning the pages of the little book by Christine de Pisan, which is called *The Path of Long Study* and was dedicated to him. He wasn't reading the learned polemics of that allegorical parliament which had undertaken to find out what sort of prince would be worthy of ruling over the whole earth. The book always opened for him at the simplest passages: where it spoke of the heart which, for thirteen years, had stood like a retort over the fire of grief, its only function to distill the water of bitterness for the eyes; he understood that true consolation only began when happiness had vanished and was gone forever. Nothing was more precious to him than this solace. And while his glance seemed to embrace the bridge beyond, he liked to see the world through Christine's heart, which had been caught up by the powerful Cumaean and led through the paths of heaven— liked to see the world of those days: the dared-upon seas, the strange-towered cities held shut by the pressure of distances, the ecstatic solitude of the assembled mountains, and the skies that were explored in fearful doubt and were only now closing like an infant's skull.

But when anyone entered, the King got frightened and slowly his mind grew dim. He allowed them to lead him away from the window and give him something to do. They had gotten him used to spending hours over illustrations, and he was satisfied with that. Only one thing annoyed him: that in turning the pages you could never have several pictures in front of you at the same time; they were firmly bound into the folios, so that you couldn't move them back and forth. Then someone remembered a deck of cards that had been completely forgotten, and the King showered his favor on the man who brought it, so delighted was he with these pieces of cardboard, which were painted with bright colors and separable and full of images. And while card-playing became the fashion among the courtiers, the King sat in his library and played alone. Just as he now turned up two kings, side by side, so God had recently brought him and Emperor Wenceslaus together; sometimes a queen died, and then he would put an ace of hearts on her that was like a tombstone. It didn't surprise him that in this game there were several popes; he placed Rome over there at the edge of the table, and here at his right hand was Avignon. He wasn't interested in Rome; for some reason or other he imagined it as round, and dropped the matter at that. But he knew Avignon. And hardly had the thought occurred to him, when his memory repeated the high, hermetic palace and overexerted itself. He closed his eyes and had to take a deep breath. He was afraid he would have bad dreams that night.

But on the whole it was really a soothing occupation, and they were right to bring him back to it again and again. Such hours confirmed him in the opinion that he was the King, King Charles VI. This is not to say that he exaggerated his own importance; he was far from thinking that he was anything more than one of those pieces of paper; but he had a growing certainty that he too was a definite card—perhaps a bad one, one that was played in anger, and that always lost: but always the same card: but never any other. And yet, when a week had passed this way, in the regular confirmation of his own existence, he would begin to feel a certain tightness inside him. The skin grew tense across his forehead and at the back of his neck, as if all at once he felt his own too-distinct outline. No one knew what temptation he gave in to then, when he asked about the Mysteries and could hardly wait for them to begin. And when the time came at last, he lived more on the rue Saint Denis than in his palace at Saint-Pol.

The fatal thing about these drama-poems was that they continually enlarged and extended themselves, growing to tens of thousands of verses, so that the time in them ultimately became real time; rather as if someone were to make a globe as big as the earth. The concave stage, with hell underneath it, and above it—attached to a pillar—the unrailed scaffolding of a balcony, representing the level of paradise, only served to weaken the illusion. For this century had in fact brought both heaven and hell to earth: it lived on the powers of both, in order to survive itself.

These were the days of that Avignonese Christendom which, a generation earlier, had drawn together around John XXII, with so much instinctive desire for shelter that at the site of his pontificate, immediately after he settled there, the mass of this palace had arisen, closed and heavy, like a last, emergency body for the homeless soul of all. But he himself, this small, transparent, spiritual old man, still lived out in the open. When, shortly after he arrived, he began to act swiftly and concisely in every direction, dishes spiced with poison appeared on his table; the first cup always had to be poured out, since the piece of unicorn was discolored when the cupbearer took it out again. Perplexed, not knowing where to hide them, the seventy-year-old man carried around the wax images of him that his enemies had made, to destroy him; and he was continually being scratched by the long needles that had been stuck through them. They might have been melted down; but these secret simulacra had filled him with such terror that, against his own powerful will, he repeatedly found himself thinking that this procedure would prove to be fatal and he would vanish like the wax in the flames. His shrunken body became even more dry with horror, and more enduring. And now they were even daring to attack the body of his empire; from Granada the Jews had been incited to exterminate all Christians, and this time they had hired more terrible accomplices. No one, from the very first rumor, doubted the conspiracy of the lepers; already several people had seen them throwing bundles of their horrible decomposition into the wells. It wasn't out of any light credulity that people thought this possible; faith, on the contrary, had become so heavy that it had dropped from those trembling creatures and fallen to the bottom of the wells. And once again the zealous old man had to hold off the poison from the blood. During his fits of superstition, he had prescribed the Angelus for himself and his entourage, against the demons of twilight; and now every evening, throughout the whole agitated world, they rang the bells for that calming prayer. But with this exception, all the bulls and epistles that he gave out resembled spiced wine more than medicinal tea. The Empire had not entrusted itself to him for treatment; but he never tired of overwhelming it with proofs of its sickness; and already people were coming from the farthest East to consult this imperious physician.

But then the incredible happened. On All Saints' Day he had preached longer and more fervently than usual; gripped by a sudden need, as if to see it again himself, he had manifested his faith; had lifted it slowly, with all his strength, out of its eighty-five-year-old tabernacle, and displayed it in the pulpit: and immediately they began to cry out against him. All Europe cried out: this was an evil faith.

Then the Pope disappeared. Day after day he did nothing; he remained on his knees in his oratory and explored the mystery of those who by taking action do harm to their souls. Finally he reappeared, exhausted by the heavy meditations, and recanted. He recanted over and over. It became his mind's senile passion to recant. He would even have the cardinals awakened at night in order to talk with them about his repentance. And perhaps what prolonged his life beyond all bounds was in the end just the hope of abasing himself before Napoleone Orsini, who hated him and refused to come.

Jacques of Cahors had recanted. And it appeared as if God himself had wanted to prove the Pope's error, since, so soon afterward, he took up to himself that son of the Count of Ligny who seemed to await his coming-of-age on earth only so that he could enjoy the soul's sensuous delights in heaven as a grown-up man. Many were alive who remembered this radiant boy in the days of his cardinalate, and how at the threshold of his adolescence he had become a bishop and had died when he was barely eighteen, in an ecstasy of consummation. Because of him the dead came back to life: for around his tomb the air, filled with the sheer life that he had freed, had a long and powerful effect on the corpses. But wasn't there something desperate even in that precocious sanctity? Wasn't it an injustice to all, that the pure fabric of this soul had only been pulled through life, as if just to brightly dye it in the bubbling scarlet vat of the age? Didn't people feel something like a counter-blow when this young prince leaped away from the earth into his passionate ascension? Why didn't these luminous spirits linger among the laborious candle-makers? Wasn't it this darkness that had brought John XXII to declare that *before* the Last Judgment there could be no perfect blessedness, not anywhere, not even among the blessed? And indeed how much stubborn tenacity was needed to imagine that, while such dense confusion reigned here, somewhere there were faces already basking in the light of God, re-clining on angels and soothed by the inexhaustible vision of him.

— ••• —

Here I sit in the cold night, writing, knowing all this. I know it perhaps because I met that man, when I was little. He was very tall; even astonishingly tall, I think.

As unlikely as it may seem, I had somehow managed to get away from the house alone, toward evening. I was running; I turned the corner of a street, and at the same instant I ran into him. I don't understand how what happened now could have taken place within about five seconds. It will take much longer than that to tell the story, however concise I may be. I had hurt myself in the collision; I was little, and I thought I already deserved a lot of credit for not crying; also, I was involuntarily expecting to be comforted. Since he wasn't doing anything, I supposed that he was embarrassed; probably he couldn't find the right sort of joking remark to relieve the situation. I didn't mind helping him, but for that I would have to look him in the face. I said that he was tall. Now he hadn't bent down to me, as would have been natural; so that he was standing at a height that I wasn't prepared for. In front of me there was still nothing but the smell and the peculiar roughness of his suit, which I had felt. Suddenly his face appeared. What was it like? I don't know, I don't want to know. It was the face of an enemy. And beside this face, right beside it, on the level of his terrifying eyes, like a second head, was his fist. Even before I had time to lower my own face, I was already running; I dodged past him on the left and ran straight down an empty, horrible street, a street in an alien city, a city in which nothing was ever forgiven.

It was then that I experienced what I now understand: that heavy, massive, desperate age. An age when the kiss of reconciliation between two men was just a signal for the murderers who were standing nearby. They drank from the same cup, they mounted the same horse before all eyes, and it was said that they would sleep in the same bed that night: and through all these contacts their aversion for each other became so strong that whenever one of them saw the pulsing veins of the other, a sickening disgust made him pull back, as at the sight of a toad. An age when brother attacked brother and held him prisoner because he had received the larger share of their inheritance. True, the king did intercede on behalf of the imprisoned brother and had his freedom and possessions restored to him; and the elder brother, taken up with adventures in other, distant lands, granted him peace and in his letters repented of his injustice. But after he was released he could never regain his composure. The century shows him in pilgrim's clothes going from church to church, inventing vows that grew more and more peculiar. With amulets hanging from his neck, he whispered his fears to the monks of Saint-Denis, and for a long time the hundred-pound wax candle which he dedicated to Saint Louis was inscribed in their registers. He never got back to a life of his own; to the end of his days he felt his brother's envy and anger as a grimacing constellation over his heart. And that Count of Foix, Gaston Phoebus, admired by all—hadn't he openly killed his cousin Ernault, the English king's captain, at Lourdes? But what was this obvious murder in comparison with the horrible accident that happened because he had forgotten to put down his sharp little pen-knife when, in quivering reproach, he reached out his famously beautiful hand to seize the naked throat of his son lying on the bed? The room was dark; lights had to be brought in to see the blood that had come from so far away and was now leaving a noble family forever, as it secretly issued from the tiny wound of this exhausted boy.

Who in that age could be strong enough to refrain from murder? Who didn't know that the worst was inevitable? Here and there someone whose glance had during the day met the savoring glance of his murderer, would be overwhelmed by a strange foreboding. He would withdraw and shut himself in, would write his will, and at the end would order the litter of willow twigs, the Celestine cowl, and the strewing of ashes. Foreign minstrels appeared in front of his castle, and he gave them princely rewards for their song, which seemed to confirm his vague presentiments. The eyes of the dogs, as they looked up at him, were filled with doubt, and they grew less and less sure of his commands. From the motto that had served him all his life, a secondary meaning quietly emerged. Many long-established customs appeared antiquated, but there didn't seem to be any substitutes to take their place. If projects came up, you managed them without really believing in them; on the other hand, certain memories took on an unexpected finality. Evenings, by the fire, you meant to abandon yourself to them. But the night outside, which you no longer knew, all at once became very loud in your hearing. Your ear, experienced in so many safe or dangerous nights, distinguished separate pieces of the silence. And yet it was different this time. Not the night between yesterday and today: one night. Night. Beau Sire Dieu, and then the Resurrection. Even the song in honor of a beloved could hardly penetrate into these hours: the women were all disguised in albas and sirventes; had become incomprehensible under long, trailing, gaudy names. At most, in the dark, like the full upward glance, almost feminine in its softness, of a favorite bastard son.

And then, before the late supper, this pensiveness over the hands in the silver washbasin. Your own hands. Could any coherence be brought into what they did? any order or continuity in their grasping and releasing? No. All men attempted both the thing and its opposite. All men canceled themselves out; there was no such thing as action.

There was no action except at the mission brothers' church. The King, when he had seen them move and gesture, devised the charter for them himself. He addressed them as his "dear brothers"; no one had ever affected him so deeply. The decree stated explicitly that they were permitted to go around among the laity as the characters they represented; for the King desired nothing more than that they might kindle many others with their fervor and sweep them into this powerful and ordered action. As for himself, he longed to learn from them. Didn't he wear, just as they did, symbols and clothes that had a meaning? When he watched them, he believed it must be possible to learn these things: how to come and go, how to speak out and turn away, in a manner that didn't leave any doubt. Huge hopes spread over his heart. Every day he would go to this restlessly lighted, strangely indefinite hall in the Hospital of the Trinity and sit in the best seat, sometimes standing up involuntarily, as absorbed and excited as a schoolboy. Others cried; but he was inwardly filled with shining tears and only pressed his cold hands together so that he could endure it. Occasionally at critical moments, when an actor who had finished speaking suddenly stepped out of his wide gaze, the King lifted his face and was afraid: how long now had He been present: Monseigneur Saint Michael, up there, advanced to the edge of the scaffolding, in his mirror-bright silver armor?

At moments like this he sat up. He looked around him as if he were trying to make a decision. He was very close to understanding the counterpart to the play on the stage: the other one, the great, anguished, profane passion play that he himself was acting in. But all at once it was gone. All these people were moving around meaninglessly. Open torches advanced toward him, and formless shadows threw themselves onto the vault above him. Men whom he didn't know were pulling at him. He wanted to take part in the

230

play: but nothing came out of his mouth, his movements didn't result in true gestures. They crowded so strangely around him that he began to think he ought to be carrying the cross. And he wanted to wait for them to bring it. But they were stronger, and they pushed him slowly out.

— ••• —

Outside, much has changed. I don't know how. But inside and before you, Lord, inside before you, Spectator: aren't we without action? We discover, indeed, that we don't know our part; we look for a mirror; we want to rub off the make-up and remove everything that is artificial, and become real. But somewhere a piece of our disguise still sticks to us, which we forgot. A trace of exaggeration remains on our eyebrows; we don't notice that the corners of our mouth are twisted. And this is how we go around, a laughing-stock and a half-truth: neither real beings nor actors.

— ••• —

It was in the theater in Orange. Without really looking up, merely aware of the rustic fracture that now makes up its façade, I had entered by the caretaker's little glass door. I found myself among the prone bodies of columns, and little mallow shrubs, but it was just for a moment that they hid the open shell of the auditorium, which lay there, divided by the afternoon shadows, like a gigantic concave sundial. I walked toward it quickly. As I climbed up between the rows of seats, I felt how small I was becoming in these surroundings. A little higher up, a few tourists, unequally distributed, were standing around in idle curiosity; their clothes were unpleasantly distinct, but their size was negligible. For a while they looked at me, astonished at my smallness. This made me turn around.

Ah, I was completely unprepared. There was a play being performed. An immense, a superhuman drama was in progress, the drama of that powerful backdrop, whose vertical structure appeared, tripartite, resonant with grandeur, almost annihilating, and suddenly measured in its sheer immeasurability.

I felt so joyfully alarmed that I had to sit down. What was towering in front of me now, with its shadows arranged in the likeness of a face, with the darkness concentrated in the mouth at its center, bordered on top by the symmetrically curled hair of its cornice: this was the mighty, all-covering antique mask behind which the world condensed into a face. Here, in this vast, inward-bent circle of seats, there reigned an existence where everything was expectancy, emptiness, absorption: everything in the realm of happening was there inside it: gods and fate. And from it (when you looked up high) came, lightly, over the wall's rim: the eternal procession of the sky.

That hour, I realize now, shut me out of our theaters, for ever. What would I do in them? What would I do in front of a stage where this wall (the icon-screen of Russian churches) has been pulled down, because we no longer have the strength to press the gas-like action through its hardness, to come forth in full, heavy oil-drops. Now plays fall in fragments through the coarse sieve of our stages, and pile up and are swept away when we have had enough. It is the same uncooked reality that litters our streets and houses, except that there, more of it gathers than can be put into a single evening.

* [Let's be honest about it, then: we don't have a theater, any more than we have a God: for this, community is needed. Each individual has his own particular inspirations and anxieties, and he lets the others see as much of them as serves his purpose. We continually dilute our understanding so that there will be enough of it to go around, instead of crying out for the wall of a mutual distress, behind which the incomprehensible would have time to gather, in all its strength.]

— ••• —

If we had a theater, would you, most tragic of women, stand there again and again—so slight, so naked, so entirely without the pretext of a role—in front of those who please their hasty curiosity with the spectacle of your grief? You who inspire such un-

* Written on the margin of the MS.

utterable emotions, you foresaw the reality of your own suffering, that time on the stage in Verona when, still almost a child, you held a bouquet of roses in front of your face like a mask that would more intensely hide you.

It's true that you were a child of the theater, and when your parents performed, they wanted to be seen; but you weren't like that. This profession was to become for you what nunhood was for Mariana Alcoforado, even though she didn't know it: a disguise thick and durable enough to let you be unrestrainedly wretched behind it, with the same ardor that flames through the blessedness of the invisible blessed. In all the cities you visited, they described that gesture of yours; but they didn't understand how, more hopeless from day to day, over and over again you lifted up a poem to see whether you could hide behind it. You held your hair, your hands, or any other opaque object in front of the translucent places. You dimmed the transparent ones by breathing on them; you made yourself small; you hid, the way children hide, and then you couldn't stifle that momentary shriek of happiness, and only an angel should have been allowed to search for you. But when you looked up, there was no doubt that they had seen you the whole time, all the people in the ugly, hollow, eye-filled space: you, you, you, and nothing else.

And you felt like holding out your arm, foreshortened, toward them, with your fingers crossed against the evil eye. You felt like snatching back your face, which they were gnawing on. You felt like being yourself. Your fellow-actors lost courage; as if they had been caged in with a lioness, they crawled along the stage and said what they had to say, just so that they wouldn't irritate you. But you dragged them forward and stood them there and treated them as if they were real. Those loose doors, those false curtains, those props that didn't have a reverse side forced you to contradict them. You felt how your heart ceaselessly rose toward an immense reality and, frightened, you once again tried to take their looks off you, as if they were gossamer threads—: But now, in their fear of the worst, they were already breaking into applause: as if to ward off, at the last moment, something that would force them to change their life.

— ••• —

Women who are loved live poorly and in danger. If only they could surpass themselves and become women in love. Around women in love there is sheer security. No one is suspicious of them any more, and they aren't in a position to betray themselves. In them the mystery has become inviolate; they cry it out whole, like nightingales; it is no longer divided. They lament for one man; but the whole of nature joins in with their voice: it is the lament for an eternal being. They hurl themselves after the man they have lost, but even with their first steps they overtake him, and in front of them there is only God. Theirs is the legend of Byblis, who pursued Caunus as far as Lycia. The urgency of her heart drove her through many lands on his track, until at last she came to the end of her strength; but so powerful was the mobility of her innermost being that, sinking to earth, she reappeared, beyond death, as a fountain, hurrying, as a hurrying fountain.

What else happened to the Portuguese nun than have come down to us: Gaspara Stampa, Countess Héloïse? or to all you women in love whose laments have come down to us: Gaspara Stampa, Countess of Die, and Clara of Anduze; Louise Labé, Marceline Desbordes, Elisa Mercoeur? But you, poor, fugitive Aïssé, you began to hesitate and you gave in. Weary Julie de Lespinasse. Disconsolate story of the happy park: Marie-Anne de Clermont.

I still remember exactly how, one day long ago, at home, I found a jewel-case; it was two handsbreadths large, fan-shaped, with a border of flowers stamped into the dark-green morocco. I opened it: it was empty. I can say this now after so many years. But at that time, when I had opened it, I saw only what its emptiness consisted of: velvet, a small mound of light-colored, no longer fresh velvet; and the jewel-groove which, empty and brighter by just a trace of melancholy, vanished into it. For a moment this was bearable. But to those who, as women who are loved, remain behind, it is perhaps always like this.

— ••• —

Leaf back in your diaries. Wasn't there always a time, my dear, toward the approach of spring, when the bursting year struck you as a reproach? Inside you there was a desire to be happy, and yet when you stepped out into the spacious open, an astonishment arose in the air, and your steps became as uncertain as if you were on a ship. The garden was beginning; but you—that was it—, you dragged winter into it, and the year that had passed; for you, it was at best a continuation. While you waited for your soul to take part, suddenly you felt the weight of your limbs; and something like the possibility of becoming ill forced its way into your open presentiment. You thought it was because of your too-light dress; you put your shawl over your shoulders; you ran up to the end of the tree-lined driveway: and then you stood, with your heart pounding, in the center of the wide turnaround, determined to be at one with all this. But a bird rang out and was alone and denied you. Ah, should you have been dead?

Perhaps. Perhaps what is new is that we survive these: the year and love. Flowers and fruits are ripe when they fall; animals feel their own being and find one another and are satisfied with that. But we, who

237

have undertaken to achieve God, we can never become perfected. We keep postponing our nature; we need more time. What is a year to us? What are all the years? Before we have even begun God, we are already praying to him: let us survive this night. And then illness. And then love.

That Clémence de Bourges should have had to die in the dawn of her life. She who was without an equal; the most beautiful of all the instruments that she could play as no one else could, unforgettably played, even in the softest ringing of her voice. Her girlhood was so resolute in its high purpose, that a woman in love, in the torrents of her passion, could dedicate to this rising heart the book of sonnets in which every line was unfulfilled. Louise Labé wasn't afraid of frightening this child with the long sufferings of love. She showed her the nightly ascent of longing; she promised pain like a more spacious world; and she suspected that she herself, with all her deeply felt grief, remained far behind what lay darkly in store for this young girl and made her so beautiful.

— ••• —

Girls in my homeland. May the most beautiful of you, on a summer afternoon in the darkened library, find the little book that Jean de Tournes printed in 1556. May she take the cool, polished-leather volume out with her into the murmurous orchard or to the phlox beyond, in whose oversweet fragrance a sediment of pure sweetness lies. May she find it early. In the days when her eyes begin to be watchful, while her mouth, younger, is still capable of biting into an apple and filling itself with pieces that are much too big.

And then, when the time of more animated friendships comes, may it be your secret, girls, to call one another Diké and Anaktoria, Gyrinno and Atthis. May someone, a neighbor perhaps, an older man who traveled a great deal when he was young and has long been considered an eccentric, reveal these names to you. May he sometimes invite you to his house, to taste his famous peaches or to go up to the white hallway and look at the Ridinger engravings illustrating horsemanship, which are talked about so much that one ought to have seen them.

Perhaps you will persuade him to tell a story. Perhaps there is a girl among you who can induce him to bring out his old travel-diaries; who can tell? The same girl who one day gets him to disclose that certain passages of Sappho's poetry have come down to us, and who can't rest until she learns what is almost a secret: that this secluded man now and then liked to devote his leisure to translating these bits of verse. He has to admit that, for a long time now, he hasn't given his translations a thought, and what there is of them, he assures her, isn't worth mentioning. Yet he is happy to recite a stanza for these ingenuous friends, if they insist. He even discovers the Greek text in his memory, and says it aloud, because the translation really doesn't do it justice, and because he wants to show the young people this authentic fragment of the massive, gorgeous language that was wrought in so intense a fire.

All of this warms him again to his work. Beautiful evenings come and he feels almost young again; autumn evenings, for example, which have long, silent nights before them. Then the lamp burns late in his study. He doesn't always sit bent over his pages; often he leans back and closes his eyes over a line he has been reading again, and its meaning spreads through his blood. Never has he been so certain of antiquity. He could almost smile at the generations that have mourned it as if it were a lost play that they would have liked to act in. Now he instantaneously grasps the dynamic significance of that early world-unity, which was something like a new and simultaneous gathering-up of all human work. It doesn't trouble him that that consistent civilization, with its almost totally visualized ideals, seemed to many later onlookers to form a whole and to be wholly past. There, it is true, the celestial half of life really was fitted against the semicircular bowl of earthly existence, the way two full hemispheres connect to form a complete golden ball. Yet hardly had this occurred when the spirits confined inside it felt that this absolute realization was just a parable; the massive star lost weight and rose into space, and its golden sphere hesitantly reflected the sadness of everything that still couldn't be mastered.

As he thinks this, solitary in his night, as he thinks and understands, he notices a bowl of fruit lying on the window seat. Involuntarily he takes an apple from it and puts it in front of him on the table. How my life is standing around this fruit, he thinks. Around everything that is perfected, the unfinished ascends and intensifies.

And then, beyond the unfinished, there rises before him, almost too quickly, that small figure straining out into the infinite, whom (according to Galen's testimony) they all had in mind when they said "the poetess." For just as after the labors of Hercules, the destruction and rebuilding of the world stood up, demanding to be fulfilled: so, from the storehouse of being, all the ecstasies and despairs which the ages would have to manage with, crowded toward the deeds of her heart, so that they might be lived.

All of a sudden he knows this resolute heart, which was ready to achieve the whole of love, to the end. It doesn't surprise him that people misunderstood it; that in this woman in love, who so utterly belonged to the future, they saw only excess, not the new unit of measure for love and heart-grief. That they interpreted the inscription above her life only as it was credible at that time; that finally they ascribed to her the death of those women whom the god incites, singly, to pour themselves out in a love that cannot be requited. Perhaps even among the girls formed by her there were some who didn't understand: how at the height of her activity she lamented, not for one man who had left her embrace empty, but for the no longer possible one who had grown vast enough for her love.

Here he stands up from his meditations and walks to his window; his high-ceilinged room is too close to him; he would like to see stars, if that is possible. He has no illusions about himself. He knows that this emotion fills him because among the young girls of the neighborhood there is one who matters to him. He has wishes (not for himself, no, but for her); for her sake he understands, during a passing hour of the night, the exigency of love. He promises himself not to tell her anything about it. It seems to him that the most he can do is to be alone and wakeful and for her sake to think how right that poetess had been: when she knew that sexual union means nothing but increased solitude; when she broke through the temporal aim of sex and reached its infinite purpose. When in the darkness of embracing she delved not for fulfillment but for greater longing. When she despised the thought that of two people one had to be the lover and one the beloved, and the frail beloved women whom she led to her couch were kindled into women in love, who left her. By such supreme partings her heart became a force of nature. Above fate, she sang the epithalamia of her most recent favorites;

exalted their nuptials for them; magnified the approaching bridegroom, so that they might prepare themselves for him as for a god and survive *his* magnificence as well.

— ••• —

One more time during these last years I felt your presence and understood you, Abelone, unexpectedly, after I had long stopped thinking of you.

It was in Venice, in the autumn, in one of those salons where passing foreigners gather around the lady of the house, who is as foreign as they are. These people stand around with their cups of tea and are delighted whenever a well-informed neighbor turns them quickly and surreptitiously toward the door and whispers a name that sounds Venetian. They are prepared for the strangest names; nothing can surprise them; for, as frugal as they may otherwise be in experience, in this city they nonchalantly abandon themselves to the most extravagant possibilities. In their usual existence they constantly confuse what is extraordinary with what is forbidden, so that the expectation of something marvelous, which they now permit themselves, appears on their faces as an expression of coarse licentiousness. The emotion which at home they feel only momentarily, at concerts or when they are alone with a novel—now, in these flattering circumstances, they exhibit it openly, as a legitimate condition. Just as, completely unprepared, unconscious of any danger, they let themselves be excited by the almost deadly confessions of music as if by physical indiscretions: so, without even beginning to master the existence of Venice, they surrender themselves to the lucrative swoon of gondolas. Couples who are no longer newlyweds and who during their whole trip have had just nasty words for each other sink into silent compatibility; the husband is overcome with the pleasant weariness of his ideals, while she feels young again and nods encouragingly to the lazy natives, smiling as if she had teeth made of sugar that were constantly melting. And if you listen in, it turns out that they will be leaving tomorrow or the day after tomorrow or at the end of the week.

So I stood among them and was happy that I didn't have to leave. Soon it would be cold. The soft, opiate Venice of their preconceptions and demands vanishes with these somnolent foreigners, and one morning the other Venice is there, the real one, awake, lucid and brittle as glass, not in the least imaginary: this city willed into existence, on sunken forests, in the midst of the void; this enforced and in the end so thoroughly present Venice. Hardened body—reduced to the bare necessities—through which the sleepless arsenal drove the blood of its work; and this body's penetrating, continually expanding spirit, which was stronger than the fragrance of aromatic lands. Inventive state that bartered the salt and glass of its poverty for the treasures of the nations. Beautiful counterweight of the world, which, down to its very ornaments, stands full of latent energies that spread out like finer and finer nerves—: this Venice.

The awareness that I knew this city overcame me among all these self-deluding people and filled me with such a sense of opposition that I looked up, wondering how I could communicate what I was feeling. Was it possible that in these rooms there was not one person who was unconsciously waiting to be enlightened about the nature of his surroundings? Some young person who would immediately understand that what was being offered here wasn't an enjoyment, but rather an example of willpower, more demanding and more severe than could be found anywhere else? I walked around; this truth of mine made me restless. Since it had seized me here among so many people, it brought with it the desire to be expressed, defended, proved. The grotesque idea arose in me that the next moment I would start clapping my hands out of hatred for all their chattered misunderstanding.

In this ridiculous mood I caught sight of her. She was standing by herself in front of a luminous window and was watching me; not really with her eyes, which were serious and thoughtful, but, it seemed, with her mouth, which was ironically imitating the obviously irritated expression on my face. I immediately felt the impatient tension in my features and put on a calm face; at that, her mouth became natural and

haughty. Then, after a brief interval of consideration, we smiled to each other at the same moment.

She reminded me of a certain youthful portrait of
the beautiful Benedicte von Qualen, who played a
part in Baggesen's life. You couldn't see the dark
silence of her eyes without guessing the lucid darkness of her voice. Furthermore, her braided hair and
the neckline of her bright-colored dress were so
reminiscent of Copenhagen that I made up my mind
to speak to her in Danish.

But before I had gotten close enough to do that, a
stream of people pushed toward her from the other
side of the room; our guest-happy Countess herself, in
her warm, enthusiastic distractedness, rushed upon
the young woman, with a number of supporters, intending to carry her off, on the spot, to sing. I was
sure that she would excuse herself by saying that no
one there could possibly be interested in listening to
songs in Danish. This is what she in fact did, when
they gave her a chance to reply. The crowd around the
bright figure became more urgent; someone knew that
she also sang in German. "And Italian," a laughing
voice added, with malicious assurance. I didn't know
of any excuse that I could have lent her in my mind,
but I didn't doubt that she would be able to resist
them. Already an expression of mortification and
dryness was spreading over the faces of the persuaders,
exhausted by their prolonged smiling; already the
good Countess, to preserve her authority, had taken a

step backward, with a look of pity and dignity—and then, when there was no longer any need at all, she gave in. I felt myself grow pale with disappointment; my eyes filled with reproach, but I turned away; there was no use letting her see that. She disengaged herself from the others, though, and all at once was beside me. Her dress shone upon me; the flowery smell of her warmth enveloped me.

"I really am going to sing," she said in Danish, close to my cheek; "not because they demand it, not for appearance's sake: but because I *must* sing."

Through her words the same irritated intolerance burst out which she had just saved me from.

I slowly followed the group of people which she had rejoined and which was now moving into another room. But near a high door I stayed behind, allowing people to move around and get settled. I leaned against the black-mirroring doorway and waited. Someone asked me what was happening, whether there was going to be a recital. I pretended I didn't know. While I was telling the lie, she had already begun to sing.

I couldn't see her. Space gradually formed around one of those Italian songs that foreigners think are very authentic because they are so plainly conventional. And she, though she sang it, didn't believe in it. She lifted it up with great effort; she took it much too heavily. You could tell when it was finished by the applause in front. I felt sad and ashamed. People began to move, and I decided that when anyone left, I would join them.

But all at once the room was silent. It was a silence which, a moment before, no one would have thought possible; it continued, it intensified, and now, inside it, arose that voice. (Abelone, I thought. Abelone.) This time it was strong, full, and yet not heavy; of one piece, without a break, without a seam. She was singing an unknown German song, in a strangely simple manner, like something inevitable. She sang:

> *You whom I don't tell that every night,*
> *for your sake, I cannot rest;*
> *you who make me as soft and light*
> *as a babe on its mother's breast;*
> *you who for my sake do not reveal*
> *that you reach out for sleep in vain:*
> *shall we continue to feel*
> *this glorious pain*
> *or shall we make ourselves numb?*

(a brief pause, then hesitantly:)

> *Look at lovers: whenever they start*
> *confessing what is deep in their heart,*
> *what liars they soon become.*

Again the silence. God knows who made it. Then the people stirred, jostled one another, apologized,

248

coughed. They were about to pass on into a general, obliterating hubbub when suddenly the voice burst out, resolute, wide, and urgent:

> When you leave me alone, you are part of
>   the world for me.
> You change into all things: you enter the
>   sound of the sea
> or the scent of flowers in the evening air.
> My arms have held them and lost them,
>   again and again.
> You, only, are always reborn; and the
>   moment when
> I let go of you, I hold on to you everywhere.

No one had expected it. They all stood bowed, as it were, beneath that voice. And in the end there was such a vast confidence inside her that it seemed as if she had known for years that at that precise moment she would have to start singing.

— ••• —

I had sometimes wondered, before that, why Abelone didn't direct toward God the calories of her magnificent emotion. I know that she longed to purify her love of anything transitive, but could her truthful heart be deceived in thinking that God is only a direction, and not an object, of love? Didn't she know there was no reason to be afraid that he would love her in return? Wasn't she aware of the restraint of this superior beloved, who calmly defers pleasure so that we, since we are so slow, may achieve our whole heart? Or did she want to elude Christ? Was she afraid that, detained by him halfway along, she would become a beloved? Was that why she didn't like to think of Julie Reventlow?

I almost believe it, when I remember how women in love as simple as Mechthild, as passionate as Teresa of Avila, as wounded as Blessed Rose of Lima, could swoon, yielding yet beloved, into this alleviation of God. But he who was a helper for the weak is an injustice for these strong souls; when they were expecting nothing but the endless path, once again in the suspense-filled space before heaven a palpable figure comes to meet them, pampering them with shelter and troubling them with maleness. His heart's powerfully refracting lens once again gathers their already parallel heart-rays, and they, whom the angels were hoping to keep intact for God, flame up and are consumed in the dryness of their longing.

* [To be loved means to be consumed in flames. To love is to give light with inexhaustible oil. To be loved is to pass away; to love is to endure.]

It is nevertheless possible that in later years Abelone tried to think with her heart, so that she could unobtrusively and directly come into relation with

* Written on the margin of the MS.

God. I can imagine that there are letters of hers which recall the attentive inner contemplation of Princess Amalie Gallitzin; but if these letters were addressed to someone whom for years she had been close to, how he must have suffered from her change. And she herself: I suspect that more than anything else she was afraid of that ghostly alteration that we don't notice because its proofs seem so alien to us that we are constantly letting them slip from our fingers.

— ••• —

It would be difficult to persuade me that the story of the Prodigal Son is not the legend of a man who didn't want to be loved. When he was a child, everyone in the house loved him. He grew up not knowing it could be any other way and got used to their tenderness, when he was a child.

But as a boy he tried to lay aside these habits. He wouldn't have been able to say it, but when he spent the whole day roaming around outside and didn't even want to have the dogs with him, it was because they too loved him; because in their eyes he could see observation and sympathy, expectation, concern; because in their presence too he couldn't do anything without giving pleasure or pain. But what he wanted in those days was that profound indifference of heart which sometimes, early in the morning, in the fields, seized him with such purity that he had to start running, in order to have no time or breath to be more than a weightless moment in which the morning becomes conscious of itself.

The secret of that life of his which had never yet come into being, spread out before him. Involuntarily he left the footpath and went running across the fields, with outstretched arms, as if in this wide reach he would be able to master several directions at once. And then he flung himself down behind some bush and didn't matter to anyone. He peeled himself a willow flute, threw a pebble at some small animal, he leaned over and forced a beetle to turn around: none of this became fate, and the sky passed over him as over nature. Finally afternoon came with all its inspirations; you could become a buccaneer on the isle of Tortuga, and there was no obligation to be that; you could besiege Campeche, take Vera Cruz by storm; you could be a whole army or an officer on horseback or a ship on the ocean: according to the way you felt. If you thought of kneeling, right away you were Deodatus of Gozon and had slain the dragon and understood that this heroism was pure arrogance, without an obedient heart. For you didn't spare yourself anything that belonged to the game. But no matter how many scenes arose in your imagination, in between them there was always enough time to be nothing but a bird, you didn't even know what kind. Though afterward, you had to go home.

My God, how much there was then to leave behind and forget. For you really had to forget; otherwise you would betray yourself when they insisted. No matter how much you lingered and looked around, the gable always came into sight at last. The first window up there kept its eye on you; someone might be standing there. The dogs, in whom expectation had been growing all day long, ran through the hedges and drove you together into the one they recognized. And the house did the rest. Once you walked in to its full smell, most matters were already decided. A few details might still be changed; but on the whole you were already the person they thought you were; the person for whom they had long ago fashioned a life, out of his small past and their own desires; the creature belonging to them all, who stood day and night under the influence of their love, between their hope and their mistrust, before their approval or their blame.

It is useless for such a person to walk up the front steps with infinite caution. They will all be in the living room, and as soon as the door opens they will all look his way. He remains in the dark, wants to wait for their questions. But then comes the worst. They take him by the hands, lead him over to the table, and all of them, as many as are there, gather inquisitively in front of the lamp. They have the best of it; they stay in the shadows, and on him alone falls, along with the light, all the shame of having a face.

Can he stay and conform to this lying life of approximations which they have assigned to him, and come to resemble them all in every feature of his face? Can he divide himself between the delicate truthfulness of his will and the coarse deceit which corrupts it in his own eyes? Can he give up becoming what might hurt those of his family who have nothing left but a weak heart?

No, he will go away. For example, while they are all busy setting out on his birthday table those badly guessed presents which, once again, are supposed to make up for everything. He will go away forever. Not until long afterward would he realize how thoroughly he had decided never to love, in order not to put anyone in the terrible position of being loved. He remembered this years later and, like other good intentions, it too had proved impossible. For he had loved again and again in his solitude, each time squandering his whole nature and in unspeakable fear for the freedom of the other person. Slowly he learned to let the rays of his emotion shine through into the beloved object, instead of consuming the emotion in her. And he was pampered by the joy of recognizing, through the more and more transparent form of the beloved, the expanses that she opened to his infinite desire for possession.

Sometimes he would spend whole nights in tears, longing to be filled with such rays himself. But a woman loved, who yields, is still far from being a woman who loves. Oh nights of no consolation, which

returned his flooding gifts in pieces heavy with tran-
sience. How often he thought then of the Troubadours, who feared nothing more than having their
prayers answered. All the money he had acquired and
increased, he gave away so as not to experience that
himself. He hurt them by so grossly offering pay-
ment, more and more afraid that they might try to
respond to his love. For he had lost hope of ever
meeting the woman whose love could pierce him.

Even during the time when poverty terrified him
every day with new hardships, when his head was
the favorite toy of misery, and utterly worn ragged
by it, when ulcers broke out all over his body like
emergency eyes against the blackness of tribulation,
when he shuddered at the filth to which he had been
abandoned because he was just as foul himself: even
then, when he thought about it, his greatest terror
was that someone would respond to him. What were
all the darknesses of that time, compared to the thick
sorrow of those embraces in which everything was
lost? Didn't you wake up feeling that you had no
future? Didn't you walk around drained of all meaning, without the right to even the slightest danger?
Didn't you have to promise, a hundred times, not to
die? Perhaps it was the stubbornness of this most
painful memory, which wanted to reserve a place in
him to return to again and again, that allowed him,
amid the dunghills, to continue living. Finally, he

found his freedom again. And not until then, not until his years as a shepherd, was there any peace in his crowded past.

Who can describe what happened to him then? What poet has the eloquence to reconcile the length of those days with the brevity of life? What art is broad enough to simultaneously evoke his thin, cloaked form and the vast spaciousness of his gigantic nights?

This was the time which began with his feeling as general and anonymous as a slowly recovering convalescent. He didn't love anything, unless it could be said that he loved existing. The humble love that his sheep felt for him was no burden; like sunlight falling through clouds, it dispersed around him and softly shimmered upon the meadows. On the innocent trail of their hunger, he walked silently over the pastures of the world. Strangers saw him on the Acropolis, and perhaps for many years he was one of the shepherds in Les Baux, and saw petrified time outlast that noble family which, in spite of all their conquests under the holy numbers seven and three, could not overcome the fatal sixteen-rayed star on their own coat-of-arms. Or should I imagine him at Orange, resting against the rustic triumphal arch? Should I see him in the soul-inhabited shade of Alyscamps where, among the tombs that lie open as the tombs of the resurrected, his glance chases a dragonfly?

It doesn't matter. I see more than him: I see his whole existence, which was then beginning its long love toward God, that silent work undertaken without thought of ever reaching its goal. For though he had wanted to hold himself back forever, he was now once again overcome by the growing urgency of his heart. And this time he hoped to be answered. His whole being, which during his long solitude had become prescient and imperturbable, promised him that the one he was now turning to would be capable of loving with a penetrating, radiant love. But even while he longed to be loved in so masterful a way, his emotion, which had grown accustomed to great distances, realized how extremely remote God was. There were nights when he thought he would be able to fling himself into space, toward God; hours full of disclosure, when he felt strong enough to dive back to earth and pull it up with him on the tidal wave of his heart. He was like someone who hears a glorious language and feverishly decides to write poetry in it. Before long he would, to his dismay, find out how very difficult this language was; at first he was unwilling to believe that a person might spend a whole life putting together the words of the first short meaningless exercises. He threw himself into this learning like a runner into a race; but the density of what had to be mastered slowed him down. It would be hard to imagine anything more humiliating than this apprenticeship. He had found the philosopher's stone, and now he was being forced to cease-lessly transform the quickly produced gold of his happiness into the gross lead of patience. He, who had adapted himself to infinite space, had now be-come like a worm crawling through crooked passage-ways, without exit or direction. Now that he was learning to love, learning so laboriously and with so much pain, he could see how careless and trivial all the love had been which he thought he had achieved; how nothing could have come of it, because he had not begun to devote to it the work necessary to make it real.

During those years the great transformations were taking place inside him. He almost forgot God in the difficult work of approaching him, and all that he hoped to perhaps attain with him in time was "sa patience de supporter une âme." The accidents of fate, which most men cling to, had long ago fallen away from him; but now even the necessary pleasures and pains lost their spicy aftertaste and became pure and nourishing for him. From the roots of his being grew the sturdy evergreen plant of a fruitful joyous-ness. He became totally absorbed in mastering what constituted his inner life; he didn't want to omit anything, for he had no doubt that in all this his love existed and was growing. Indeed, his inward composure went so far that he decided to retrieve the most important of the experiences which he had been unable to accomplish before, those that had merely been waited through. Above all, he thought of his childhood, and the more calmly he recalled it, the more unfinished it seemed; all its memories had the vagueness of premonitions, and the fact that they were past made them almost arise as future. To take all this past upon himself once more, and this time really, was the reason why, from the midst of his estrangement, he returned home. We don't know whether he stayed there; we only know that he came back.

Those who have told the story try at this point to remind us of the house as it was then; there, only a short time has passed, a short period of counted time, everyone in the house knows exactly how much. The dogs have grown old, but they are still alive. It is reported that one of them let out a howl. All the daily tasks stop. Faces appear in the window, faces that have aged or grown up and touchingly resemble how they used to look. And in one old face, grown suddenly pale, recognition breaks through. Recognition? Is it really just recognition? —Forgiveness. Forgiveness of what? —Love. My God: it is love.

He, the one who was recognized, had no longer thought, preoccupied as he was, that love could still exist. It is easy to understand how, of everything that happened then, only this has been handed down to us: his gesture, the incredible gesture which had never been seen before, the gesture of supplication with which he threw himself at their feet, imploring them not to love. Dizzy with fright, they made him stand up, embraced him. They interpreted his outburst in their own way, forgiving him. It must have been an indescribable relief for him that, in spite of the desperate clarity of his posture, they all misunderstood him. He was probably able to stay. For every day he recognized more clearly that their love, of which they were so vain and to which they secretly encouraged one another, had nothing to do with him. He almost had to smile at their exertions, and it was obvious how little they could have him in mind.

How could they know who he was? He was now terribly difficult to love, and he felt that only One would be capable of it. But He was not yet willing.

p.   3,   *maison d'accouchement:* Maternity hospital.

p.   4,   *Asile de nuit:* Overnight shelter (for the poor).

p.   4,   *Ah tais-toi, je ne veux plus:* Oh be quiet, I've had
enough!

p.   7,   *Hôtel-Dieu* (literally, God's hotel): Large hospital
near the cathedral of Notre-Dame on the Île de la
Cité. It was built in 1868–78, on the site of one of
the oldest hospitals in Europe, dating from the
seventh century.

p.   8,   *Duke of Sagan:* Albrecht Wenzel Euscbius von
Wallenstein, duke of Friedland, Sagan, and Meck-
lenburg (1583–1634), German general and statesman; commander of one of the greatest Imperial
armies during the Thirty Years' War. He is the
subject of Schiller's dramatic trilogy *Wallenstein.*

p.   8,   *Cité:* One of two islands in the river Seine at the
center of Paris; the oldest part of the city.

p.   8,   *King Clovis* (466–511): Founder of the Frankish
empire.

p.   9,   *Voilà votre mort, monsieur:* There is your death,
monsieur.

p. 17,   *Tuileries:* Public garden between the Louvre and
the Place de la Concorde.

p. 18,   *Pont-Neuf:* Bridge over the Seine, connecting the
western tip of the Ile de la Cité with both the Left
and Right Banks.

p. 31,   *Anna Sophie:* Anna Sophie Reventlow (1693–
1743). In 1712 King Frederick IV eloped with her

and married her bigamously. When the legitimate queen died nine years later, Frederick married Anna Sophie a second time and made her queen.

p. 31, *Frederick IV* (1671–1730): King of Denmark and Norway, 1699–1730.

p. 31, *Roskilde:* A twelfth-century cathedral in eastern Denmark where members of the Danish royal family were buried.

p. 41, *another poet:* Francis Jammes (1868–1938).

p. 45, *Chou-fleur:* Cauliflower.

p. 48, *crémerie:* Small dairy restaurant.

p. 50, *Duval:* A chain of fairly inexpensive restaurants, of a higher quality than the crémeries.

p. 52, *when there shall not be left one word upon another:* Cf. Mark 13:2.

p. 53, *"Mécontent de tous . . . ":* From Baudelaire's prose-poem "A une heure du matin": "Dissatisfied with everyone and dissatisfied with myself, I want to redeem myself and be a little proud of myself in the silence and solitude of the night. Souls of those I have loved, souls of those I have sung, strengthen me, support me, keep far away from me the lies and the corrupting vapors of the world. And you, Lord my God, grant me the grace to create a few beautiful poems which will prove to me that I am not the lowest of men, that I am not inferior to those whom I despise."

p. 54, *"The children of despised men . . . ":* Job 30:8–9, 12–13, 16–18, 27, 31.

p. 54, *Salpêtrière:* A large hospital near the Jardin des Plantes, especially known for its electrotherapeutic treatment of psychological disorders. Freud studied there in 1885–1886, with the neurologist J. M. Charcot.

p. 57, *chapeau à huit reflets:* An elegant top hat of that period.

p. 61, *"Riez! . . . ":* "Laugh! Go on, laugh, laugh!"

p. 61, *"Dites-nous . . .":* "Say for us the word *before.* . . . We can't hear a thing. Once again . . ."

p. 71, *Panthéon:* A church where many of France's famous men are buried. The reference is to Puvis de Chavannes' mural of St. Genevieve, patron saint of Paris.

p. 72, *"Une Charogne":* The poem describes a putrid, maggot-eaten animal carcass.

p. 72, *"Saint Julien l'Hospitalier":* One of Flaubert's *Three Tales.*

p. 76, *mouleur:* Molder (of plaster casts).

p. 76, *young drowned woman:* The famous death-mask of a beautiful young woman who had drowned in the Seine.

p. 76, *his face:* Beethoven's death-mask.

p. 80, *obstinate man:* Henrik Ibsen (1828–1906).

p. 83, *a rabbit . . . :* These details are taken from Ibsen's *The Wild Duck, Ghosts,* and *Brand.*

p. 102, *Admiral Juel:* Niels Juel (1629–1697). In July 1677, having overwhelmingly defeated the Swedish fleet in the Battle of Køge Bay, one of the greatest sea victories in Danish history, he was acclaimed as a national hero and raised to the highest naval rank.

p. 104, *bautta* (pronounced ba-oot'-ta): Venetian mask, covering the lower part of the face.

p. 104, *dominos:* Venetian cloaks, worn chiefly at masquerades.

p. 104, *Pierrot:* Character in French pantomime.

p. 109, *Lavater:* Johann Kaspar Lavater (1741–1801), Swiss poet and theologian; chiefly remembered for his work on physiognomy.

p. 114, *Christian IV* (1577–1648): King of Denmark and Norway, 1588–1648.

p. 114, *Kirstine Munk* (1598–1658): Christian's second, morganatic wife, and mother of twelve of his children. Her affair with a German cavalry officer, Count Otto Ludwig von Salm, became a major scandal and caused the King intense mortification.

p. 114, *Ellen Marsvin* (1572–1649): Friend of Christian IV and mother of Kirstine Munk. Her husband was the head of one of the most ancient and powerful families in Denmark.

p. 114, *the "incomparable" Eleonore:* Leonora Christina (1621–1698), daughter of Christian IV and Kirstine Munk. She was imprisoned in the Blue Tower of the royal castle in Copenhagen from 1663 until 1685. (See the wonderful story in *Letters of Rainer Maria Rilke*, translated by Jane Bannard Greene and M. D. Herter Norton, New York: Norton, 1948, vol. 2, pp. 363 ff.)

p. 114, *the Gyldenløves* (literally, golden lions): Gyldenløve was the official surname given to the many illegitimate children of Christian IV.

p. 114, *Hans Ulrik* (1615–1645): Naval officer and statesman. He was at the Spanish court on a diplomatic mission.

p. 114, *Ulrik Christian* (1630–1658): Served with distinction in the Spanish and French armies, where he was Condé's chief of staff. In 1655 he was promoted to the rank of major-general and became his half-brother Frederick III's foremost military advisor.

p. 114, *the Ulfelds:* Children of Leonora Christina and her husband Count Corfitz Ulfeld.

p. 114, *Henrik Holck* (1599–1633): Danish mercenary. He served with great distinction on the Protestant side in the Thirty Years' War under Duke Christian of Brunswick, then in 1630 changed sides and served in the Imperial army. He was Wallenstein's chief of staff and most trusted officer, and became famous not only for his courage and military skill but also for his brutality in laying waste the Saxon countryside during the campaign of 1633.

p. 115, *Duke Ulrik* (1611–1633): The talented third (and favorite) son of Christian IV and Queen Anna

Cathrine. He served as an officer under King Gus-
tavus Adolphus of Sweden in the Thirty Years' War
and was killed by a sniper's bullet during a truce.

p. 115, *Otte Brahe* (1579–1611): Danish officer, killed
during the siege of Kolmar.

p. 115, *Claus Daa* (1579–1641): Danish admiral and
statesman.

p. 115, *Sten Rosensparre* (1588–1612): Danish officer,
killed in battle at Skjellinge Heath, a few days after
his betrothal.

p. 119, *an Erik Brahe who was executed:* This Count Erik
Brahe (1722–1756) was a member of the Swedish
branch of the family who was executed for his role
in a plot to extend the powers of the king.

p. 120, Prince *Felix Lichnowsky* (1814–1848): Conserva-
tive member in the Frankfurt National Assembly,
was murdered during the democratic revolts against
the conduct of the German-Danish war over
Schleswig-Holstein.

p. 127, *tapestries:* The famous sixteenth-century tapestries
representing "The Lady with the Unicorn." Rilke
saw some of them at the Musée de Cluny in Paris.

p. 129, *'À mon seul désir':* 'To my only desire.'

p. 131, *Dame à la Licorne:* Lady with the Unicorn.

p. 131, *Boussac:* Castle in central France owned by Pierre
d'Aubusson.

p. 131, *Delle Viste:* The tapestries were an engagement
present to Claude le Viste.

p. 131, *Pierre d'Aubusson* (1423–1503): Grand Master of
the Order of St. John of Jerusalem (Knights of
Malta).

p. 134, *Gaspara Stampa* (1523–1554): An Italian noble-
woman who wrote of her unhappy love for Count
Collaltino di Collalto in a series of some two hundred sonnets. She is mentioned in the First Duino
Elegy.

p. 134, *the Portuguese nun:* Mariana Alcoforado (1640–

1723), who was thought to have written the *Lettres portugaises* to her unfaithful lover, Noël Bouton, Marquis de Chamilly. Rilke's translation of these letters was published in 1913.

p. 136, *Points d'Alençon . . . Valenciennes . . . Binche:* Types of French and Belgian lace.

p. 147, *Bredgade:* Broadway (in Copenhagen).

p. 149, *Swedenborg:* Emanuel Swedenborg (1688–1772), Swedish scientist, mystic, and theosophist.

p. 150, *Eckernførde:* Town in Schleswig where Saint-Germain died.

p. 150, *Saint-Germain:* The Comte de Saint-Germain (1710–1784), also known as the Marquis d'Aymar, de Betmar, de Belmare, etc. Adventurer, diplomat, composer and violinist, chemist, and Freemason, who exercised great influence at the court of Louis XV, in Russia, and in Germany. Among his other achievements, he was supposed to have developed secret processes for removing flaws from diamonds and for transmuting metals, and a liquid that could prolong life (he maintained that he himself was over a thousand years old).

p. 152, *Jardin d'Acclimatation:* Parisian amusement park with zoo.

p. 153, *the Bernstorff circle:* The group of political and intellectual figures around Count Johann Hartwig Ernst von Bernstorff (1712–1772) and his nephew Count Andreas Peter von Bernstorff (1735–1797), Hanoverians who became leading statesmen in the service of the Danish crown.

p. 154, *Julie Reventlow:* Countess Friederike Juliane Reventlow (1762–1816) belonged to the Bernstorff circle and was famous for her beauty and spirituality.

p. 157, *perforation of the heart:* A precaution against a death-like trance and subsequent burial alive; at the time, quite common in Central Europe.

p. 159, *shattering of the helmet:* Traditionally, when the

last representative of a noble family died, his helmet was broken.

p. 160, *Langelinie:* Street in downtown Copenhagen (as are the Amaliengade and Dronningens Tvaergade).

p. 167, *Félix Arvers* (1806–1850): French poet, chiefly remembered as the author of a sonnet beginning "Mon âme a son secret, ma vie a son mystère."

p. 168, *Jean de Dieu:* Juan de Dio (1495–1550), Portuguese saint, founder of a charitable order.

p. 184, *those strange pictures:* The reference is to the paintings of Pieter Bruegel the Elder or of Hieronymus Bosch.

p. 188, *Grishka Otrepyov* (ca. 1582–1606): The "False Dmitri." Dmitri Ivanovich, the youngest son of Ivan the Terrible, died (or was murdered) under mysterious circumstances in 1591, at the age of nine. This made it possible for Boris Godunov, the brother-in-law of the weak and childless Tsar Feodor I, to ascend the throne upon Feodor's death in 1598. Otrepyov surfaced in Poland in 1603, claiming that he was Dmitri Ivanovich, the rightful tsar, who had survived an attempted murder twelve years before. Having secretly converted to Roman Catholicism and promised large concessions to Poland, he received support from the Polish nobility and the Jesuits, and was allowed to recruit an army and advance into Russia. After the sudden death of Boris Godunov in 1605, he marched into Moscow at the head of a Polish-Cossack-Muscovite army, was declared tsar, and during his brief reign distinguished himself by his diplomatic skill, his enlightened concern for the peasantry, and his toleration in religious matters. He was killed during an uprising in 1606.

p. 189, *Maria Nagoi:* Seventh wife of Ivan the Terrible, and mother of Dmitri Ivanovich. After his death she became a nun.

p. 189, *Marina Mniszech* (1588 or 1589–1614): Daughter

of a Polish nobleman who had supported Otrepyov. They were married by proxy in November 1605, and crowned on May 8, 1606, nine days before the uprising. Two years later she acknowledged as her husband a second False Dmitri.

p. 190, *streltsy* (literally, archers): Bodyguards of the tsar.

p. 190, *Ivan Grozny:* Ivan the Terrible (1530–1584).

p. 190, *Shuisky:* Prince Vasily Ivanovich Shuisky (1552–1612), formerly a general under Boris Godunov; head of a conspiracy of ultra-conservative, xenophobic boyars who incited the uprising. The previous summer he had been sentenced to death for plotting against the new tsar, but at the last moment Otrepyov had pardoned him. Shuisky was proclaimed tsar on May 19, 1606, and reigned for four years.

p. 191, *the last days of a man:* Charles the Bold (1433–1477), Duke of Burgundy. Under his rule, Burgundy attained the height of its power and then, immediately, its dissolution. Charles had conquered Lorraine in 1475; but a year later he suffered two humiliating defeats at Granson and Morat, and on October 6 he lost Nancy, the capital of Lorraine. In a last effort to repossess the city, he besieged it with a newly formed army in the middle of that particularly severe winter, and lost many of his troops through exposure. Only a few thousand soldiers remained by the time the vastly superior army of allied Lorrainers and Swiss, led by René, Duke of Lorraine, came to the relief of the starved and "wretched" city on January 5, 1477. The Burgundians were routed in a "remarkably short" battle.

p. 193, *Uri:* A Swiss canton. It is reported that when the Swiss troops marched into battle, blowing a bloodcurdling battle music on their enormous horns, Charles remembered the battles of Granson and Morat, and felt "chilled to the depths of his heart."

p. 193, *Epiphany:* January 6, the day after the battle of Nancy, in which Charles was killed.

p. 195, *Louis-Onze* (Louis the Eleventh): The nickname was intended as ridicule of the French king Louis XI, who was Charles's enemy.

p. 196, *Olivier de la Marche* (1425 or 1426–1502): Charles's chamberlain and, later, his chronicler; author of a famous book of memoirs on life in the Burgundian court.

p. 196, *the Roman:* Gian-Battista Colonna, who came from an old Roman family.

p. 201, *Baggesen:* Jens Immanuel Baggesen (1764–1826), Danish poet, best known for his comic poems and satires.

p. 201, *Oehlenschläger:* Adam Gottlob Oehlenschläger (1779–1850), Danish romantic poet and dramatist, many of whose works were based on Norse sagas and history. In 1829 he was crowned Scandinavian poet laureate.

p. 201, *Schack-Staffeldt:* Adolf Wilhelm Schack von Staffeldt (1769–1826), Danish poet.

p. 204, *Bettina:* Elisabeth (Bettina) von Arnim, née Brentano (1785–1859), German writer; sister of Clemens Brentano and, after 1811, wife of Ludwig Achim von Arnim—two of the leading German romantic poets; and a close friend of Beethoven. Goethe had been in love with her mother a generation before, and by the time Bettina met him in 1807 her feeling for him had become adoration. The great man, for his part, didn't take her passion very seriously, and regarded her as an enchanting and sometimes irritating enfant terrible. In 1835, three years after his death, she published *Goethe's Correspondence with a Child,* based on their actual letters, though these were treated with great freedom of imagination.

p. 206, *with both hands:* Rilke had seen a painting by Hans

Memling—the left shutter of his triptych representing the mystic marriage of Saint Catherine, in the Hospital of St. John at Bruges—in which the apostle, rapt before the vision of the Apocalypse, is writing with his left hand while with his right hand he dips another pen into an ink bottle.

p. 207, *"performed the angels' function"*: A quotation from Bettina.

p. 207, *the chariot of his fiery ascension*: Cf. II Kings 2:11.

p. 207, *Héloïse* (1101–1164): The student and mistress of the famous scholastic philosopher Abelard, to whom she bore a son. After their secret marriage and brutal separation, Héloïse became a nun and, later, abbess of a convent. Abelard's *Historia Calamitatum* moved her to write her three *Letters,* which are generally considered to be among the most beautiful love letters ever written.

p. 207, *the Portuguese nun:* See note on pp. 265–66.

p. 208, *Jardin du Luxembourg:* Public garden in Paris, on the Left Bank.

p. 209, *Pietà:* A scene representing Mary or Mary Magdalene mourning over the dead body of Jesus.

p. 210, *Saint-Sulpice:* Church in Paris, north of the Jardin du Luxembourg.

p. 214, *as if with a lamp that has grown cold:* Cf. Matthew 25:1 ff.

p. 214, *he, even though he was a king:* Charles VI of France (1368–1422; reigned from 1380). He had his first attack of insanity in 1392 and gradually declined into extreme feeble-mindedness.

p. 215, *Jean Charlier de Gerson* (1363–1429): Theologian and chancellor of the University of Paris.

p. 215, *parva regina* (little queen): Odette (or Odinette) de Champdivers (?–1424 or 1425, though Rilke's source apparently gave an earlier date), a young Burgundian lady who in 1407 had become the

King's concubine and rescued him from the wretched state of neglect he had fallen into. According to the chronicles, "She calmed his ill tempers, sweetened his blood, and eased his pains by her beauty, her charm, and her good nature." She had two daughters by Charles, the elder of whom was later legitimized.

p. 216, *Juvénal:* Jean Juvénal des Ursins (1369–1431), a skilled administrator and magistrate, and one of Charles's most faithful supporters. His son wrote *History of Charles VI and of the Memorable Events during the Forty-two Years of His Reign.*

p. 216, *his brother:* Louis, Duke of Orleans (1372–1407), murdered at the instigation of his cousin, John the Fearless, Duke of Burgundy. His death precipitated the civil war between the Armagnacs and the Burgundians.

p. 216, *Valentina Visconti* (1370 or 1371–1408): Wife of the Duke of Orleans; daughter of Gian Galeazzo Visconti, Duke of Milan, and of Princess Isabelle of France.

p. 217, *Saint-Pol:* The Hôtel de Saint-Pol, a large conglomerate of mansions situated on the easternmost part of the Right Bank. Nothing of it remains today.

p. 217, *the day of Roosebeke:* This battle (1382) had crushed a revolt of several cities in Flanders.

p. 218, *Brotherhood of the Passion:* A society founded in Paris in 1402 for the performance of the passion play and other Mysteries. Charles was its chief patron.

p. 219, *Christine de Pisan* (1363 or 1364–ca. 1430): French poet and feminist. Her father, an Italian, had been Charles V's personal physician and astrologer. After his death and the death of her beloved husband in 1389, she found herself without a protector, and with three small children to support. She began to write prolifically, and became

perhaps the first woman to earn her living by literature. Her long, learned poems include several
Defenses of women.

p. 219, *the powerful Cumaean:* The Cumaean sibyl, who in
a dream had taken her through heaven.

p. 220, *Wenceslaus* (1361–1419): King of Bohemia and
head of the Holy Roman Empire. He and Charles
had met at Rheims in 1397 to discuss the crisis in
the papacy.

p. 220, *several popes:* In 1378, four months after choosing
Urban VI as pope, the College of Cardinals an-
nounced that their decision was invalid, and elected
Clement VII. This "anti-pope" was recognized as
the legitimate one by France, Scotland, Savoy,
Spain, and Portugal, while the German Empire,
England, Hungary, Poland, Denmark, Sweden, and
most of Italy remained loyal to Urban. For the next
thirty years, during the period known as the Great
Schism, there was one pope in Rome and another
(anti-pope) in Avignon. In 1409 the Council of
Pisa deposed both popes, as being supporters of the
Schism and heretics, and elected yet a third pope,
Alexander V. This chaotic situation lasted until the
Council of Constance in 1417.

p. 222, *Avignonese Christendom:* In 1309, for political
reasons, the French pope Clement V had trans-
ferred his residence to the Provençal town of Avignon, which remained the papal seat until 1377.

p. 222, *John XXII:* Jacques Duèse of Cahors (1244–1334),
elected pope in 1316; the second pope to live in
Avignon. Because he opposed the Empire and tried
to increase the political power of the Church, Dante
has Saint Peter denounce him in the *Paradiso*
(xxvii, 58).

p. 222, *piece of unicorn:* A piece of what was thought to be
a unicorn's horn, which was dipped into food or

drink before tasting it; any discoloration showed that the food had been poisoned.

p. 222, *wax images:* John reported in a letter that his enemies had made these images of him and several cardinals "to attack our life by sticking them full of magic spells and demonic invocations; but God has preserved us and made three of these images fall into our hands."

p. 223, *Granada:* A Moslem kingdom at the time.

p. 224, *he had manifested his faith:* The Pope's thesis was that the souls of those who have died in a state of grace go into Abraham's bosom and don't enjoy the beatific vision of God until after the Last Judgment and the Resurrection.

p. 224, *Napoleone Orsini* (1263–1342): The senior Cardinal, and one of John's bitterest enemies. He was opposed to papal absolutism and in favor of a "spiritual papacy," with a strong alliance between the Church and the French monarchy.

p. 224, *son of the Count of Ligny:* Pierre of Luxembourg-Ligny (1369–1387).

p. 227, *brother attacked brother:* The Count of Vendôme and the Count of la Marche, cousins of the King.

p. 227, *Count of Foix:* Gaston III Phoebus of Foix-Béarn (1331–1391). The Count suspected his son of being party to a conspiracy by his uncle, Charles II, King of Navarre, to poison him, and had locked him in a room, where the boy threw himself on a bed, face to the wall.

p. 229, *Beau Sire Dieu:* Dear Lord God.

p. 229, *albas:* Aubades, a genre of poem popular in the age of the Troubadours. Their theme is the parting from the beloved at dawn, after a night together.

p. 229, *sirventes:* Another genre, whose theme was the worshipful homage that the poet/servant paid to his lady.

p. 231, *the theater in Orange:* The second-century Roman amphitheater in this Provençal town.

p. 233, *most tragic of women:* The reference is to Eleonora Duse (1859–1924), one of the greatest actresses of her time.

p. 234, *Mariana Alcoforado:* See note on pp. 265–66.

p. 236, *Byblis:* She fell in love with her brother Caunus, who rejected her advances and fled to Lycia in Asia Minor. Byblis pursued him; when her strength gave out, she cried so much that she was totally consumed in her tears and became a fountain under the dark oaks.

p. 236, *Héloïse:* See note on p. 270.

p. 236, *Gaspara Stampa:* See note on p. 265.

p. 236, *Countess of Die* (12th–13th century): The earliest of the women Troubadours. Some scholars identify her as Béatrice, daughter of Guigne IV, Dauphin of Viennois in the mid-twelfth century; others as Flotte Béranger, wife of Guillaume of Poitou, Count of Valentinois (either Guillaume I, ca. 1158–ca. 1189, or his grandson Guillaume II, 1202–ca. 1227). The five poems of hers that survive are complaints about the coldness of her lover, possibly the Troubadour Rambaut of Orange (died ca. 1173).

p. 236, *Clara of Anduze* (13th century): Provençal poet. Nothing is known about her life, and only one poem of hers has survived.

p. 236, *Louise Labé* (ca. 1520–1566): French poet, known as "La Belle Cordière." Her *Oeuvres* (1555), which were probably inspired by her love for the poet Olivier de Magny and her grief at his absence in Italy, contain poems remarkable for their passion and clarity.

p. 236, *Marceline Desbordes-Valmore* (1786–1859): French actress, opera singer, and later poet and novelist. She had an unhappy love affair with a man whose name she never revealed.

p. 236, *Elisa Mercoeur* (1809–1835): French poet.

p. 236, *Aïssé*: Charlotte Haydée (1694–1733), daughter of a Circassian chief whose palace was raided by Turks. She was bought at the age of four in the slave market of Constantinople by the French ambassador, the Comte de Ferriol, and brought to Paris, where her great beauty and romantic history made her a central attraction in the salons.

p. 236, *Julie de Lespinasse* (1732–1776): Close friend of d'Alembert and other Encyclopedists, who gathered in her salon. She fell in love with the Comte de Guibert, a young man who was later to become famous as a military strategist, and she died of grief a few years after his marriage. Her letters to Guibert, in which she gives voice to her intense passion, were published by his widow in 1809.

p. 236, *Marie-Anne de Clermont*: Marie-Anne de Bourbon-Condé, Princesse de Clermont (1697–1741). Her meeting with Louis de Melun, Duc de Joyeuse, in the forest of Chantilly and their secret marriage were followed by his sudden death in a hunting accident.

p. 238, *Clémence de Bourges* (1535–1561): Friend of Louise Labé, who dedicated the Sonnets to her; known for her great beauty and intelligence. She died of grief when her fiancé was killed at the siege of Beaurepaire.

p. 238, *Jean de Tournes* (1504–1564): Printer in Lyon. The book is the second edition of Louise Labé's *Works*.

p. 239, *Diké and Anaktoria, Gyrinno and Atthis*: Women friends of Sappho, mentioned in her poems.

p. 239, *Ridinger*: Johann Elias Ridinger (1698–1767), German painter and etcher, known for his portrayal of animals.

p. 241, *that small figure*: Sappho.

p. 241, *Galen's testimony*: Claudius Galenus (ca. 130–ca.

200), Greek physician; he also wrote books on logic, ethics, and grammar.

p. 246, *Benedicte von Qualen* (1774–1813): The poet Baggesen had met her in 1795; two years later, shortly after the death of his wife, he proposed marriage and was refused.

p. 250, *Julie Reventlow:* See note on p. 266.

p. 250, *Mechthild:* Mechthild of Magdeburg (ca. 1212–ca. 1282), German mystic, author of *The Light of My Godhead Flowing into All Hearts That Live without Guile* (commonly called *The Flowing Light of Godhead:* 1250–1264). Some scholars think that her descriptions of hell, purgatory, and heaven were a principal source for Dante's *Divine Comedy,* and identify her with the Matelda in *Purgatorio* xxvii–xxxiii.

p. 250, *Teresa of Avila* (1515–1582): Spanish Carmelite nun, Doctor of the Church, one of the leading figures in the Catholic Reformation. Her two main treatises are *The Way of Perfection* (1565) and *The Interior Castle* (1577).

p. 250, *Rose of Lima* (1586–1617): Peruvian ascetic and mystic; the first American to be canonized (1671).

p. 251, *Princess Amalie Gallitzin* (1748–1806): Daughter of a Prussian general, wife of the Russian ambassador to Paris, Turin, and The Hague, and an intimate friend of Voltaire and Diderot. A severe illness in 1786 led her back to the Roman Catholic church, and her house became the center of Catholic activity in Westphalia.

p. 252, *Tortuga:* Island off northwest Haiti. In the seventeenth century, it was a base for the French and English pirates who ravaged the Caribbean.

p. 252, *Campeche:* Port in southeastern Mexico, frequently raided by pirates during the seventeenth century.

p. 252, *Vera Cruz:* City in east-central Mexico; the country's chief port of entry. It was looted by pirates in 1653 and 1712.

p. 252, *Deodatus of Gozon:* A fourteenth-century member of the Order of the Knights of Saint John of Jerusalem (Knights of Malta). Because so many had lost their lives trying to kill the famous dragon of Rhodes, the Grand Master of the Order had forbidden all knights even to approach its cave. Deodatus went ahead and killed the dragon, but because of his disobedience he was stripped of his knighthood. Later he was pardoned, and in 1346 he himself became Grand Master.

p. 256, *Les Baux:* A small village in Provence. In the Middle Ages it was a flourishing town; the church, the eleventh-century castle, and many of the houses were hollowed out of the white friable limestone on which they stand. Now it is almost completely deserted, and there is nothing left but ruins.

p. 256, *that noble family:* The Princes of Les Baux, a Provençal family that reached the height of its power during the fourteenth and fifteenth centuries. They traced their origin to King Balthazar, one of the three wisemen of the Gospel, and took for their coat-of-arms the star of Bethlehem. Unfortunately, the star had sixteen rays—an extremely unlucky number, which they tried to counteract by having their possessions in threes and sevens, or multiples of these two lucky numbers.

p. 256, *Alyscamps:* The ancient cemetery near Arles, with its uncovered sarcophagi.

p. 258, *"sa patience de supporter une âme":* "his patience in enduring a soul." The quotation is probably from Saint Teresa of Avila.

ABOUT THE TRANSLATOR

STEPHEN MITCHELL was born in Brooklyn, New York, in 1943, and studied at Amherst, the University of Paris, and Yale. His books include *The Selected Poetry of Rainer Maria Rilke*, *The Book of Job*, *Tao Te Ching*, *The Enlightened Heart*, *Parables and Portraits*, *The Enlightened Mind*, and *The Gospel According to Jesus*. He lives with his wife, Vicki Chang, an acupuncturist and healer, in Berkeley, California.